In merry England long ago, when good King Henry the Second ruled, a famous outlaw lived in Sherwood Forest near the town of Nottingham.

His name was Robin Hood, and no archer was his equal, nor was there ever such a band as his hundred and forty merry men. They lived carefree lives in the forest; they passed the time competing at archery or battling with the quarterstaff; they lived on the King's deer and washed it down with strong October ale. They were outlaws, of course, but the common people loved them—for no one who came to Robin in need went away empty-handed.

A Note about
The Merry Adventures of Robin Hood

No one knows for certain if Robin Hood really existed. He is a legendary character who has shown up in ballads, poems, and stories for more than six hundred years. He is said to have been born about 1160. The kings who are mentioned in this book, Henry II, Richard the Lion-Hearted, and John, as well as Queen Eleanor, really did exist and rule England during the period of time covered in the story.

In 1883, the American writer and illustrator Howard Pyle took the various tales of Robin Hood that existed in ballads, poems, and stories and combined them into the a book he called *The Merry Adventures of Robin Hood*. It is Howard Pyle's portrait of Robin Hood that created the vivid image of this entertaining outlaw that exists today.

The story is set in England more than eight hundred years ago. At that time, the rich nobility and church officials often did not worry much about the common people. These powerful people had large groups of men (free landowners, or yeomen) who enforced their laws. The laws prohibited such things as hunting on the king's land. There were strict punishments for anyone who was caught disobeying these laws. Many of the noblemen and church officials were more concerned about their own welfare than about the welfare of those less fortunate. Common people and lesser noblemen were sometimes driven into poverty by the heavy taxes and the greedy land grabs of the rich and powerful. This is the world in which Robin Hood lived and carried out his adventures.

The Merry Adventures of Robin Hood

HOWARD PYLE

Edited by Jonathan Kelly,
with an Afterword by Bill Blauvelt

 THE TOWNSEND LIBRARY

THE MERRY ADVENTURES
OF ROBIN HOOD

TP **THE TOWNSEND LIBRARY**

For more titles in the Townsend Library,
visit our website: **www.townsendpress.com**

Townsend Press, Inc.
1038 Industrial Drive
West Berlin, New Jersey 08091

ISBN 1-59194-043-5

Library of Congress Control Number
2004117885

CONTENTS

How Robin Hood Came to Be an Outlaw

In merry England long ago, when good King Henry the Second ruled, a famous outlaw lived in Sherwood Forest near the town of Nottingham. His name was Robin Hood, and no archer was his equal, nor was there ever such a band as his hundred and forty merry men. They lived carefree lives in the forest; they passed the time competing at archery or battling with the quarterstaff; they lived on the King's deer and washed it down with strong October ale. They were outlaws, of course, but the common people loved them—for no one who came to Robin in need went away empty-handed.

Robin Hood had not always been an outlaw. Before he became Robin Hood the outlaw, he was known as Robin of Locksley.

One day, when Robin of Locksley was a strong and bold young man of eighteen, the Sheriff of Nottingham announced an archery match. The prize was to be a keg of ale. "Now, that is my kind of prize," Robin said to himself. Taking his sturdy longbow of yew wood and a quiver of arrows, he set off from Locksley Town through Sherwood Forest toward Nottingham.

It was an early May morning, when flowers bloom and birds sing and people clean their homes. The sun threw playful shadows on the path and Robin whistled as he walked, thinking about winning the prize.

As he strode merrily along, he came upon some fifteen of the King's foresters seated beneath an oak tree. They were yeomen: that is to say, free men of the working class; they were able to handle weapons but ranked below the nobility. The job of the King's foresters was to protect the King's forests from trespassers and make sure that no one hunted the King's deer, for that was against the law. These particular foresters were taking time from their work to feast and make merry. They helped themselves to a huge meat pie, washing it town with ale from a nearby barrel. Then one, with his mouth full, called out to young Robin, "Hello, lad, where are you taking that toy bow and those cheap arrows?"

Robin grew angry, for no young man likes that kind of talk.

"My bow and arrows are as good as yours," he said. "I go to the shooting match at Nottingham Town; there I will shoot against other strong yeomen, to win a keg of good ale."

Then a man holding a horn of ale cried out, "Why, boy, your mother's milk is barely dry on your lips. You talk of competing with good strong men at archery—yet you can hardly draw a man's bow!"

"I'll bet your best archer fifteen pounds," bold Robin said, "that I hit the target at three hundred yards."

At this all laughed aloud, and one said, "It is easy for you to brag and offer bets, boy. You know that there are no targets around here, so we cannot hold you to your words."

Another mocked, "Soon he will be mixing ale with his milk."

At this Robin grew infuriated. "Listen, and look," he said. "I see a herd of deer far away at the edge of the clearing, even more than three hundred yards away. I will bet you fifteen pounds that I can slay the best of the herd."

"Done!" cried the forester who had spoken first, pulling out golden coins. "And here are fifteen pounds. I bet that you will not kill a single deer, let alone the best of the herd."

Robin took his longbow in his hand, strung

it easily, and placed a broad English arrow trimmed—'fletched,' as they say—with gray goose feathers. He raised, aimed, pulled the string back to his ear, and in the next moment the bowstring sang. The arrow sped down the clearing like a sparrow hawk. A magnificent buck, with the largest antlers in the herd, leaped with the impact and fell dead in the green grass.

"Ha!" cried Robin "How do you like that shot, good fellow? I would have won this bet even had it been three hundred pounds."

All the foresters were filled with rage, but the angriest was the one who had lost the bet.

"No!" he cried. "It was a silly bet. Get out of here, right now, or I'll spank you so hard you'll never walk again."

"Do you not know," said another, "that you just killed one of the King's deer? According to the law of our good King Henry, your ears should be cut off for this!"

"Catch him!" cried a third.

"No," said a fourth, "let him go. He is just a child."

Robin said nothing but glared at the foresters—especially the one who refused to pay his bet. He turned on his heel and strode away with the bitter anger of any hot-tempered youth who gets disrespect from his elders.

It would have been far better for the loser of the bet had he left Robin alone, but he had drunk more than his share. Before anyone could interfere, he sprang to his feet and fitted an arrow to his bow. "Yes, and I'll give you reason to hurry!" he said, and sent the arrow whistling after Robin.

Had the forester been sober, Robin would never have taken another step, but fortunately the older man's head was spinning with the ale. Even so, the arrow came within three inches of Robin's head. Robin turned, quickly drew his own bow, and sent back an arrow in reply.

"You said I was no archer," he cried. "Say so now!"

The shaft flew straight. The man fell forward with a cry and lay face down in the grass. His arrows spilled rattling from his quiver, wet with the blood of his heart. Then, before the others could gather their wits, Robin vanished into the depths of the forest. Some started after him but with no enthusiasm, for each feared the same fate. Soon they all came back, lifted their dead comrade up, and carried his body away to Nottingham.

Meanwhile Robin ran through the green wood. All the joy and brightness was gone from everything for his heart was sick with the realization that he had slain a man. "Poor devil," he cried, "your wife will weep today and because of me! I wish you had never said a word to me, or that I had never come your way, or even that my right forefinger had been cut off before this! I shot in haste, but I will grieve forever!"

And so he came to be called Robin Hood and to live in the forest. Gone forever were the happy, carefree times with his friends in Locksley Town. He had committed two crimes: murder and shooting the King's deer. A reward of two hundred pounds was offered for his capture. The Sheriff of Nottingham swore to bring this renegade Robin Hood to justice. He wanted the reward money but he also wanted revenge, for the slain forester was a relative of his.

Robin Hood hid in Sherwood Forest for the next year, during which he gathered around him many other outcasts. Some had gotten hungry in wintertime and been spotted shooting deer, yet escaped; others had lost their lands and property to powerful nobles or even to the King himself. Sherwood became a refuge for those who had been wronged or were on the run from the law. Over a hundred strong yeomen came to Sherwood that year, and they chose Robin Hood as their chief.

They vowed to treat their oppressors as they had been treated. Barons, abbots, knights, nobles, and squires all got rich—at the expense of the poor—with burdensome taxes, high rents, and wrongful fines. Robin's merry men would steal from them in turn. They would help the poor, giving them back what had been unfairly taken from them. They vowed never to harm a child or wrong any woman. Many a poor family came to

Sherwood in need and found kindness and help. Soon the common people felt that Robin was one of their own, and they praised and admired him.

One merry morning, when all the birds were singing among the leaves and his men were washing in the cold stream, Robin said to them, "For fourteen days we have had no sport, and I am going out to seek adventure. Wait here, my merry men, and listen well. If I am in trouble, I will sound three blasts of my horn—come quickly!"

With that he strode away through the leafy forest and soon came to the edge of Sherwood. There he wandered for a long time, on highways and side roads, through woods and fields. He joked and laughed with lovely young maidens and tipped his cap to dignified ladies on carriages. He saw fat monks on heavily laden donkeys, gallant knights with flashing armor and lances, pageboys in crimson, and merchants from Nottingham Town—but no adventure. Finally he came to a wide, rocky stream with only a single great log for a bridge. As he approached, he saw a tall stranger coming from the other side. Each hurried, thinking to cross first.

"Stand back," Robin said, "and let the better man cross first."

"Then stand back yourself," answered the stranger, "for I am the better man."

"We will see," Robin replied. "Meanwhile, stay back, or I will welcome you to Nottingham with an arrow in the ribs."

"Now," the stranger said, "if you even dare touch your bowstring, I will beat you until your hide is as many colors as a beggar's cloak."

"You talk like a donkey for I could put this arrow clear through that proud heart of yours before a friar could say 'grace.'"

"And you sound like a coward," answered the stranger. "There you stand with a good yew bow to shoot at me, while I have only a plain blackthorn staff to fight you with."

"I have been called many things but never a coward," replied Robin. "Very well; I will set aside my bow and arrows, and go cut myself a staff. Then we will see what kind of man you are. Wait here."

"With pleasure," the stranger said, leaning on his strong staff.

Then Robin Hood stepped into the forest, picked out a small oak tree, and quickly cut away the limbs and roots. Before long he had a six-foot quarterstaff, just thick enough to fill his strong hands. As he worked, he kept an eye on the new-comer, for never before had he seen such a huge, stout fellow. Robin was tall, but this man was at least seven feet tall—and even broader in the shoulders than Robin.

"Even so," Robin said to himself, "I will give you a merry beating, my good fellow." Then, aloud: "Here is my staff. Now meet me on the log—if you are not afraid, of course—and we will fight until one of us falls into the stream."

"A fine plan!" cried the stranger, twirling his staff over his head until it whistled.

In a moment Robin met the stranger on the bridge, faked in one direction, then launched a blow at the stranger's head that would have sent him right into the water. But the stranger skillfully blocked the blow, answering with one just as powerful; this Robin also blocked. So they stood, neither backing off, trading blows and blocks and bruises for over an hour. Neither thought of giving up. Sometimes they stopped to rest, each thinking that he had never in all his life seen such great skill with the quarterstaff.

At last Robin gave the stranger a belt in the ribs that made dust fly from his jacket like smoke. The bigger man nearly fell off the bridge but regained his balance and replied with a thwack that caught Robin along the head, drawing blood. Robin grew angry and swung with all his might, but the stranger successfully blocked this blow. Then he got through Robin's guard with one more mighty swing, bowling him head over heels into the water with a splash.

"And where are you now, young man?" shouted the stranger, roaring with laughter.

"Oh, in the drink!" cried Robin, laughing at his sorry state. Then he got to his feet and waded ashore.

"Shake my hand," cried Robin, when he had reached the bank. "I must say, you are a strong and brave man, and very good with the cudgel. My head is humming like a hive of bees in June." Then he clapped his horn to his lips and sounded a blast that echoed through the forest. "No one between here and Canterbury Town could have done this to me."

"And you," laughed the stranger, "know how to take your cudgeling like a true yeoman."

But now the woods rustled, and suddenly forty good men in Lincoln green burst into view, led by merry Will Stutely.

"Good master," cried Will, "how is this? You are soaked to the skin."

"Yes, indeed," answered jolly Robin. "That fellow over there has not only tumbled me into the water, but given me a good beating."

"Then he shall have a ducking and a beating himself!" cried Will Stutely. "Have at him, lads!"

Will and twenty yeomen leaped on the stranger, but he was ready. He struck left and right with his staff, and even though he was brought down by sheer numbers, many of Robin's men were soon rubbing sore heads.

"No, stop!" cried Robin, laughing until his sore sides ached again. "He is a good, brave man, and we will not harm him. Now listen, newcomer: will you join my band? You will have three suits of Lincoln green each year, as well as a salary of twenty-five pounds, plus a share of anything else good that we find. You will dine on fresh deer meat and drink stout ale, and you will be my right-hand man, for never in my life did I see such skill with the staff. Will you be one of my merry men?"

"I do not know," growled the stranger, for he was angry at being roughed up. "If you handle a bow no better than you do a staff, you would not be called yeomen where I come from. But if any of you can outshoot me, then I will reconsider."

"You have a lot of nerve," Robin said, "but I will humor you. Will Stutely, cut a piece of white bark four fingers wide, and set it eighty yards away on that oak. Now, stranger, hit that with an arrow and call yourself an archer."

"I will," he answered. "Give me a good stout bow and a fair arrow, and I will."

He chose the sturdiest bow among them all, next to Robin's own, and an arrow with perfect gray-goose fletching. Then he stepped up to the mark. All the band sat to watch him shoot. The newcomer drew the arrow to his cheek and let it fly, sending it so straight that it hit the bark in the very center. "Aha!" he cried. "Beat that, if you can!" The yeomen clapped their hands at so fine a shot.

"A good shot indeed," answered Robin. "I cannot beat it, but perhaps I can ruin it."

Then Robin took his own bow, chose and drew an arrow, and shot with all his skill. The arrow flew straight, so truly that it hit the end of the stranger's arrow and splintered it. All the yeomen leaped to their feet and cheered their master's amazing shot.

"I swear on my honor," cried the stranger, "I have never seen or even heard of anything like that in my whole life! I will be one of your men."

"Then I have gained a good man this day," Robin said. "What is your name, good fellow?"

"Men call me John Little," answered the stranger.

Then Will Stutely, who loved a good joke, eyed the huge man and said, "No, my friend, I think you should have another name. You should be baptized Little John!"

Robin Hood and his band laughed aloud until the stranger began to grow angry.

"Make fun of me," John Little said to Stutely, "and you will have sore bones—and soon."

"Do not be angry, good friend," Robin Hood said, "for the name fits. From this day you shall be called Little John. Come, my merry men: we must prepare a feast to baptize the little one!"

They turned and plunged into the forest again to their camp. It was deep in the woods;

they had built huts of bark and branches, with couches and beds of deerskin stuffed with grasses. There was a great spreading oak tree, under which Robin Hood usually sat on a seat of green moss. Here they found the rest of the band, some of whom had been hunting and had brought in two fat does. They built great fires and roasted the deer, opening a barrel of strong ale.

When the feast was ready they all sat down, but Robin sat Little John on his right, for he was to be second in command. The band ate, joked, and drank merrily for an hour. When the feast was done, Will Stutely spoke up. "It is now time to christen our lovely baby, is it not?"

"Yes! Yes!" everyone cried, laughing till the woods echoed.

"The child must have seven sponsors," said Will Stutely, and from the band he chose the seven biggest and strongest men.

"By Saint Dunstan," cried Little John, springing to his feet, "lay a finger on me, and plenty of you will regret it."

But they rushed him without warning, seizing him by his legs and arms and holding him too tightly to struggle. The seven carried him forth while the rest stood around to watch. Then one man, who had been chosen to play the priest because he was bald-headed like a traveling friar, came forward with a full pot of ale. "Who brings the baby for baptism?" he asked, soberly.

"I do," answered Will Stutely.

"And what name do you give him?"

"I call him Little John."

"Now, Little John," said the mock priest, "you have not really lived before, but merely gotten along; you were called John Little. From this day, you will truly live. I baptize you 'Little John.'" And with that, the bald man emptied the pot of ale on Little John's head.

All shouted with laughter as they saw the brown ale stream over Little John's beard and trickle from his nose and chin, his eyes blinking with the sting. His first impulse was to be angry, but the merriment of the others swayed him and he laughed along. Then Robin took him, clothed him from head to toe in Lincoln green, gave him a good sturdy bow, and so made him a member of the merry band.

And that is how Robin Hood became an outlaw and gained a band of merry companions, including his right-hand man Little John.

Robin Hood and
the Tinker

Tales of Robin Hood's deeds spread far and wide, but few tried to claim the two hundred pounds offered for his capture. The Sheriff of Nottingham swore to capture Robin himself. The reward money and the chance to avenge his relative's murder were reason enough. But to make matters worse, the band's actions were making the Sheriff look weak and foolish.

The Sheriff had no idea how many men Robin had with him and thought that he could simply serve an arrest warrant on him like any other lawbreaker. He offered thirty pounds to anyone who would serve the warrant, but the men of Nottingham Town knew more of Robin and his doings than the Sheriff did. Two weeks later, no one had volunteered. The Sheriff complained to his men, "I have offered a fine reward to anyone who will serve my warrant, but no one even dares try!"

One of his men said, "Good master, you do not realize how many men Robin Hood has, or how little he cares about warrants, whether from king or sheriff. No one wants broken bones."

"Then every man in Nottingham is a coward," said the Sheriff. "If no man here is brave enough to win thirty pounds, I will look elsewhere. There must be daring men somewhere in England."

Then he called up a trusted messenger and told him to ride to Lincoln Town to see if anyone there would serve the warrant and win the reward. The messenger left that very morning.

It was a bright sunny day on the dusty road from Nottingham to Lincoln, and the messenger got tired. A little more than halfway to Lincoln Town, he was glad to see the Sign of the Blue Boar Inn, and he decided to stop for a pot of ale in the cool shade of the oak trees.

A merry party was seated beneath the oak tree in front of the door, for it was common to drink outside. There were a tinker who made his living mending broken pots and pans, two barefoot friars with curly beards who wandered the land ministering to the people, and a party of six King's foresters. All were drinking strong ale and singing merry ballads, joking and laughing, but the tinker laughed loudest and sang best. His bag and hammer hung on the oak tree, and near-by was his sturdy quarterstaff, thick as his wrist.

"Come!" cried one of the foresters to the tired messenger. "Join us for a drink and a song. Landlord! A fresh pot of ale for each man!" The messenger gladly joined them.

"Now, what news do you bear so quickly," asked one, "and where do you ride today?"

The messenger loved a bit of gossip as much as he loved a pot of ale. Sitting down, he began his story: how Robin Hood had slain the forester, and hidden in Sherwood to escape the law, and how he lived on His Majesty's deer and charged a toll to rich people who passed by, so that none dared travel near Sherwood. He explained that the Sheriff wished to serve the King's warrant on this outlaw—though he would surely ignore it—but that no one in Nottingham was willing to serve it. He was on his way, he said, to see if the men in Lincoln were any braver.

"I come from Banbury Town," said the jolly tinker, "and no one near Nottingham—or Sherwood, either—can beat me at quarterstaff. I have never heard of this Robin Hood; he sounds strong and sly, but I am stronger and slyer. Now, by my own name—and that's Wat of the Crabstaff—I will meet this sturdy rascal. If he mocks the order of our glorious King Henry, I will beat him so that he will never move again! What do you say, my lads?"

"Then you are my man," cried the messenger. "Come back with me to Nottingham Town. Our good Sheriff has offered thirty pounds for this service."

"Then I will go with you, lad. Just wait while I get my bag and hammer and my staff. Let me see if this Robin Hood dares ignore the royal warrant." After paying the innkeeper, they started back to Nottingham, the tinker walking along beside the mounted messenger.

One bright morning soon afterward, Robin Hood started off to Nottingham Town, his eyes and his thoughts wandering. His bugle horn hung at his hip and his bow and arrows at his back, while in his hand he bore a good stout oak staff. As he walked down a shady lane he saw a tinker coming, singing merrily as he walked. On his back hung his bag and his hammer, and he carried a six-foot staff of crabapple wood.

"Hello, good friend!" cried Robin. But the tinker just kept on singing.

"Hello!" cried Robin again. But still the tinker sang on.

"Hello! Are you deaf, man?" Robin shouted.

"And who so rudely interrupts a pretty song?" demanded the tinker. "Hello, yourself, whether you are a good friend or not. You had better hope you are, because otherwise you might be sorry."

"Where do you come from, my good fellow?" asked Robin.

"I come from Banbury," the tinker answered.

"Too bad!" Robin said. "I hear there is sad news in Banbury this merry morning. I hear that two tinkers are in Banbury jail for drinking ale and beer!"

"Now a plague on you, you scurvy dog, for bringing bad news about good men," said the tinker. "But that is sad indeed, if two brave fellows are in jail."

"No, you miss the point," Robin replied with a twinkle in his eye. "What makes the news so sad is that only two tinkers are in jail, which means others are still roaming around loose."

"Now by Saint Dunstan," cried the tinker, "I have a good mind to beat you for that poor joke. But if men are thrown in jail for drinking ale and beer, I bet your own future does not look so good."

Robin laughed loudly and cried, "Well said, tinker, well said! Come with me to the Sign of the Blue Boar near here, and I will wet your throat with the best ale in Nottinghamshire."

"By my faith!" the tinker said. "You are a good fellow in spite of your bad jokes. I will go with you to this Blue Boar."

"And what is your own news, good friend?" Robin asked as they trudged along. "Everyone knows that tinkers hear all the news."

"Now, I love you as my brother, good fellow," said the tinker, "or I would not tell you; for I am very sly, and I have official business that requires all my wits. I come to seek a bold outlaw by the name of Robin Hood. I have a warrant from the Sheriff in my pouch. If I can find this same Robin Hood, I will serve it on him; if he ignores it, I will beat him black and blue. But you live hereabouts, do you not? Perhaps you know Robin Hood yourself, my good man."

"Yes, I do somewhat," answered Robin, "and I have seen him this very morning. But, tinker, men say that he is a clever thief. Be careful, for he might even steal the warrant right out of your pouch!"

"Let him try!" cried the tinker. "He may be clever, but so am I. I wish I had him here now, man to man!" He twirled his heavy staff. "But tell me, lad: what does he look like?"

"Much like myself," said Robin, laughing, "and of similar height and build and age; and he has blue eyes, too."

"Are you sure?" the tinker said. "You are just a youth. I thought he must be a great bearded man, if Nottingham men feared him so."

"Truly, he is not as old and strong as you," Robin said. "But men do say that he is good with the quarterstaff."

"That may be," the tinker replied, "but I am better. Will you lead me to him? I have been promised thirty pounds by the Sheriff to serve the warrant on this rascal. If you show me where to find him, I will give you five of them."

"I will," Robin said, "But here we are at the Sign of the Blue Boar, so first let us stop and taste some brown October ale."

There was no sweeter inn in all Nottinghamshire than the Blue Boar. None had such lovely trees or had such good beer and ale. It was Robin's men's favorite inn.

As for the host, he was no fool and knew when to keep silent. Robin and his men were excellent customers, and they always paid promptly in coin—unlike many, who wanted to drink and eat now and pay later. So, when Robin Hood and the tinker came to the door and called for two great pots of ale, the host gave no hint that he knew Robin.

"Wait here in the shade," Robin said to the tinker, "while I go and see that our host gets the ale from the right keg. I know that he has good October ale brewed by the great Withold of Tamworth." He went inside and whispered to the host to add some pure grain alcohol—of the sort often homebrewed by country folk—to the tinker's pot of good English ale. The landlord did so and brought it to them.

"By Our Lady," the tinker said, after a deep drink, "this Withold of Tamworth brews the strongest ale that ever passed the lips of Wat of the Crabstaff."

"Drink, man, drink," cried Robin. "Landlord! Bring my friend another pot of the same. And how about a song, my good man?"

"I will give you a song indeed, good fellow," said the tinker, "for I have never tasted such ale in all my days—by Our Lady, my head is already humming!" He turned to the landlady and her daughter. "Hostess, come and listen if you like, and you too, my lovely young girl, for I sing best when bright eyes are watching me."

Then he sang an ancient ballad of the time of good King Arthur. All listened as he sang of a noble knight and his sacrifice to his king. But long before the tinker came to the last verse, he began to trip over the words. His tongue grew thick, his head wagged, and at last he fell sound asleep.

Robin Hood laughed aloud and quickly fished the warrant out of the tinker's pouch, along with what money was there. "You are sly, tinker," said he, "but perhaps not yet as sly as that sly thief, Robin Hood."

He called the host over and said, "Here, good man, is half a pound for the fun you have given us today. Take good care of your guest there. When he wakes up, you can tell him I did not pay. If he cannot pay you, you can take his bag and hammer, and even his coat in payment. This is how I punish those who come to Sherwood to do me harm. As for you, good landlord, I never met a landlord who did not like to get paid twice." At this the host smiled slyly, for Robin was right.

The tinker did not awake until evening. When he had gathered his wits, he looked about for his merry companion—but he was gone. Then he thought of his stout crabapple-wood staff; it was in his hand. Finally he thought of his warrant and of the reward. He reached into his pouch, only to find it empty of paper and money. He sprang to his feet in a rage.

"Landlord!" he cried. "Where did that rascal go, the one who was just with me?"

"What rascal does Your Worship mean?" the landlord asked innocently. "I saw no rascal with Your Worship, for surely no man would dare call him that so close to Sherwood Forest. I saw a brave yeoman with Your Worship, but I thought that Your Worship knew him, for he is well known hereabouts."

"I have never been in your pigsty," growled the tinker, "so how should I know every pig in it? Who was he, then?"

"Why, he is a bold fellow whom we call Robin Hood, which same—"

"By Our Lady!" cried the tinker hastily.

Then he growled, "You saw me come into your inn, an honest craftsman, and never told me who I was drinking with, even though you knew. I have a good mind to crack your skull!" Then he raised his crabstaff as if to strike.

"But," cried the host, crouching in fear, "how was I to know that you did not know him?"

"Be thankful," the tinker said, "that I am a patient man, and will spare that bald head of yours, or you would never cheat another customer. As for this rascal Robin Hood, I am going to find him and when I do, I'll crack his head open."

"Wait," said the landlord, standing in front of him and holding out his arms—for money made him bold—"not until you pay your bill."

"Did he not pay you?"

"Not a penny; and you two drank half a pound worth of ale today. If you leave without paying me, our good Sheriff will hear of it."

"But I have nothing to pay you with, good fellow," said the tinker.

"Don't 'good fellow' me," said the landlord. "I am no 'good fellow' when it comes to half a pound! Either pay me in coin, or leave your coat and bag and hammer; they look worn, and are probably not worth half a pound, so I still lose. If you move, I will set my dog on you. Maken!" he cried to his daughter. "If this fellow takes one step, open the door and let Brian out."

"No," the tinker replied—for his travels had taught him about dogs—"take what you want, and let me go in peace, and a plague on you. But if I catch that scurvy troublemaker, I swear that he will pay me back with interest!"

With that he strode away toward the forest grumbling to himself, while the landlord and his good wife and Maken stood looking after him, laughing only when he was out of earshot. "Robin and I stripped that donkey of his load quite neatly," the landlord said.

Just about this time, Robin Hood was going through the forest toward the main road. The evening was well lit by the full moon. His oak staff was in his hand and at his side his bugle horn. As he walked up a path, whistling, down another path came the tinker, muttering and shaking his head like an angry bull. At a sharp bend, they suddenly met face to face. Each stood still for a moment. Then Robin spoke:

"Hello, my friend," said he with a merry laugh. "How did you like your ale? Will you sing me another song?"

The tinker stood still for a moment, glaring, then said: "Just the man I want to see. If I do not rattle your bones, you can put your foot on my neck!"

"With all my heart!" cried merry Robin. "Rattle them if you can!" He gripped his staff and prepared to fight.

The tinker spat on his hands, grasped his staff, and came straight at Robin. He struck two or three blows, but soon found that he had met his match, for Robin blocked all of them—then slipped a blow past the tinker's guard to hit him in the ribs. At this Robin laughed aloud, and the tinker lost his temper, swinging with all his might. Robin again blocked all three strokes, but the third mighty blow broke Robin's oak staff. "Traitor staff," cried Robin, dropping the useless pieces, "what a time to break on me!"

"Now give up," ordered the tinker, "or I will beat your head to pudding."

Robin Hood made no answer, but clapped his horn to his lips and blew three loud, clear blasts.

"Blow all you wish," the tinker said, "but you are coming with me to Nottingham Town. The Sheriff would like a word with you. Now, will you surrender or get your skull broken?"

"If I must, I must," Robin said, "but I have never surrendered to any man before, and I am not even hurt. I think I will not. My merry men! Come quickly!"

Out of the forest leaped Little John and six strong yeomen clad in Lincoln green.

"Why, good master," cried Little John, "what do you need, that you blow your horn so loudly?"

"There stands a tinker," Robin said, "that would like to take me to Nottingham to hang."

"Then he himself shall hang," cried Little John, and he and the others made to seize the tinker.

"No!" Robin said. "He is a strong and brave man who sings a lovely ballad. Say, good fellow, will you join my merry men? Each year you shall have three suits of Lincoln green, and be paid twenty-five pounds. We shall share and share alike; we live a merry, carefree life here, dining on deer and oatcakes and honey washed down with good ale. Will you come?"

"Yes, indeed, I will," said the tinker, "for it sounds like a merry life. And I like you, good master, even though you thwacked my ribs and cheated me. I must admit that you are both bolder and more clever than I, and I will serve you."

So all turned their steps to the deep forest, where the tinker lived from that day on.

The Shooting Match
at Nottingham Tower

𝕿he Sheriff was infuriated at this failure to take Robin. He knew that people laughed at the notion of serving a warrant on such a bold outlaw and no man likes to be a laughingstock. The Sheriff said to himself: "Our gracious King himself shall know how his laws and warrant are ignored by this band of rebels. As for that traitor tinker, if I catch him, he will hang from the highest tree in all Nottinghamshire."

Then he ordered all his many servants and guards to prepare to go to London Town for he was going to speak with the King. There was much bustling about with everyone busy doing this and that, and every blacksmith in town working late mending armor. After three days all was ready. At sunup the Sheriff's party headed for London. Their flashing armor and bright plumes attracted a lot of attention as they passed through the towns along the way.

Two days' travel brought into sight the spires and towers of great London Town, where King Henry and his fair Queen Eleanor held court. The Sheriff went to the palace, which was full of brave knights and richly dressed ladies. He was shown into the King's presence.

"I come to ask a favor," he said, kneeling low.

"Tell us what you wish," said the King.

"My good Lord and Sovereign," answered the Sheriff, "in Sherwood Forest, in our own shire of Nottingham, lives a bold outlaw named Robin Hood."

"Indeed," the King said, "his doings have reached even our own royal ears. He is a rebellious fellow, yet I also hear that he is quite a merry soul."

"But, my most gracious Sovereign," said the Sheriff. "I sent him a warrant with your own royal seal, and he beat the messenger and stole the warrant. He kills your deer and robs your subjects on the highways."

"Are you not my Sheriff, and are my laws not enforced in Nottinghamshire?" the King demanded angrily. "You appear to have a great force of men-at-arms. Why are you unable to defeat this single band of outlaws? Are you incompetent? Get out of here, and do not bother me again with this. And, furthermore, take note: everyone in my kingdom will obey my laws. If you cannot enforce them, I will find someone else who can."

Then the Sheriff turned away, greatly worried. He now regretted bringing such a large escort. On the way back to Nottingham he was silent, busy devising a plan to capture Robin Hood. He turned over dozens of schemes in his head and found flaws in all of them. He kept thinking about what a fearless and daring man Robin was.

"Now," thought the Sheriff, "if I could get Robin close enough to Nottingham Town that I could find him, I could surely capture him." Then he had an inspiration: a great shooting match, with a grand prize, to lure Robin Hood to come and compete.

"Aha!" he cried aloud, slapping his thigh. "I have it now! Mark my words, men: within two weeks that evil Robin Hood will be safely inside Nottingham jail."

As soon as he was back in Nottingham, he sent messengers north and south, and east and west, to announce this grand shooting match. Everyone who could draw a longbow was welcome to compete, and the prize would be an arrow of pure gold.

Robin Hood first heard the news one day

when he was in Lincoln Town. He hurried back to Sherwood, gathered his merry men and said:

"Listen, my men, to my news. Our friend the Sheriff of Nottingham is having a shooting match, and the prize is a bright golden arrow. Now I think that one of us should win it, for it is a handsome prize and we love our good Sheriff so. We will take our bows and arrows and go there to shoot, for it will be merry sport. What say you, lads?"

Then young David of Doncaster spoke up: "Good master, I have come straight from our friend Eadom of the Blue Boar, and there I heard the news of the match. Eadom overheard one of the Sheriff's men saying that this match is a trap to lure you into town. Please do not go, good master, or we may all be sorry."

"You are a wise lad who knows when to listen," Robin said. "But can we let it be said that Robin Hood—and a hundred and forty of the best archers in all England—are afraid of the Sheriff of Nottingham? No, good David, this makes me want the prize all the more; but we will be careful. Some of you will dress as friars, some as country folk, and others as tinkers or beggars—but make sure each of you has a good bow or broadsword, in case we need it. As for me, I will compete for this golden arrow. If I win it, we will hang it from our great oak tree here for all to enjoy. What do you think of my plan, men?"

"Good, good!" cried the band heartily.

On the day of the match, Nottingham Town was a sight to see. All along the green meadow outside the walls stretched a row of benches for knights and nobles and the wealthy to sit on. A rail was built on the other side, to keep the common folk from crowding into the shooting-range. The target stood in front a large mound of earth: a white ring, a black ring, and the bull's-eye. To one side of it was a raised seat, gaily decorated, for the Sheriff and his lady. The range was forty feet wide, and at the opposite end from the target was a great striped tent with kegs of ale, in case any of the archers got thirsty.

While it was still early, the benches began to fill. The rails across from them were crowded with the peasants. In the great tent the archers were gathering and chatting or inspecting their bows and arrows. The very best archers in the land had come: Gilbert of the Red Cap, the Sheriff's own head archer; Diccon Cruikshank of Lincoln Town; and Adam of Tamsworth, sixty years old but still hearty; and many other famous bowmen.

When all the benches were filled with guests, at last the Sheriff himself appeared with his lady. He rode a milk-white horse and she a brown filly, and they were dressed in bright finery, heavy with jewelry and gems. The peasants cheered as the couple rode forward. Awaiting them at their high seat were men-at-arms, in chain mail and bearing spears.

When the Sheriff and his wife had sat down, he had his herald sound three blasts on a silver horn. The archers stepped forward to their places, while all the people shouted, each calling the name of a favorite yeoman. "Red Cap!" cried some; "Cruikshank!" cried others; "Hurrah for William of Leslie!" shouted still others.

Then the herald stepped forward and loudly proclaimed the rules of the game:

"Each man will first shoot once from the mark, which is a hundred and fifty yards from the target. The ten who shoot best will shoot again twice, and of these, the best three will be chosen to shoot for the prize. Each of these will shoot three times, and he who shoots best will win the golden arrow."

Then the Sheriff leaned forward, looking hard for any sign of Robin Hood, but there was no one wearing Lincoln green. "Nevertheless," said the Sheriff to himself, "he may still be there, and I miss him among the crowd. When there are only ten men left, he will surely be among them."

The archers shot, each man in turn. The crowd had never seen such fine archery in their lives. Only two arrows hit in the white outer ring, and only four struck in the black ring inside that; the rest hit some part of the bull's-eye. Only ten men were left, six of whom were famous: Gilbert of the Red Cap, Adam of Tamsworth, Diccon Cruikshank, William of Leslie, Hubert of Cloud, and Swithin of Hertford. Two others were yeomen from Yorkshire; another was a tall stranger in blue from London Town. The last was a tattered stranger in scarlet with an eye-patch.

"Now," the Sheriff said to a nearby man-at-arms, "do you see Robin Hood among those ten?"

"No, Your Worship," answered the man. "Six of them I know well. Of the two from Yorkshire, one is too tall and the other too short to be that bold outlaw. Robin's beard is as yellow as gold, and that beggar in scarlet has a brown beard—nor is Robin blind in one eye. As for the stranger in blue, Robin's shoulders are at least three inches broader than his."

"Then," the Sheriff said, slapping his thigh angrily, "Robin Hood is not only a thief but a coward who dares not show his face among honest men."

After those ten archers had rested a short time, they stepped forward to shoot again. Each man shot two arrows while the crowd watched in silence. Only when the last had shot his second arrow did another great shout arise, and many threw their caps in the air to cheer such fine archery.

"Now by our gracious Lady fair," said old Sir Amyas, seated near the Sheriff, "I have seen the best longbowmen for sixty years and more, yet have never seen such shooting in all my days."

Now but three men were left: Gilbert of the Red Cap, the tattered stranger in scarlet, and Adam of Tamsworth. The people called aloud, some crying, "Hurrah for Gilbert of the Red Cap!" and some, "Hey for brave Adam of Tamsworth!" But not a single man in the crowd cheered the stranger in scarlet.

"Shoot well, Gilbert," cried the Sheriff, "and if you win, I shall give you a hundred silver pennies on top of the prize."

"Truly, I will do my best," Gilbert replied firmly. With that he fitted a smooth arrow to the string, drew his bow with care, and let fly. The arrow hit in the bull's-eye, an inch from the very center. The crowd shouted his name.

"Well done, Gilbert!" cried the Sheriff, clapping his hands.

Then the tattered stranger stepped forward, and the people laughed at his patched clothing and his one-eyed aim. He drew the bowstring quickly and shot without a pause, yet his arrow was half an inch closer to the center than Gilbert's.

"By all the saints in Paradise!" cried the Sheriff, "what an amazing shot!"

Then Adam of Tamsworth took his shot,

and his arrow lodged close beside the stranger's. Then all three shot again, and once more each arrow lodged within the bull's-eye, but this time Adam of Tamsworth's was farthest from the center, and again the tattered stranger's shot was the best. They then prepared to shoot for the third time.

This time Gilbert took aim, carefully measuring the distance and shooting with precision. The arrow flew straight, and the crowd shouted so loudly the noise scared up a flock of nearby birds, for it hit close to the very center.

"Well done, Gilbert!" cried the Sheriff joyfully. "I think you have just won the prize fair and square. Now, you beggar, let me see you outshoot that."

The scarlet-clad stranger was as silent as the crowd. He held his bow for five seconds, then drew, held the string a moment, and let it go. It sliced a gray goose feather from Gilbert's arrow and struck the exact center of the bull's-eye. As the feather fluttered earthward, the crowd was mute with amazement.

"I have been shooting for over forty years and done well enough," said old Adam of Tamsworth, shaking his head. "But I am finished for today. No man can match this stranger, whoever he is." He quivered his arrow and unstrung his bow without another word.

Then the Sheriff came down from his seat,

in all his silks and velvets, and went to where the
tattered stranger stood leaning upon his stout
bow, while the people crowded around to see
the incredible archer. "Here, good fellow," the
Sheriff said, handing over the golden arrow,
"you have won the prize fairly. What is your
name, and where are you from?"

"Men call me Jack of Teviotdale, and I
come from there," the stranger said in a gruff
voice.

"Then, by Our Lady, Jack, you are the finest
archer I ever saw. If you will join my service,
I will put better clothes on your back, you will

eat and drink well, and have wages of fifty pounds each Christmas. I think you shoot better than that coward Robin Hood, who dared not show his face here today. Will you accept?"

"No, I will not," said the stranger roughly. "I will do as I like, and no man in all merry England shall be my master."

"Then be gone, and a plague on you!" cried the Sheriff, his voice trembling with anger. "I should have you beaten for such disrespect!" Then he turned his back and strode away.

An odd company gathered around the great oak tree deep in Sherwood that day. There were twenty or more barefoot friars, and some tinkers, and a number of beggars and country folk. On a mossy chair sat one dressed in scarlet, with a patch over one eye, and in his hand he held the golden arrow. Then, amidst the talking and laughter, he removed the eye-patch and the scarlet rags to reveal a full suit of Lincoln green. "It is a lot easier to take off these rags than it is to get brown dye out of yellow hair." Then everyone laughed even louder, for the Sheriff had personally handed the prize to Robin Hood.

They all sat down to the woodland feast and talked about the joke that had been played on the Sheriff and of their adventures in disguise. But when the feast was done, Robin Hood took Little John aside and said, "I am angry, for the Sheriff called me a coward. I would like to show him just who won his prize, and that I am not the coward he thinks I am."

Little John said, "Good master, take me and Will Stutely, and we will send that fat Sheriff news of this by a messenger that he does not expect."

That day the Sheriff sat at dinner in the great hall of his house at Nottingham Town. Some eighty men-at-arms and servants sat at the long tables with him, talking of the day's shooting as they ate their meat and drank their ale. The Sheriff sat at the head of the table, his lady beside him.

"I was sure that lawbreaker Robin Hood would be at the game today," he said. "I did not realize he was such a coward. But who was that insolent beggar who answered me so rudely? He was lucky I did not have him beaten; but there was something odd about him. He seemed out of place in those tattered red rags."

Just as he finished speaking, something fell rattling among the dishes on the table. Those nearby jumped, wondering what it might be. After a moment one of the men-at-arms picked it up and brought it to the Sheriff. Then everyone saw that it was a blunted arrow with gray goose feathers. A small scroll of parchment was tied to it. The Sheriff opened the scroll and read it. The veins on his forehead swelled and his cheeks flushed with rage at what he saw:

"Now Heaven bless Your Grace this day
Say all in the Forest Sherwood
For you did give the prize away
To the merry thief Robin Hood."

"Where did this come from?" bellowed the Sheriff.

"Right through the window, Your Worship," said the man-at-arms.

Chapter 4

Will Stutely Rescued
by His Companions

When the Sheriff found that neither law nor trickery could overcome Robin Hood, he was stumped and said to himself, "What a fool I am! If I had not told our King of Robin Hood, I would not be in this mess. Either I capture him, or His Majesty will punish me. If I cannot arrest him or lure him, I will overcome him with force."

He gathered his sixty or so constables and gave orders: "Each of you take four men-at-arms and go to different points in Sherwood Forest. Try to ambush this Robin Hood. But if any of you find yourselves heavily outnumbered, sound a horn to summon the other groups to your aid. In this way, I think we will catch this rascal.

"Furthermore, whoever brings me Robin Hood—dead or alive—will get one hundred pounds in silver. The reward for any other outlaw is forty pounds, also dead or alive. So be bold and clever, and you will wind up richer."

Accordingly, sixty groups of five men each headed for Sherwood, eager to catch outlaws. They hunted through the forest for a full week but never saw a single man in Lincoln green, for trusty Eadom of the Blue Boar had sent word of the search to Robin.

When he first heard the news, Robin said, "If the Sheriff dares come in force, it will be a bad day for his men, for blood will flow. I would rather avoid battle; I killed a man once, and I hope never to do so again, for it gnaws at my soul. So we will lie low in Sherwood Forest, for everyone's benefit; but if we are forced into a fight, then let every man draw bow and sword and fight well."

At this many of the band shook their heads, and said to themselves, "Now the Sheriff and everyone else will think that we are cowards." But they kept quiet and did as Robin said.

They hid deep in Sherwood Forest for a week, but early in the morning of the eighth day Robin Hood called the band together and said, "Who will go and find out what the Sheriff's men are up to? They surely will not stay here forever."

A great shout arose, and each man waved his bow and asked to be the one to go. Their eager bravery made Robin Hood proud, and he said, "You are all brave and loyal, my merry men, but you cannot all go. I choose good Will Stutely, for he is as clever as an old fox."

Then Will Stutely leaped high, laughing and clapping for joy at being chosen. "Thank you, good master," he said, "and if I do not bring you news of the constables' doings, my name is not sly Will Stutely."

Then he dressed up in a friar's gown, and underneath the robe he hung a good broadsword. Soon he set forth and before long came to the highway. Twice he saw groups of the Sheriff's men, but he drew his hood closely about his face and pretended to be deep in prayer. Eventually he came to the Sign of the Blue Boar, for he knew that good Eadom would tell him all the news.

At the Blue Boar he found a band of the Sheriff's men drinking heartily. Without speaking to anyone, he sat far apart from others with his head bowed as if praying. He waited for a chance to speak to the landlord in private, but Eadom did not recognize him and left him alone.

As Stutely sat, a great house cat rubbed against his knee, raising his robe six inches or so.

Stutely pushed his robe quickly down again, but the constable saw it and also saw Lincoln green beneath the robe. The Sheriff's man thought to himself, "That is no friar, and no honest yeoman goes around dressed like a traveling priest. I do believe that this is one of Robin Hood's men." So he said aloud, "Holy Father, may I buy you a good pot of March beer to quench your thirst?"

But Stutely shook his head silently.

Then the constable said again, "Where are you going, Holy Father, on this hot summer day?"

"On a pilgrimage to Canterbury Town," Will Stutely answered, speaking gruffly to disguise his voice.

Then the constable said, for the third time, "Now tell me, Holy Father, do pilgrims to Canterbury wear good Lincoln green beneath their robes? Ha! By my faith, I think you are one of Robin Hood's own band! Stand still, or I will run you through with my sword!"

He drew his bright sword and leaped at Will Stutely, thinking to surprise him; but Stutely had his own sword out before the constable reached him. The constable struck a mighty blow, but Stutely parried the blow and swung back, catching his attacker in the head with the flat of the blade. Though the constable was dizzy with the bloody wound, he managed to get Stutely by the legs as he fell. The other men-at-arms rushed the outlaw, and after a brief struggle he was overpowered. The Sheriff's men then bound him hand and foot and prepared to take him into town along with their wounded constable.

Robin Hood stood under the great oak tree, thinking of Will Stutely and how he might be doing. Suddenly he saw two of his yeomen running down the forest path with pretty young Maken of the Blue Boar between them. Robin's heart fell, for he knew they brought bad news.

"Will Stutely has been taken," they cried.

"Did you see it happen?" Robin asked Maken.

"Indeed, I did," she gasped, panting from the run, "and I fear he is badly wounded, for one hit him very hard in the head. They have bound him and taken him to Nottingham Town. Before I left the Blue Boar I heard that he was to be hanged tomorrow."

"He shall not be hanged tomorrow," cried Robin, "or if he is, a lot of other men will also die, and many others will pay as well!"

Then he clapped his horn to his lips and blew three loud blasts. Presently his good yeomen came running, and soon a hundred and forty bold outlaws were assembled.

"Now listen!" cried Robin. "Our dear companion Will Stutely has been taken by that vile Sheriff's men. We should take bow and sword in hand to rescue him, risking life and limb for him, as he has done for us."

"Yes!" they all shouted as one.

So the next day they all left Sherwood Forest in small groups by different paths and assembled in a small woods near Nottingham Town. When they were all present, Robin said, "Now we will lie here in wait until we can get news. We must be very crafty if we are going to get our friend out of the Sheriff's clutches."

So they lay hidden until the sun stood high in the sky. The day was warm and the dusty road was mostly empty. Finally, along came an aged palmer—a religious man who had been to Jerusalem and wore a palm leaf on his clothing in remembrance. Robin called young David of Doncaster, who was wise for his years, and said, "Go, David, and speak to that palmer. See if he has news of good Stutely."

So David walked along the road. When he came up to the pilgrim, he greeted him. "Good day, Holy Father. Can you tell me when Will Stutely will be hanged on the gallows tree? I have come a long way to see such a sturdy rogue hang."

"Now, shame on you, young man," the palmer said, "for being glad when a good brave man is to hang for nothing but defending himself!" He struck his staff on the ground in anger. "It is terrible! This evening, he is to be hanged, a quarter mile from the town gate of

Nottingham where three roads meet. The Sheriff swears that it shall be a warning to all outlaws in Nottinghamshire, but I scoff at that, because Robin Hood and his men only take from the Norman nobles and fat abbots—the rich and strong. Thanks to him, every peasant family or poor widow near Sherwood has food to eat all year. In my day I was a good Saxon yeoman before I became a palmer and it breaks my heart to see a good man like Stutely die. If his master knew the situation, he might try a rescue."

"That is true," David said. "If Robin and his men are near here, I do not doubt that they will try. But farewell, holy man, and believe me: if Will Stutely dies, he will be well avenged."

He turned and strode rapidly away; but the palmer looked after him, muttering, "That is no peasant eager to see a good man die. Well, maybe Robin Hood is near enough that there will be brave deeds this day." He went on his way.

When David of Doncaster told Robin Hood what the palmer had said, Robin called the band around him.

"We must get quickly into Nottingham Town," he said. "There we will mingle with the crowd, but stay close to each other. Once they are outside the walls, get as close to the prisoner and guards as you can. Do not strike without need, because I hope to avoid bloodshed; but if you must, strike hard enough that you need not strike again. Then keep together until we return to Sherwood, and let no man leave his friends behind."

The sun was low in the western sky when a bugle note sounded from the castle wall. Then crowds filled the streets, for all knew that the famous Will Stutely was to be hanged that day. The castle gates opened wide and a great array of men-at-arms came forth with noise and clatter. The Sheriff rode at their head, in shining chain mail. In the midst of the guards was a horse-cart in which rode Will Stutely, his hands tightly bound and a halter around his neck. His face was pale with loss of blood, which had dried dark brown on his forehead. He looked through the crowd, and though he saw pity and even friendliness in some faces, he saw no one he knew. His heart sank, but he spoke up boldly.

"Give me a sword, Sir Sheriff," he said, "and despite my wound, I will fight you and all your men until I die."

"No, you rascal," the Sheriff answered, turning to glare at Will Stutely, "you will die the proper, miserable death of every thief."

"Then untie my hands and I will fight you all with only my fists. I need no weapon, just a chance to die like a man."

The Sheriff laughed aloud. "Why, are you getting scared? Say your prayers, outlaw, because

I will see you hanged today at the crossroads, where all men can watch the crows and vultures peck at you."

"Scoundrel!" cried Will Stutely, grinding his teeth at the Sheriff. "Coward! If my good master meets you, you will pay dearly for today's work. Do you not realize that your name is a joke on the lips of every brave yeoman? A low coward like you will never catch bold Robin Hood!"

"Ha!" cried the Sheriff in a rage, "Really? Am I a joke with your so-called master? Then I will make a sorrier joke of you, for I will have you cut into quarters after you hang." Then he spurred his horse forward and said no more to Stutely.

At last they came to the great town gate, through which Stutely saw the beautiful country beyond with its green hills and valleys. Far away he could see the dusky line of Sherwood's edge.

When he saw the long shadows and heard the birds singing their evening songs and the sheep bleating, his heart grew heavy; he kept his head bowed so that no one would see the tears in his eyes. Only when they were outside the town walls did he raise his head, and when he did, his heart leaped for pure joy: in the crowd was one of his companions of Sherwood. Glancing quickly around, he saw well-known faces on all sides crowding in on the men-at-arms. The blood rushed to his cheeks: there, for a moment, was Robin Hood himself! The whole band must be there—but between him and his companions was a line of armed and armored men.

"Now, stand back!" yelled the Sheriff, for the crowd pressed around on all sides. "Get back, you peasants! Stop pushing in on us!"

Then came a racket, and a huge fellow tried to push between the men-at-arms and reach the cart. Stutely saw that it was Little John.

"Stand back, you!" cried one of the men-at-arms as he was elbowed by Little John.

"Stand back yourself," Little John replied and gave the man a blow that would have flattened a bull. He then leaped onto the cart where Stutely sat.

"I suggest you leave your friends before you die, Will," he said, "or maybe I will die with you, for I could not ask for better company." Then with one sword-stroke he cut the ropes that bound his comrade, and he and Stutely jumped down from the cart.

"I know that man," cried the Sheriff. "He is a rebel! Take him! Don't let him get away!"

He spurred his horse toward Little John, rose in the stirrups, and swung with all his might, but Little John ducked underneath the horse's belly. The blow whistled harmlessly overhead.

"Excuse me, Sir Sheriff," cried Little John, standing up again. "I must borrow Your Worship's sword." He yanked the weapon out of the Sheriff's hand and handed it to his friend, saying, "Here, Stutely, the Sheriff has agreed to lend you his sword! Back to back, man, and defend yourself, for help is here!"

"Down with them!" bellowed the Sheriff in a voice like an angry bull. He spurred his horse at the two, so angry he forgot he had no weapon with which to defend himself.

"Stand back, Sheriff!" cried Little John. Even as he spoke, a bugle horn sounded shrilly and an arrow hissed within an inch of the Sheriff's head. There was a tremendous commotion of oaths, cries, groans, the clash of steel, the flash of swords, and the whistling of arrows through the air. Some cried: "Help, help!" but others, "A rescue, a rescue!"

"This is treason!" cried the Sheriff in a loud voice. "Fall back! Retreat, or we will all die!" With that he reined his horse backward, plowing carelessly through the crowd.

Robin Hood and his band might have killed half of the Sheriff's men had they wished, but they let them escape, only sending a couple of dozen arrows after them to hurry them along.

"Wait, Sir Sheriff!" shouted Will Stutely. "You will never catch bold Robin Hood if you run away from him!" But the Sheriff only bent lower and put the spurs to his horse.

Will Stutely turned to Little John, weeping for joy, and embraced him saying, "Little John!

My true friend, whom I love better than anyone in the world! I never expected to see your face today or ever again except in Heaven." Little John could not speak but wept also.

Then Robin Hood gathered his band closely together with drawn weapons, and they moved slowly toward Sherwood. Soon they were gone, leaving ten of the Sheriff's men lying wounded on the ground, some badly hurt—yet no one knew who had struck them down.

And that is how the Sheriff of Nottingham tried and failed, three times, to take Robin Hood. He realized how near he had come to dying, so he said to himself, "These men fear neither God, nor man, nor King, nor King's officers. I would sooner lose my job than my life, so I will leave them alone." He stayed in his castle for many days, too ashamed to show his face in public.

Robin Hood Turns Butcher

After the Sheriff had tried three times to capture Robin Hood, Robin said to himself, "If I get the chance, I will make our worshipful Sheriff pay handsomely for bothering me. Maybe we should have him here for a merry feast." When Robin Hood caught a rich nobleman or bishop, he brought them to the great oak tree and feasted them—after which, of course, they had to pay.

But in the meantime Robin Hood and his band kept a low profile, for Robin knew that the authorities were still angry with them. His men lived merrily in the forest, spending the days practicing archery. The woods rang with joking and laughter. They also wrestled and fought with quarterstaffs, and so grew in skill and strength.

This lasted for nearly a year, during which Robin Hood considered ways to get even with the Sheriff. Finally he grew restless, and one day he took up his stout cudgel and set out for adventure toward to the edge of Sherwood.

As he rambled along the sunlit road, he met a hearty young butcher riding a horse-cart loaded with meat, whistling merrily.

"Good morning, jolly fellow," Robin said. "You seem happy today."

"How could I not be?" the jolly butcher replied. "I am to marry the prettiest girl in all Nottinghamshire on Thursday in sweet Locksley Town."

"Locksley?" Robin said. "I know every hedge and stream there, even every fish, for I was born and raised there. Where are you taking your meat, good friend?"

"To the market at Nottingham Town, for sale," the butcher answered. "But who are you?"

"I am a yeoman. People call me Robin Hood."

"I know your name well," cried the butcher, "for your deeds are told far and wide. But Heaven forbid that you should rob me! I am an honest man and have never wronged man or woman."

"Heaven forbid, indeed!" Robin said. "I would not take a single penny from you, kind fellow, for you have a fine Saxon face and come from Locksley and are about to be married. But tell me: how much do you want for your horse and cart and all this meat?"

"All together, they are worth three pounds," the butcher replied.

Then Robin Hood reached into his purse and said: "Here are five pounds. I would like to be a butcher for the day and sell meat in Nottingham Town. Will you sell me your outfit?"

"May all the saints bless you, honest fellow!" the butcher cried joyfully, as he leaped down from his cart and took Robin's money.

Robin laughed loudly. "Many wish me well, but few call me honest. Now get back to your girl, and give her a sweet kiss from me." With that, he put on the butcher's apron, climbed into the cart and drove off toward Nottingham Town.

When he came to Nottingham, he entered the butchers' area of the market and set up his stand. Then he took his meat-cleaver and sharpening-steel in hand and clattered them together, crying: "Come, young maidens and wives, and buy your meat from me! Today I am selling three pennies' worth of meat for just one penny. I have the finest lamb and beef and mutton. Who'll buy?" he shouted, banging the tools some more.

Everyone gaped at him in amazement. Then he called out: "I have four prices. For a fat friar or priest, three pennies' worth of meat costs six pennies for I do not want their business. For businessmen I charge three pennies, for I do not care if they buy or not. For pretty wives I sell three pennies' worth for just one penny, because I like their business very much. But for a pretty maiden who likes handsome butchers, I charge only a kiss, because I like her business best of all."

Then all began to stare and wonder and crowd around, laughing, for they had never heard of such a strange pricing scheme. When they came to buy, they found that he was serious. Wives paid one penny and got three times the meat anyone else would have given them for that sum. If a widow or poor woman came, he charged her nothing. But when a merry young maiden came, and gave him a kiss, he also charged her nothing—and many came, because his eyes were as blue as June skies, and he laughed so merrily. He sold his meat so fast that no butcher that stood near him could sell anything.

The other butchers began to grumble among themselves. Some said, "This must be a thief who has stolen a butcher's outfit." Others said, "When did you ever see a thief give away money like that? This is some young fellow who has sold his father's land and plans to live merrily while the money lasts." This was the majority view, and one by one the others were convinced.

Then some of the butchers came to him to get acquainted. "Come, brother," said the leader. "Will you feast with us? Today the Sheriff has invited the Butcher's Guild to dine with him at the Guild Hall. We are butchers, so you know there will be good meat and plenty to drink—I would guess that you are fond of both."

"Now, down with anyone that would deny a butcher," said jolly Robin. "I will be glad to come feast with you, my merry lads." Having sold all his meat, he closed his stall and went with them to the great Guild Hall.

The Sheriff was already present at the Hall, along with many butchers. When Robin and his butcher comrades came in, all laughing at a merry joke of his, those near the Sheriff whispered to him, "That one is a madman, for he sold meat for a third of our price." Others said, "Surely he has just inherited a lot of money and means to enjoy it while it lasts."

Then the Sheriff called Robin to him, not recognizing him in his butcher's costume, and had him sit on his right. The Sheriff loved free-spending young men, especially if their money might find its way into his own pockets. Therefore, he paid Robin plenty of attention, laughing and talking more with him than the others.

When dinner was about to be served, the Sheriff invited Robin to say grace. Robin stood up and said, "Now Heaven bless us all, and also good meat and good wine, and may all butchers always be as honest as I am."

Everyone found this a merry joke, especially

the Sheriff, whose hopes of handsome profit rose every time Robin did or said something careless. The Sheriff slapped him on the back, saying, "You are a jolly young fellow, and I love your company."

Then Robin laughed loudly too. "Yes," he said, "I know how fond you are of jolly young men, for did you not have jolly Robin Hood at your shooting match, and gladly give him a bright golden arrow?"

The Sheriff stopped laughing, as did the guild of butchers, though a few winked slyly.

"Come, pour some wine!" cried Robin. "Let us be merry while we can, for no one lives forever. Do not look so glum, Sir Sheriff. Who knows; maybe you will catch Robin Hood yet, if you get rid of some of that extra fat from your waist and the dust from your brain. Be merry, man!"

Then the Sheriff laughed again, but without any pleasure, while the butchers said to one another, "He is the funniest fellow we have ever seen—but he may make the Sheriff angry."

"Be merry, my brothers," Robin cried, "and do not worry about money, because I am paying for this entire dinner, even if it costs two hundred pounds. None of you shall pay one penny for this feast."

"You are most generous," said the Sheriff. "You must have many horned beasts on many acres of land, to spend money so freely."

"That I do," said Robin, laughing loudly again. "My brothers and I have five hundred or more horned beasts, and we've been unable to sell any, or I would not have become a butcher. As for my land, I have never asked my manager how many acres I have."

At this the Sheriff's eyes twinkled, and he chuckled to himself. "Well, good youth," he said, "maybe I can give you a helping hand. How much do you want for your cattle?"

"Well," Robin replied, "they are worth at least five hundred pounds."

"No," answered the Sheriff slowly and thoughtfully, "I like you and would like to help you, but that is a lot more money than I have to spend. I will give you three hundred pounds for them all."

"You old miser!" Robin said. "You know good and well that so many horned cattle are a bargain at seven hundred pounds or more. Yet you, with your gray hairs and one foot in the grave, would take advantage of a wild youth."

The Sheriff scowled at Robin. "Do not look at me as though you just drank sour beer, man," Robin said. "I will take your offer, because my brothers and I need the money to have fun. But be sure that you bring the full three hundred pounds with you, because I am not sure I trust someone who drives such a hard bargain."

"I will bring the money. But what is your

name, good youth?"

"Men call me Robert of Locksley," bold Robin said.

"Then, good Robert of Locksley," the Sheriff said, "I will come this day to see your horned beasts. But first my clerk shall draw up a sales contract, because you will not get my money unless I get your animals."

Robin Hood laughed again and shook the Sheriff's hand. "So be it. Surely my brothers will be grateful." So the bargain was arranged, but many of the butchers thought ill of the Sheriff for swindling an innocent young man in this way.

Later that afternoon the Sheriff mounted his horse and joined Robin Hood, who stood outside waiting for him, having sold his horse and cart to a trader. They set forth, Robin trotting beside the Sheriff's horse. The two men laughed and joked like old friends. But the Sheriff said to himself, "Laugh now, young fool, for your little joke about Robin Hood will cost you about four hundred pounds." He was sure that he would make at least that much profit from the cattle deal.

They journeyed on until they came close to Sherwood Forest. Here the Sheriff looked all around him and grew quiet. "Now," said he, "may Heaven protect us from a bandit named Robin Hood."

Robin laughed aloud. "Relax," he said, "for I know Robin Hood well. You are as safe from him today as you are from me."

At this the Sheriff looked sideways at Robin, saying to himself, "You seem too familiar with this outlaw, young man. I wish I were far from Sherwood Forest."

But they traveled deeper into the forest, and the deeper they went, the quieter the Sheriff grew. At last they came to a sudden bend in the road, and a herd of deer came running across the path. Robin Hood pointed and said, "These are my horned beasts, good Master Sheriff. How do you like them?"

At this the Sheriff reined up quickly. "I want out of this forest. Those are the King's deer, not yours to sell. You go your way, good friend, and let me go mine."

But Robin only laughed and caught the Sheriff's bridle rein. "Wait!" he cried. "Stay and meet my brothers." He put his horn to his mouth and blew three times. Soon a hundred strong yeomen came up the path with Little John in the lead.

"What do you want, good master?" asked Little John.

"Are you blind?" scolded Robin. "Can you not see that I have brought an important guest to feast with us? Shame on you! Do you not recognize our good Sheriff of Nottingham? Take his bridle, Little John, for he is our guest of honor today."

Then all removed their hats humbly, seeming quite sincere, while Little John took the bridle rein and led the Sheriff's horse deeper into the forest. Robin Hood walked beside the Sheriff, hat in hand. The Sheriff was silent and bewildered at first, but as they went deeper into Sherwood, his heart sank, for he thought, "Surely I will be robbed or even killed, for I have tried hard to kill them more than once." But they all seemed polite and humble, and they made no threat of any sort.

At last they came to the great noble oak with the mossy seat in the heart of Sherwood, and Robin sat down, giving the Sheriff the seat of honor on his right. "Now, get busy, my merry men," he said, "and bring our best meat and wine. His Worship the Sheriff has feasted me today in Nottingham Guild Hall, and I must return the favor."

Nothing had been said of the Sheriff's money, so he began to take heart. "Maybe," he said to himself, "Robin Hood has forgotten all about it."

While chicken and deer and meat pies cooked over open fires, filling the air with wonderful smells, Robin entertained the Sheriff. First, several pairs of men battled with quarterstaffs, fighting so skillfully that the Sheriff—who loved all such yeomanlike sports—forgot where he was. "Well struck, you with the black beard!" he cried, not realizing that he was cheering for the tinker who had tried to serve his warrant on Robin Hood.

Then several yeomen came forward and spread cloths on the green grass and set out a royal feast. Others opened kegs of ale and barrels of wine and filled drinking-horns. Everyone sat down and feasted and drank merrily together until the sun was low and the half-moon glimmered through the leaves of the trees overhead.

Finally the Sheriff stood up and said, "I thank you, good yeomen, for the merry entertainment you have given me. Your courtesy to me shows much respect for our glorious King and his deputy in Nottinghamshire. But the shadows are long, and I must be going, or I will get lost in the dark."

"If you must go, worshipful sir, you must," Robin said. "But you have forgotten something."

"No, I have not," the Sheriff replied; yet his heart sank.

"Oh, but you have," Robin said. "We keep a merry inn here in the green wood, but every guest must of course pay his bill."

Then the Sheriff laughed hollowly. "Well, jolly boys, even if you had not asked me, I would have given you twenty pounds for this evening's fine entertainment."

"No," Robin said seriously, "we would not insult Your Worship with such a tiny bill. By my faith, Sir Sheriff, I would be ashamed to show my face if I charged the King's deputy a penny less than three hundred pounds. Right, my merry men?"

"Yes!" they cried loudly.

"Three hundred!" roared the Sheriff. "What makes you think that your beggarly feast was worth three pounds, let alone three hundred?"

"Be careful what you say, Your Worship," Robin said gravely. "I like you, as you know, but some here are not so fond of you. If you will look over there, you will see Will Stutely, who has less than pleasant memories of you. Two others you would not recognize, but they were wounded by your men near Nottingham Town, one badly. Take my advice, good Sheriff: pay your bill without any more complaining, or you may regret it."

As he spoke the Sheriff's red cheeks grew pale, and he looked downward. Slowly he drew out his fat purse and threw it down in front of him.

"Now take the purse, Little John," instructed Robin Hood, "and count the money. We would not doubt our Sheriff, of course, but if he found that he had underpaid us, he would be embarrassed."

Then Little John counted the money; it was indeed three hundred pounds in silver and gold. For the Sheriff, each clink of a coin was like a drop of blood from his veins. When he saw it all counted out in a heap, he turned away and silently mounted his horse.

"You are the most distinguished and generous guest we have ever had," Robin said, "and it is getting late. I will send one of my young men to guide you out of the forest."

"I can find my own way," the Sheriff said hastily.

"Then I will guide you myself," said Robin. Taking the Sheriff's horse by the bridle, he led him onto the main forest path. Before he let him go, he said, "Farewell, good Sheriff, and the next time you think to take advantage of some young fool, remember your feast in Sherwood

Forest. Once more, farewell!" Robin gave the horse a mild slap on the rear, and off went horse and Sheriff through the forest.

And so the Sheriff bitterly regretted the day he first meddled with Robin Hood, for he became the subject of many jokes and ballads. Everyone in the country soon knew how he had come to Sherwood intending to fleece a carefree young man and was instead fleeced himself—as so often happens to greedy men.

Little John Goes
to Nottingham Fair

$\mathcal{S}$ince the Sheriff's feast in Sherwood, spring and summer had given way to mellow October. Everyone was busy with the harvest. Most people had forgotten about the trick Robin had played on the Sheriff—but the Sheriff had not. The mere mention of Robin Hood's name sent him into a rage.

Every five years in October, Nottingham Town held a great fair, bringing people from near and far. Archery was always the most popular event, for Nottinghamshire yeomen were the best archers in merry England. This year, the Sheriff hesitated to announce the fair for fear that Robin Hood and his band might attend. He was tempted not to hold the fair, but he realized that people would guess why and laugh at his fear of Robin Hood. Then he had an idea. He would hold the fair, but the archery prize would be something that Robin's men would consider boring. Normally it was a half dozen pounds, or a keg of ale; this year, he announced that the best archer would win two fat steers.

When Robin Hood heard of this, he grumbled, "Only cowherds and butchers would shoot for a prize like this. I would have loved to compete again at merry Nottingham Town but not to win a couple of cattle."

Then Little John spoke up: "But listen, good master. Today Will Stutely, young David of Doncaster, and I were at the Sign of the Blue Boar, and we heard that the Sheriff chose this prize just so that we will stay away. If we do, he wins. Therefore, if you will allow me, I will go and shoot even for this poor prize."

"I don't know, Little John," Robin said. "You are a brave man but not so cunning as Stutely. I think it too dangerous. But if you insist on going, disguise yourself well so you won't be recognized."

"So be it, good master," Little John said. "A good suit of scarlet will be disguise enough. I will keep my hood up, to hide my brown hair and beard, and no one will recognize me."

"If you must, go ahead," Robin Hood said. "But be careful, Little John. I cannot afford to lose my right-hand man."

So Little John dressed in scarlet, slung his stout bow and arrows, and started off to the fair. He found Nottingham a merry sight, for the green in front of the town gate was dotted with booths and tents decorated with flowers and streamers. There was music and dancing, and sweet cakes and barley sugar, and ale and beer. Minstrels sang old ballads and played the harp. Wrestlers competed in a sawdust ring, but the greatest attraction was a raised platform where men battled with quarterstaffs. Many gaped at Little John, who was a head taller than any other man and six inches broader in the shoulders. The young women in particular thought him quite pleasant to look at.

First he went to the booth where stout ale was sold and stood up on a bench, calling everyone to come drink with him. "Hey, good lads!" he cried, "who will drink with a brave yeoman? Come, good yeomen, for I am buying!" All crowded around, laughing, while the brown ale flowed. They called Little John a great fellow, for everyone likes free entertainment.

Then he strolled to the platform where cudgel play was held, for he loved a game at quarterstaff as he loved meat and drink.

In the ring was the famous Eric of Lincoln, who had beaten every man who challenged him. When Little John reached the ring, bold Eric was walking up and down the platform, swinging his staff and shouting, "Now, who will come and fight against a good Lincolnshire yeoman? Step up! Or are the girls' eyes here too dull to inspire you to brave deeds? Is the blood of Nottingham yeomen sluggish and cold? Lincoln against Nottingham, I say! So far today, I have not faced a single man whom we of Lincolnshire would call a cudgel player."

At this, one would nudge another with his elbow, saying, "Go, Ned!" or "Go, Thomas!" but no one was eager for a cracked skull.

When Eric saw Little John standing among the others, head and shoulders above them all, he called to him loudly, "Hey, you long-legged lout in scarlet! Your shoulders are as thick as your head. Maybe your girl is not pretty enough to make you eager for manly sports? Honestly, I believe that Nottingham men have no courage at all! Come on, you big oaf, will you not defend the honor of Nottingham?"

"I would," Little John said, "if I had my own good staff here. I would love to crack such a loud-mouthed skull, for you need a good beating." Little John was slow to anger, but once it started, it was like a big rock rolling down a hill. When he finished speaking, he was infuriated.

Then Eric of Lincoln laughed aloud. "Not bad for someone who is afraid to meet me fairly, man to man," he said. "You have a big mouth yourself. If you step onto these boards, I will rattle your bragging tongue between your teeth."

Little John then addressed the crowd: "Will anyone here lend me a good staff so that I can give this braggart what he wants?" Ten or so men offered staves, and Little John took the heaviest one. "This is only a little straw, but it will have to do," he said, climbing into the ring. They stood and glared at each other until the referee cried, "Play!" The combatants stepped forward, and so began the grandest game of quarterstaff ever seen in Nottingham Town.

At first Eric of Lincoln stepped forward arrogantly, winking at the crowd in expectation of a speedy win, but it was not so easy. He struck with great skill and speed, but he had met his match in Little John. The big fellow turned away three straight blows, then answered with a rap to Eric's head that made his ears ring. The Lincoln man stepped back to gather his wits, and the crowd shouted for joy that Nottingham had won the first bout of the game.

Then presently the referee cried, "Play!" and they came together again; but now Eric's overconfidence had given way to wariness. Both played carefully—especially Eric, who was not eager for another knock on the head. Neither could penetrate the other's guard. After a time they stepped back, ending the second bout.

Then for the third time they came together, and at first Eric was as crafty as before. But soon he became frustrated and lost control. He began to rain blows so fast they rattled like hail on a solid roof, but none got past Little John's guard. Seeing an opening, Little John smacked Eric above the ear. Then before the Lincoln man could recover, Little John brought the staff back around from the other side and hit Eric of Lincoln so hard in the head that he fell unconscious and lay as though he would never rise again.

Then the people shouted so loud that folk came running to see what had happened. Little John leaped down from the stand and gave the staff back. This ended the famous bout between Little John and Eric of Lincoln.

It was time for the archery competition, so the people flocked to the targets. The Sheriff sat near the targets, surrounded by the rich and noble. When the archers were at their places, the herald announced the rules: each man would shoot three times, and the best shot would win two fat steers. Among the twenty or so competitors were some of the best archers in Lincolnshire and Nottinghamshire. "Who is that stranger in scarlet?" asked some, and others answered, "The man who just gave Eric of Lincoln a good thwack in the head." The news spread rapidly, reaching even the Sheriff's ears.

Each man stepped forward and shot in turn. Everyone shot well, but Little John was the best of all, for he struck the bull's-eye with all three shots—once within half an inch of the center. "Hurray for the tall archer!" shouted the crowd, and some shouted, "Hey for Reynold Greenleaf!" for this was the name that Little John had chosen for the day.

Then the Sheriff stepped down from the raised seat and came to where the archers stood, while all removed their caps in respect. He looked closely at Little John but did not recognize him. But after a moment he said, "You know, good fellow, there is something familiar about you."

"Maybe," Little John replied, "for I have often seen Your Worship." He met the Sheriff's eyes steadily, so as not to look suspicious.

"You are a brave yeoman," the Sheriff said, "and I hear that you truly upheld the skill of Nottinghamshire against that of Lincoln today. What is your name, good fellow?"

"Men call me Reynold Greenleaf, Your Worship," Little John replied.

"Reynold Greenleaf," the Sheriff said, "you are the finest archer I have ever seen, except for that cowardly rascal Robin Hood. Will you join my service, good fellow? You will have three suits of clothes each year, good food, all the ale you can drink, and twenty-five pounds every September."

"Then, as a free man, I will gladly join your household," Little John said, for he thought he might find merry adventure working for the Sheriff.

"You have won the fat steers," said the Sheriff, "and I will throw in a barrel of good March beer to celebrate your recruitment; for I think you shoot as well as Robin Hood himself."

"Then," Little John said, "to celebrate my new job, I will give the fat steers and brown ale to all these good people for a merry feast." A great shout arose, many throwing their caps high in appreciation of the gift.

Then some built great fires and roasted the steers, and others opened the ale, and everyone had a fine feast. When they had eaten and drunk all they could, they danced around the fires to the sound of bagpipes and harps. But long before the feast was over, the Sheriff and his new servant Reynold Greenleaf were in Nottingham Castle.

Chapter 7

How Little John Lived at the Sheriff's

Little John found the Sheriff's service an easy life. As the Sheriff's right-hand man, he sat next to the Sheriff at meals, with rich food and fine wine. He spent his time hunting with the Sheriff and often slept late. He grew as fat as an ox. One day, though, things went wrong.

That morning the Sheriff set out with a hunting party. He looked all about him for his good man, Reynold Greenleaf, but in vain. This annoyed him for he wished to show off Little John's skill to his noble friends.

Little John lay snoring until almost noon. Finally he opened his eyes and looked around. It was a beautiful spring morning, the air sweet with the scents of flowers.

Just then he heard, faint and far away, a distant bugle note sounding thin and clear. The sound was small, but, like a little pebble dropped into a glassy pool, it shattered his peace of mind. His spirit seemed to awaken, and he remembered the merry greenwood life—how the birds were singing in Sherwood, and how his loved companions and friends were feasting and making merry. What might they be saying about him? That he was no longer their friend, perhaps? At first he had joined the Sheriff's service as a joke; but the hearthstone was warm during the winter, and the food was good, and he had put off returning to Sherwood for six long months. But now he thought of his good master and of his best friend Will Stutely and of young David of Doncaster, whom he had trained so well in manly sports. His heart filled with a great and bitter longing for them all, and his eyes filled with tears. He said aloud, "I am getting fat, and my manliness flees while I loaf here. I will go back to my dear friends, and I will never again leave them as long as I live." So saying, he leaped from bed, for he hated his sluggishness now.

When he came downstairs he saw the steward standing near the pantry door—a great, fat man with a huge key ring at his belt. Little John said, "Hello, Master Steward. I have eaten nothing all morning. Get me breakfast."

The steward looked grimly at him and rattled the keys, for he was jealous of Little John's favor with the Sheriff. "So, Master Reynold Greenleaf, you are hungry, are you?" he said. "Well, young man, if you live long enough, you will learn that sluggards who sleep late go without breakfast."

"You great ball of fat!" cried Little John, "I am not asking you for a fool's wisdom but for bread and meat. Who are you to deny me breakfast? You had better tell me where my breakfast is unless you want broken bones."

"Your breakfast, Master Sluggard, is in the pantry," answered the steward.

"Then bring it!" cried Little John angrily.

"Go get it yourself," replied the steward. "Am I your slave, to fetch and carry for you?"

"I say, go and bring it to me!"

"I say, fetch it yourself!"

"All right, I will!" Little John said furiously. He tried the pantry door but found it locked. The steward laughed and rattled his keys. Then Little John's temper boiled over, and he brought back his fist and put it clear through the pantry door. It shattered, leaving so large an opening he could easily walk through.

The steward went mad with rage. As Little John bent to look inside the pantry, the steward seized him from behind by the nape of the neck and began to pound him over the head with his heavy key ring. Ears ringing, Little John turned and punched the steward in the head so hard he fell unconscious to the ground. "There," Little John said, "remember that next time you try to get between a hungry man and a good breakfast."

He crept into the pantry and looked about, finding a great meat pie and two roast chickens, plus a platter of eggs and flasks of wine: a sweet sight to a hungry man. He took them down from the shelves and sat down to eat.

The cook, in the kitchen across the courtyard, heard the commotion. He came running across the court and up the stairway to the steward's pantry, carrying a roast still on its cooking-spindle. Meanwhile, the steward had come to and risen to his feet. The cook arrived to find the steward glaring through the broken pantry door at Little John.

When the steward saw the cook, he came to him, put one arm over his shoulder, and said, "My good man! See what that worthless Reynold Greenleaf has done? He broke into our master's goods and hit me so hard in the ear I thought I was dead. Good cook, I like you very much. I think you should have a flask of our master's best wine each day, considering your long and faithful service to him. I also have half a pound for you. But can you stand to watch an upstart like this Reynold Greenleaf acting so important?"

"Yes, I see," the cook said boldly, for he liked the steward's promise of wine and money. "Go to your room, and I will drag this rascal out by the ears." He laid aside the roast and drew his sword; the steward left in a hurry, for he hated the sight of drawn steel.

Then the cook, a tall strong fellow, walked straight to the broken pantry door, through which he saw Little John tucking a napkin beneath his chin and preparing to eat.

"What is this, Reynold Greenleaf?" the cook said. "You are no better than a thief. Come out here, man, or I will carve you up like a pig."

"Good cook, be careful, or I will come out and you will be sorry. Most of the time I am as peaceful as a lamb, but if anyone gets between me and my meat, I become a raging lion."

"Lion or no lion," the bold cook replied, "come out, or you are a coward as well as a thief."

"Ha!" cried Little John. "No one calls me a coward. Get ready, good cook, for the roaring lion is coming out."

Then he drew his own sword and came out of the pantry, and they prepared to fight. Suddenly Little John lowered his weapon. "Wait, good cook!" he said. "It is silly for us to fight with so much good food so nearby. Let us eat first, then fight. What do you say?"

At this speech the cook scratched his head and thought, for he loved good feasting. At last he sighed and said to Little John, "I like your plan. Let us indeed feast, for it may be the last meal for one of us."

Each thrust his sword back into the scabbard and entered the pantry. After they had seated themselves, Little John drew his dagger and cut a piece of the meat pie. The cook did the same, and they began to stuff themselves.

After some time, the cook sighed in satisfaction and wiped his hands on the napkin, for he was full. Little John had also had enough, for he pushed the pie aside. Then he took the flask of wine, and said, "Now, good fellow, I swear that you are the best companion at eating I have ever had. To your health!" With that he put the flask to his lips and tipped it high in the air, drinking deeply, then passed it to the cook. He in turn said, "And to your own, good fellow!" and drank as deeply.

"Good cook," Little John said, "your voice is that of a man who sings a lovely ballad."

"I do, now and then," said the cook, "yet I do not sing alone."

"Of course not," said Little John, "that would be rude of me. Sing away, and afterward I will try and sing one to match it."

The cook took another deep drink, cleared his throat, and sang the sweet tune he had promised. It was the lament of a woman whose man had left her for another in the springtime; she wept beneath a fair willow tree until a young man came to console her; and so it had a joyous ending.

"By my faith," cried Little John, "a fine song!"

"Glad you like it, my lad," the cook said. "Now you sing one, for no man should make merry alone or sing and then not listen to the other fellow."

"Then I will sing of a good knight of Arthur's court and how he cured his broken heart," Little John said. "So listen while I sing."

He gave the cook a song called "The Good Knight and His Love," which told of a good knight who loved a woman who would not have him. He went far away and wept for some time, even wasted away for lack of appetite, but found that self-denial gave him no comfort whatsoever. So he went home to his friends and good wine and merry company, and only then did his heart heal.

"In truth," cried the cook, as he rattled the flask on the table, "I like that song very much and especially its moral, which is good advice to anyone."

"Ah, you are a man of taste and perception," Little John said, "and I love you as a brother."

"And likewise," the cook said. "But it is getting late. I have to cook before our master comes home, so let us go and settle this fight."

"Yes, and quickly," Little John replied, "for I have never been less willing to fight than to eat and drink. Come into the passageway, where there is room to swing a sword, and I will do my part."

Then they both stepped forth into the broad passage that led to the steward's pantry. Here each man drew his sword and began trying to carve the other limb from limb. Their swords clashed noisily, throwing showers of sparks. They fought up and down the hall for an hour and more, but both were so skilled that neither was able to score a hit. From time to time they would stop to catch their wind, then go at it more fiercely than ever. At last Little John cried, "Hold on a moment, good cook!" and each leaned upon his sword, panting.

"I swear," Little John said, "you are the very best swordsman I have ever seen. I thought for sure I would have killed you by now."

"And I thought the same," the cook said, "but I was wrong."

"I wonder," Little John said, "why are we fighting?"

"I do not know," the cook said. "I have no liking for that weakling steward, but I thought that we had agreed to fight and so we must."

"Well," Little John replied, "it seems to me that instead of trying to cut one another's throats, we should be good friends. Jolly cook, will you go with me to Sherwood Forest and join Robin Hood's band? You will live a merry life there, with a hundred and forty good companions including myself. You shall have three suits of Lincoln green and twenty-five pounds in pay each year."

"You are a man after my own heart!" cried the cook. "Yes, that is the life for me. I will gladly go with you. Give me your hand, good fellow; what is your name?"

"Men call me Little John."

"What? Robin Hood's own famous right-hand man? I have heard much about you but never imagined I would meet you!" The cook gaped at his companion in amazement.

"I am Little John, indeed, and today I will bring Robin Hood a brave fellow to join his merry band. But before we go, good friend, I think that the Sheriff would like to give Robin Hood a present. Perhaps we should carry back some of his silver, as a gift from his worship."

"A good idea," the cook said. And so they hunted about and took as many silver plates and wine goblets as they could find. When they had a full bag, they headed for Sherwood Forest.

Plunging into the woods, they came at last to the great oak tree, where they found Robin Hood and sixty of his merry men relaxing on the fresh green grass. When Robin and his men saw who it was, they leaped to their feet. "Welcome back, Little John!" cried Robin Hood. "We have not heard from you in a long time, though we knew that you had joined the Sheriff's service. How have you been doing?"

"I have lived merrily at the Lord Sheriff's," answered Little John. "I have just come from there. See, good master! I have brought you his cook and even his silver plates and goblets." Then he told of everything that had happened since he had left for Nottingham Fair. Everyone laughed loudly—except Robin Hood, who looked grave.

"No, Little John," he said. "You are a brave and trusty man, and I am glad you have come back and brought us such a fine companion as the cook, whom we all welcome to Sherwood. But I do not like that you have swiped the Sheriff's silver like some low thief. We have punished the Sheriff and charged him three hundred pounds when he sought to cheat someone; but he does not deserve to have his silver stolen."

Little John was annoyed but tried to pass it off with a joke. "Well, good master," he said, "if you do not believe that the Sheriff gave us the plates, I will fetch him so he can tell you himself." He leaped to his feet and was gone before Robin could call him back.

Little John ran for five miles until he came to where the Sheriff of Nottingham and a merry company were hunting near the forest. Little John approached the Sheriff and removed his cap and knelt. "God save you, good master," he said.

"Why, Reynold Greenleaf!" cried the Sheriff, "where did you come from?"

"I have been in the forest," answered Little John, speaking as though amazed, "and there I saw the strangest sight! There was a young deer, green from head to toe, and around him were sixty other deer—also green. But I dared not shoot one, good master, for fear they might kill me."

"Green deer! Reynold Greenleaf," the

Sheriff said, "have you gone mad or had too much to drink?"

"I am not mad, nor have I been drinking," Little John said. "Come with me and I will show you. But you must come alone, good master, in order not to scare the deer away."

So the party all rode forward, and Little John led them into the forest.

"Now, good master," he said at last, "we are near the spot."

Then the Sheriff dismounted and told his party to wait. Little John led him forward through dense forest until suddenly they came to a great open space, at the end of which Robin Hood sat in the shade of the great oak tree with his merry men all about him. "See, good Master Sheriff," Little John said, "there are the green deer I told you about."

At this the Sheriff turned to Little John and said bitterly, "Long ago I thought I remembered your face, but now I know you. A plague on you, Little John, for you have betrayed me today."

Robin Hood came up to them. "Welcome, Master Sheriff," he said. "Have you come today to feast with me again?"

"Heaven forbid!" the Sheriff said earnestly. "I am not hungry."

"Nevertheless," Robin said, "you might be thirsty. I am sure you will have some wine with me. Too bad you will not feast with me; you could have your food done just the way you like it—for there stands your cook."

Then he led the Sheriff to the seat beneath the oak tree. "Hey, lads," Robin cried, "fill our good friend the Sheriff a full cup of wine for he is faint and weary."

One of the band brought the Sheriff a goblet of wine, bowing low as he handed it to him. But the Sheriff could not touch the wine, for he saw it served in one of his own silver goblets on one of his own silver plates.

"Do you not care for our new silver dishes?" Robin said. "We have gotten a bag of them this very day." And he held up the bag that Little John and the cook had brought with them.

Then the Sheriff felt bitter but dared not say anything, only gazing upon the ground.

Robin looked closely at him for a time before he spoke again. Then he said, "Master Sheriff, the last time you came to Sherwood Forest, you came to cheat a poor spendthrift, and you were cheated yourself. This time you came in peace, nor do I know of anyone you have harmed. I take money from fat priests and lordly squires to help those from whose work they profit, but I have never heard of you wronging your tenants. Therefore, take back your silver, nor will I take from you even a penny today. Come with me, and I will lead you back to your people again."

Then, slinging the bag on his shoulder, he turned away. The Sheriff followed him, too stunned to speak. They went forward until they came within a couple of hundred yards of where the Sheriff's companions waited. Robin Hood gave the sack of silver back to the Sheriff. "Take what is yours," he said, "and with it, good Sheriff, take some advice. Before you hire servants, investigate them better." With that Robin walked away, leaving the bewildered Sheriff standing there holding the sack.

The company awaiting the Sheriff were all amazed to see him come out of the forest bearing a heavy sack on his shoulders. They asked for an explanation, but he would not answer. Without a word he loaded the bag onto his horse, mounted, and rode away as if in a dream, lost in his own thoughts.

Little John and
the Tanner of Blyth

One fine day not long after Little John quit working for the Sheriff, Robin Hood and ten of his men were relaxing under the great oak tree. With most of the band out on missions and errands, they passed the time in storytelling and joking.

Suddenly Robin Hood slapped his knee.

"I almost forgot!" he said. "It is nearly Midsummer Day, and we have run out of Lincoln green cloth. That is no good. Little John, stir up your lazy bones and go to our friend, the cloth dealer Hugh Longshanks of Ancaster. Order four hundred yards of Lincoln green cloth from him; have him send them as soon as he can. Maybe the journey will work off some of the fat you picked up from lazing around at our dear Sheriff's."

"Well," muttered Little John—for he was getting tired of being made fun of—"maybe I have more flesh than before. But I bet that I could still hold my place on a narrow bridge against any yeoman in Sherwood—or Nottinghamshire for that matter—even if he had no more fat on him than you, good master."

A great shout of laughter went up, and all looked at Robin Hood, for each man knew the story.

"No, thanks," Robin Hood said, laughing loudest. "I do not care for a taste of your staff, Little John. I must admit that some of my men handle a staff better than I, though no man in all Nottinghamshire can match me at archery. Even so, a journey to Ancaster will do you no harm. Therefore, do as I say; go this very evening. Since you have lived at the Sheriff's, many people might recognize you, so you are less likely to get in trouble traveling in the twilight and dark. Wait here while I bring the money for you to pay good Hugh. I think we are his best customers." So saying, Robin headed away into the forest.

Nearby was a great rock into which a chamber had been cut. It had a massive oak door eight inches thick, studded with spikes and fastened with a great padlock. This was the band's treasure house. Robin unlocked the door and took out a bag of gold coins. This he brought back to where the men waited. Little John put the bag into his tunic, took a stout quarterstaff in his hand, and set forth.

He strode whistling along the leafy forest path until he came to where the path branched. One fork led toward Ancaster; the other, as Little John well knew, led to the merry Blue Boar Inn.

Little John halted in the middle of the path and stopped whistling to think. Two voices began to speak in his head. One said, "There lies the road to the Blue Boar Inn, a pot of brown October ale, and a merry evening." The other voice said, "There lies a long walk to Ancaster." The first of these two voices was the louder, for Little John had grown used to good living at the Sheriff's. He looked up into the blue sky and saw bright clouds sailing across. He said to himself, "It might rain this evening, so I'll just stop at the Blue Boar until it passes, for surely my good master would not want me drenched." Then he strode off down the path toward the Blue Boar.

Four merry fellows were at the Blue Boar Inn: a butcher, a beggar, and two barefoot friars. Little John could hear them singing as he walked through the mellow twilight. When he arrived, they were glad to welcome such a bold yeoman. Fresh pots of ale were brought, and they all joked and sang and told tales as the hours slipped away. No one thought of the time until it was so late that Little John decided to stay over at the inn and leave in the morning.

He rose at dawn the next day, took his quarterstaff in his hand and set out once more, as if to make up for lost time.

In the good town of Blyth there lived a tanner named Arthur of Bland. He was famous for his great strength, as demonstrated in many tough contests at wrestling and the quarterstaff. For five years he had held the mid-country champion belt for wrestling, until the great Adam of Lincoln threw him in the ring and broke one of his ribs; but at quarterstaff he had never yet met his match. He was also a fine shot with the longbow and loved a sly trip to the forest when the moon was full and deer were about. The King's rangers kept a careful eye on him.

Arthur had been to Nottingham Town to sell some tanned cowhides the day before Little John left Sherwood. At dawn the next day, not long before Little John left the inn, Arthur started home for Blyth. His way led past the edge of Sherwood, where the birds were welcoming the lovely day with a great chorus of song. His stout quarterstaff was slung across his shoulders, and he wore a stiff cap of doubled, boiled cowhide that was tough enough to turn even a broadsword—it was almost as good as a helmet.

As he came to the part of the road that cut through a corner of Sherwood, Arthur said to himself: "This is the time when the deer come down from the deep forest toward the open meadows. Maybe I will see some of them this early in the morning." He loved to watch them, even when he could not shoot one. So the tanner left the path, and with the stealth of a hunter, began to sneak through the woods to see if he could catch a glimpse of the herd.

Meanwhile Little John stepped merrily along, thinking only of the beauty of the morning. As luck would have it, he passed near the spot where Arthur of Bland was peeping through the leaves. Hearing a rustling of the branches, Little John stopped and soon spotted the brown cowhide cap of the tanner moving among the bushes.

"I wonder," Little John said to himself, "what this sneak is up to. I bet he is a thief, come after our own and the good King's deer. I had better look into this." He left the road and began spying on Arthur.

For a long time they stalked, Little John after the tanner and the tanner after the deer. At last Little John stepped on a twig with a crisp snap! Hearing the noise, the tanner turned quickly and spotted him. Little John put a bold face on the matter.

"Hey!" he said. "What sort of mischief are you up to, sneaking around in Sherwood? Who are you, anyway? You have an evil look about you, and I think you are a thief, come to steal our good King's deer."

"No," Arthur said boldly, for though taken by surprise, he was not a easily intimidated. "You lie. I am no thief but an honest craftsman. As for my face, it is what it is; and, for that matter, your own is not so handsome either."

"Ha!" bellowed Little John. "You dare talk back to me? I have a good mind to crack your skull for you. I will have you know that I am, in a way, one of the King's foresters." Then he added to himself, "Well, sort of."

"I do not care who you are," answered the bold tanner. "It will take a lot more men than you to make Arthur of Bland ask for mercy."

"Really?" cried Little John in a rage. "Now, you loudmouth, your tongue has led you into trouble! I will give you such a beating as you have never had in your whole life. Unsling that staff, you braggart, and prepare to fight!"

"A plague on you!" cried the tanner, for he, too, had talked himself into a fury. "Big words never killed even a mouse. Who are you, to speak of cracking the head of Arthur of Bland? If I do not tan your hide today, split my staff into pieces and call me a coward! Get ready!"

Each gripped his staff in the middle, and, with angry looks, they came slowly together.

In the meantime, word had reached Robin Hood that Little John had spent the evening and night at the Blue Boar instead of going straight to Ancaster. Annoyed, he set forth at dawn to find Little John and give him a piece of his mind for delaying. He was putting together the words he would use to scold Little John when suddenly he heard loud and angry voices of men making threats. Robin Hood stopped and listened. "That is Little John's voice, and in anger," he said to himself. "I do not recognize the other. Heaven forbid that my trusty Little John should have fallen into the hands of the King's rangers. I must see about this." All Robin's anger was gone at the thought of his right-hand man in mortal danger. He sneaked rapidly through the bushes toward the voices.

Soon he came to where the two men were closing to fight. "Ha!" Robin said to himself, "this will be good sport. I would give a pound for that bold fellow to give Little John a good thumping for being disobedient. There is not much chance of that though, I fear." With that, Robin Hood stretched out on the ground to watch the fight in comfort.

The two sturdy yeomen circled like two dogs preparing to fight, each looking for an opening to get in the first blow. At last Little John struck like a flash, and—rap!—the tanner parried the blow, then struck back at Little John, who also turned the blow; and so the mighty battle began.

Up and down and back and forth they fought, the blows falling so thick and fast that it sounded like ten men fighting. This went on for half an hour, until the ground was all plowed up and they were winded—especially Little John, being out of shape.

All this time Robin Hood lay hidden, enjoying the fine bout. "I never thought to see Little John so evenly matched in all my life," he said to himself. "Before he went to the Sheriff's, though, I bet he would have won by now."

At last Little John saw his chance. Throwing all his remaining energy into a blow that might have felled an ox, he struck at the tanner's head. And now the tanner's cowhide cap served him well, for without it his skull would have been smashed. As it was, the blow merely sent him staggering across the clearing. Had Little John not been so exhausted, it would have gone badly for Arthur, but the tanner had time to recover. He swung back, and this time he got past Little John's guard and dealt him a mighty blow in the chest. Robin Hood's right-hand man sprawled on the churned grass, his cudgel flying from his hands. Arthur raised his staff and gave him another blow in the ribs.

"Hold on!" roared Little John. "Do you hit a man when he is down?"

"With pleasure, if he is a braggart!" the tanner said, giving him another thwack with his staff.

"Stop!" roared Little John. "Help! I give up! I surrender, good fellow!"

"Have you had enough?" asked the tanner grimly, holding his staff high.

"Yes, more than enough."

"And you admit that I am the better man?"

"Yes, truly, and a plague on you!" said Little John, the first aloud and the last to his beard.

"Then you can go; and thank your patron saint that I am a merciful man," the tanner said.

"A plague on your kind of mercy!" Little John said, sitting up and feeling his ribs where the tanner had cudgeled him. "My ribs feel as though every one of them were broken. I tell you, good fellow, I did not think any man in all Nottinghamshire could do this to me."

"Nor did I!" cried Robin Hood, bursting out of the thicket and laughing till the tears ran down his cheeks. "Oh, man!" he said between gales of laughter, "you went over like a bottle knocked off a wall. I saw it all, and I never thought to see you surrender like that, hand and foot, to any man in all merry England. I was planning to give you a piece of my mind for not doing as I said, but you have been paid in full for it, with a handsome tip!" Robin collapsed into more laughter. "You stood there panting, and he got you with a full swing and knocked you flat!"

All the while Little John sat on the ground, looking as though he had gotten sour beer.

"What is your name, good fellow?" Robin asked, turning to the tanner.

"Men call me Arthur of Bland," the tanner said boldly, "and what is yours?"

"Arthur of Bland!" said Robin. "I have heard of you; you knocked out a friend of mine at the Ely fair last October. People there call him Jack of Nottingham; we call him Will Scathelock. As for this poor fellow you have beaten up, he is reckoned the best hand at quarterstaff in all merry England, and his name is Little John. Mine is Robin Hood."

"What?" cried the tanner. "The great Robin Hood! And is this the famous Little John? If I had known, I would never dared lift a hand against you. Let me help you up, good Master Little John, and brush the dust from your coat."

"No, thank you," Little John said testily, getting gingerly to his feet. "I can help myself, good fellow. And let me tell you, had it not been for that cursed cowskin cap of yours, you would have had a bad day."

At this Robin laughed again, then turned to

the tanner and said, "Will you join my band, good Arthur? I swear, you are one of the boldest men I have ever seen."

"Will I?" cried the tanner joyfully. "Indeed I will! Hurray for a merry life!" cried he, leaping into the air and snapping his fingers. "Away with tanning bark and filthy vats and foul cowhides! I will follow you to the ends of the earth, good master, and every herd of deer in Sherwood shall know the twang of my bowstring."

"As for you, Little John," Robin said, turning to him and laughing, "you will start once more for Ancaster, and this time we will go part way with you, for I do not want you taking any more detours. There are other inns around here, and I know them as well as you." And so they left the forest for the highway and set out on their business.

Chapter 9

Robin Hood
and Will Scarlet

Down the sunny road they traveled, three of the bravest fellows in all merry England. Many stopped to admire the strong, confident-looking trio.

Robin Hood asked Little John, "Why did you not go straight to Ancaster yesterday, as I told you? You would not have gotten into such a mess."

"It looked like rain," Little John said sullenly, for he was tired of Robin's reminders.

"Rain!" cried Robin, stopping suddenly to stare at Little John. "Why, you big oaf! For three days there has been not a drop of rain—not even a hint of it!"

"Nevertheless," growled Little John, "if God chose, he could have brought rain even from a clear sky. Would you want me soaked?"

At this Robin Hood burst into a roar of laughter. "O Little John! How can anyone stay angry with a ninny like you?" And they all traveled on.

It was warm out and the road was dusty. Robin Hood soon grew thirsty. He knew a nearby spring, so they crossed the hedge and came to where the fresh, cool water bubbled up. They cupped their hands, drank their fill, then lay down in the shade to rest awhile. Around them were tender fields of young corn and the scents of purple violets and wild thyme. The setting was so pleasant that no one spoke for some time. Eventually Robin—who had been keeping a casual eye out—broke the silence.

"Hey!" he exclaimed. "That is a brightly feathered bird."

The others looked and saw a young man walking slowly down the highway. He cut a fancy figure in a scarlet silk jacket and stockings; his expensive sword's hilt extended above a gold-inlaid scabbard; he wore a red velvet cap with a single broad feather. His long blond hair curled down onto his shoulders, and he sniffed daintily now and then at a rose in his hand.

"By my life!" said Robin Hood, laughing. "Did you ever see such a brightly dressed, mincing fellow?"

"Truly, his clothes are a bit too pretty," Arthur of Bland agreed. "But his shoulders are broad. And look at his arms. They do not dangle like spindles, but hang stiff and bend at the elbow, like those of a strong yeoman."

"I think you are right, friend Arthur," Little John said. "I think that yonder fellow is not nearly as dainty as he looks."

"Bah!" Robin Hood said. "The mere sight puts a nasty taste into my mouth! Look how he holds that rose, as if to say, 'Good rose, I believe I can tolerate you for a little while.' I think you are both wrong. If a furious mouse were to cross his path, he would faint. I wonder who he is."

"Some great baron's son, no doubt," answered Little John, "with good men's money lining his purse."

"No doubt," Robin agreed. "What a pity that people like that boss around good men whose shoes they are not fit to tie. It angers me to see Norman French lords stepping on the necks of good Saxon Englishmen who owned this land before their great-grandfathers were born! I will have all of their ill-gotten gains from them even if I hang for it!"

"Why, master," said Little John, "what has gotten your temper all a-boil? For all you know, he may be a brave, decent fellow."

"No," Robin replied, "he is what I say. Both

of you stay here and watch how I handle this fellow." Robin Hood stepped from the shade of the beech tree, crossed the hedge, and stood in the middle of the road blocking the stranger's path. The oncoming stranger had been walking slowly, seeming not to see Robin.

"Hold on!" cried Robin, when at last the other had come close to him. "Stay where you are!"

"Why should I stop, good fellow?" the stranger asked in a soft and gentle voice. "But if you wish, I shall stop for a short time to hear what you have to say to me."

"Since you reply so politely to me, I will return the courtesy," Robin said. "I would have you know, fair friend, that I am somewhat of a follower of Saint Wilfred. You may recall how he took the gold from the heathen and melted it into candlesticks. For this reason, I charge a toll to travelers through these parts, which I hope to use for a better purpose than to make candlesticks. Therefore, good fellow, kindly deliver to me your purse so I can look into it and judge whether you have more wealth than our law allows."

All this time the youth had been sniffing at the rose. "No," he said with a gentle smile. "But I love to hear you talk, good fellow. Please finish, before I must be on my way."

"I have finished," Robin said. "And now, if

you will hand over your purse, I will see what is inside and let you go unhindered. If you have little, I will take nothing from you."

"I am grieved, dear sir," the other replied, "that I cannot do as you wish. I have nothing to give you. Let me go, I pray you, for I have done you no wrong."

"You are not going anywhere," Robin said, "until you show me your purse."

"Good friend," the other said gently, "I have business elsewhere. I have listened patiently to you and given you much time. Please let me depart in peace."

"I will tell you one more time," Robin said sternly. "You are going nowhere until you do as I tell you." With that, he raised his quarterstaff to a threatening position.

"How this grieves me," said the stranger sadly. "I fear that I must kill you, poor fellow!" With that he drew his sword.

"Put that away," replied Robin. "I will not take advantage of you. An oak staff like this could snap that sword like a twig. Over there is a thicket of young oak trees; go cut yourself a cudgel and defend yourself, if you have a taste for a good beating."

The stranger looked at Robin's staff. "You are right, good fellow. My sword is no match for that heavy cudgel of yours. Wait while I get myself a staff." He tossed aside the rose, put his sword back into the fine scabbard, and walked to the little clump of oaks. Finding a sapling to his liking, he rolled up his sleeves a bit, braced himself, and with one mighty pull brought the young tree up by the very roots. Then he came back, trimming the small branches and roots from it with his sword as though he had done nothing odd.

Little John and the tanner had been watching all this, but when they saw the stranger drag the sapling up from the earth, the tanner whistled softly. "Did you see that, Arthur?" said Little John. "I think our poor master is in for it. He plucked up that tree as if it were a blade of grass."

Whatever Robin Hood thought, he stood his ground, and now he and the stranger in scarlet stood face to face. The battle began.

They fought this way and that, back and forth, Robin's skill against the stranger's strength. The dust of the highway rose up around them in a cloud, so that Little John and the tanner could sometimes only hear the rattle of the staves against one another. Robin Hood struck the stranger three times, once on the arm and twice in the ribs, and had parried all the other's blows—any one of which would have laid Robin low in the dust had it hit.

At last the stranger struck Robin's cudgel so fairly in the middle that he could hardly hold his staff in his hands; again he struck, and Robin

bent beneath the blow; a third time he struck, and now not only beat down Robin's guard, but gave him such a rap that he was bowled over into the dusty road.

"Hold on!" cried Robin Hood, when he saw the stranger raising his staff once more. "I yield!"

"Stop!" cried Little John, bursting from cover, with the tanner at his heels. "Stop, I say!"

"No," the stranger answered quietly "If you two are as strong as this good fellow, I seem to have my hands full. Nevertheless, come on, and I will do my best to serve you all."

"Halt!" Robin Hood cried, "we will fight no more. I say, this is a bad day for you and me, Little John. I think my whole arm is paralyzed."

Then Little John turned to Robin Hood.

"Why, good master," he said soberly, but with a sly twinkle in his eyes. "What a mess you are—your coat is all dusty! Let me help you up."

"Forget it! A plague on your aid!" fumed Robin. "My coat has been dusted enough already, without your help." Turning to the stranger, he said, "What is your name, good fellow?"

"My name is Gamwell," he answered.

"Ha!" cried Robin, "is it? I have close relatives by that name. Where are you from, fair friend?"

"I was born and bred in Maxfield," the stranger answered. "I come to seek my mother's young brother, whom men call Robin Hood. So, if you could perhaps direct me—"

"Ha! Will Gamwell!" cried Robin, placing both hands upon the other's shoulders and holding him off at arm's length. "I might have known you by that pretty maiden air and dainty walk. Do you not recognize me, lad? Look closely."

"By my word!" cried the other. "My own Uncle Robin!" They embraced as long-lost kinsmen.

Then once more Robin held his nephew off at arm's length and looked at him. "What has happened? Some eight or ten years ago I left you a boy, with big joints and clumsy limbs, and now here you are, as strong a fellow as I have ever seen! Do you remember, lad, how I showed you the proper way to hold the bow and arrow? You showed promise of being a great archer. And have you forgotten that I am the one who taught you to attack and parry with the cudgel?"

"I remember," young Gamwell said, "and you have always been my hero. Had I recognized you, I would never have dared lift my hand against you. I hope I did you no serious harm."

"No, no," Robin said hastily, looking sideways at Little John, "you did not, but I hope never again to feel a blow like that. My arm is still tingling from fingernail to elbow. Nephew, you are the strongest man I have ever seen. When I saw you yank up that green tree like that, I knew I was in trouble. But tell me: why did you leave Sir Edward and your mother?"

"It is a sad story," young Gamwell answered. "My father's steward, whom we hired after old Giles Crookleg died, was a good manager but rude and insolent. I do not know why my father put up with him. I was annoyed to hear him speak so disrespectfully to my father, who as you know is a very patient man and slow to anger. Well, one day he was so offensive to my father that I could no longer stand it. I punched him in the ear—and he died on the spot! They said I broke his neck or something. So they told me to find you, to escape the law. I was on my way to do that when you saw me."

"For someone running from the law, you were taking your sweet time," Robin Hood said. "Who ever saw a man, wanted for murder, mincing along the highway like a fair maiden and sniffing at a rose?"

"Good uncle," Will Gamwell answered, "too much haste can also get one in trouble. Plus, I do believe that I am too musclebound to maneuver or run very fast. Why, you just gave me three raps, and I never got through your guard at all, except by overbearing you with my strength."

"Let us say no more of that," Robin said, a bit too quickly. "I am delighted to see you, Will, and you will be a fine addition to my merry band. But you must change your name, for there will soon be warrants for your arrest. Because of your clothing, from this day you will be called Will Scarlet."

"Will Scarlet," said Little John, stepping forward and shaking hands. "The name fits you well. Welcome! I am called Little John; and this is Arthur of Bland, who has just joined us. You will be famous, Will. The story of how Robin Hood showed us his quarterstaff methods will live on in ballads and merry stories in Sherwood."

"No, good Little John," said Robin gently, for he did not care to be made fun of. "Why should we say anything of the matter? I suggest we keep today's doings to ourselves."

"If you prefer," Little John said. "But, good master, I thought that you loved merry stories, because you have so often joked about a certain increase of fat on me, gathered while living with the Sher—"

"No, good Little John," Robin said hastily. "I think I have said enough about that."

"Good," said Little John, "for I tire of it myself. But I do recall, you also seemed to dismiss the threat of rain last night, so—"

"No," Robin Hood said testily, "I was mistaken. I now remember that it did look like rain."

"So I thought myself," Little John said. "Therefore, no doubt, it was wise of me to spend the night at the Blue Boar Inn instead of going out in such stormy weather, do you not agree?"

"A plague on you!" cried Robin Hood. "You were correct to use your own judgment, all right?"

"Good," said Little John. "As for myself, I have been blind this day. I did not see you beaten up, nor tumbled head over heels in the dust, and if any man says you were, I can rattle his lying tongue between his teeth with a clear conscience."

The others could not keep from laughing. Robin just bit his lower lip for, with such sore bones, the last thing he wished to do was laugh.

Then he said, "Come. We will go no farther today, but will return to Sherwood, and you shall go to Ancaster another time, Little John." They turned back toward Sherwood, anticipating an uneventful journey.

The Adventure with Midge, the Miller's Son

When the four yeomen were nearing Sherwood, in the afternoon, they grew hungry. Robin Hood said, "I would like a good loaf of bread and some cheese, washed down with strong ale. A feast for a king."

"So would I," Will Scarlet said, "now that you mention it."

"I know a house nearby," Arthur of Bland said, "and if I had the money, I would bring you everything you have mentioned."

"Good master, I have money," Little John said.

"So you do, Little John," Robin said. "How much money will it take, good Arthur, to buy us food and drink?"

"I think that six pennies will buy enough food for a dozen men," the tanner replied.

"Then give him six pennies, Little John," Robin said, "for I could eat enough for three men right now. Take the money and go see to it, Arthur. We will wait over in that nice shady spot."

So Little John gave Arthur the money, and the others went to the thicket to wait for the tanner.

Soon he returned with a great brown loaf of bread, a large round cheese, and a goatskin full of strong March beer slung over his shoulders. Then Will Scarlet cut the loaf and the cheese into four fair portions, and each man helped himself. Robin Hood took a deep drink of the beer. "Ah!" he exclaimed, "never have I tasted better."

After this no one spoke, but munched away at his bread and cheese, with now and then a drink of the beer.

At last Will Scarlet looked at a small piece of bread he still held in his hand, and said, "This is for the sparrows." He tossed it away and brushed the crumbs off his red jacket.

"I have had enough, too," said Robin. Little John and the tanner had eaten every crumb of their own food. "I feel like a new man," continued Robin, "and would like a song before traveling on. As I recall, Will, you used to have a pretty voice. Will you sing us one?"

"I do not mind singing," answered Will

Scarlet, "if others will."

"They will. Sing away, lad," Robin said.

"Very well," Will Scarlet replied. "I remember a song that a certain minstrel used to sing in my father's hall, though I forget the title." Then clearing his throat, he sang a beautiful tune about the springtime, and the singing of birds and the bloom of flowers and the romance that the spring often brings—and of the wish that romance could be found all year, just as robins sing all year round.

"Well sung," Robin said, "but, cousin, honestly, I would rather hear a brave fellow like you sing some lusty ballad than a finicky song of flowers and birds and what not. Even so, that was well sung. Now, Little John, your turn."

"No," Little John protested, "I have nothing as fair as what Will Scarlet gave us, and my voice is out of tune today."

At this, they all clamored for Little John to sing, and after declining for a reasonable time— as is customary for those asked to sing—he gave in. He said, "Well, if you insist, I will give you what I can. My song has no title, but here goes." And he began to sing a bawdy song about a young couple in a spring meadow, but before he got very far, Robin Hood interrupted him.

"Who is that coming down the road?" Robin said.

"I do not know," Little John said in a surly voice. "But I do know that it is very rude to interrupt a good song."

"No, Little John," Robin said, "I meant no offense. I have been watching him, bent with the weight of that great bag on his shoulder, since before you started singing. Take a look and see if you recognize him."

Little John looked. "I think that fellow is a certain young miller I have seen now and then around the edge of Sherwood. A very poor reason to spoil a good song, I might add."

"Now that you mention it," Robin Hood said, "I seem to recall seeing him before myself. Does he have a mill over beyond Nottingham Town, near the Salisbury road?"

"That is the man," Little John said.

"A good strong fellow," Robin said. "I saw him thwack Ned of Bradford's head at quarter-staffs about two weeks ago. A fine display of skill."

By this time the young miller was in plain sight. His clothes were dusty with flour, and over his back he carried a great sack of it, across which was a thick quarterstaff. He was broad-shouldered and sturdy, with rosy cheeks and blond hair, and the downy golden beard of a young man.

"A good honest fellow," Robin Hood said. "Let us have a merry joke with him. We will act as though we were common thieves, and pretend to rob him of his honest gains. Then we will take him into the forest and give him such a feast as he never had before in all his life. We will flood his throat with fine wine and send him home with a gold coin for every penny he has. What do you say, lads?"

"A merry thought," Will Scarlet said.

"Indeed," Little John agreed, "but all the saints preserve us from any more beatings today! My poor bones ache so that I—"

"Hush, Little John," Robin said. "Your foolish tongue will get us both laughed at."

"My foolish tongue, indeed," growled Little John to Arthur of Bland. "I wish it could keep our master from getting us into another pickle this day."

By now the miller had come near where they lay hidden. All four of them ran at him and surrounded him.

"Hold, friend!" cried Robin. The miller turned slowly under his heavy burden to look at each nan in turn. He was a bit bewildered, for quick its were not among his gifts.

"Who says so?" the miller said in a deep, gruff voice like the growl of a great dog.

"I do," Robin said. "And let me tell you, friend, you had better obey me."

"And who are you, good friend?" the miller asked, putting down the great sack of meal, "and who are those with you?"

"We are four good Christian men," Robin replied, "who want to help you carry this heavy load."

"I thank you all," the miller said, "but I can carry my bag myself."

"No, you misunderstand," Robin said, "I meant that perhaps you might have some heavy coins on you, of copper or silver or even gold. We would be glad to lighten this load for you."

"What is this?" cried the miller. "I haven't even a penny, much less silver and gold. Let me go in peace. And let me tell you: you are on Robin Hood's territory, and if he finds you trying to rob an honest craftsman, he will cut your ears off and whip you all the way to the walls of Nottingham."

"I fear Robin Hood no more than I do myself," jolly Robin said. "Give me every penny you have on you, and if you move an inch to do anything else, I will cudgel you."

"No!" cried the miller, throwing up his elbow as though he feared the blow. "Search all you wish, but you will find nothing."

"Really?" said Robin Hood, eyeing him closely. "I believe you are putting us on and have got something in the bottom of that sack of flour. Good Arthur, dump the bag out, for I suspect you will find a shilling or two in there."

"Please!" cried the miller, falling to his knees, "do not spoil all my good meal! It will ruin me, and will not help you. Spare it, and I will give up the money in the bag."

"Ha!" Robin said, nudging Will Scarlet. "I have a wondrous nose for coins. I thought that I smelled gold and silver under there. Bring it out, miller."

Then slowly the miller got to his feet. He reluctantly untied the bag and slowly thrust his hands into the meal and began fumbling about with his arms buried to the elbows in the barley flour. The others gathered round him, bent over the sack, wondering what he would bring out.

But while he pretended to be searching for the money, the miller gathered two great handfuls of meal. "Ha," he said, "here they are, the beauties." As the others leaned further forward to see what he had, he suddenly threw the meal into their faces, filling their eyes and noses and mouths with the flour, blinding and half choking them. Arthur of Bland was the worst off, for his mouth was wide open in anticipation. A great cloud of flour flew down his throat, leaving him coughing until he could scarcely stand.

All four stumbled about, roaring with the sting of the meal in their eyes. They rubbed their eyes till the tears made great channels on their faces through the meal. As they did, the miller seized another handful of flour and another and another, throwing it in their faces. Even if they had been able to see a little bit before, they were now as blind as any beggar ever was, with hair and beards and clothes as white as snow.

Grabbing his great crabstaff, the miller began to pound them as though he had gone mad. They skipped in every direction, but could not see to protect themselves, much less run. Thwack! thwack! went the miller's cudgel across their backs, and at every blow great white clouds of flour rose in the air from their jackets.

"Stop!" roared Robin at last. "Enough, good friend, I am Robin Hood!"

"Lying bandit," cried the miller, giving him a rap on the ribs that sent up a great cloud of flour like a puff of smoke. "Brave Robin never robbed an honest tradesman. Ha! Thought to rob me, did you?" And he gave him another blow. "Hey, you long-legged thief, you are not getting your share. Share and share alike," and he belted Little John across the shoulders so hard it sent him skipping across the road. "No worries, black beard—your turn!" He gave the tanner a crack that made him roar for all his coughing. "By my faith, you thief, your pretty red coat is all dusty. Let me help you!" he cried, hitting Will Scarlet in the shoulder blades.

He gave them merry words and blows until they could scarcely stand, and whenever he saw one about to clear his eyes he threw more flour in his face. At last Robin Hood found his horn, put it to his lips, and blew three loud blasts.

Will Stutely and a party of Robin's men happened to be in the woods not far from where this merry sport was taking place. Hearing the hubbub of voices and blows that sounded like wheat being threshed in a barn, they stopped to listen and wonder. Will Stutely said, "Unless I am mistaken, there is a grand battle with cudgels going on. Let us go see." The whole party headed for the noise. When they had come near the sounds, they heard the three blasts of Robin's bugle horn.

"Quick!" cried young David of Doncaster. "Our master is in need!" They dashed forward and burst onto the road.

What a sight they saw! The road was all white with meal, and five men stood there, white from head to toe—for much of the barley flour had fallen back on the miller.

"What do you need, master?" cried Will Stutely. "And what is all this mess about?"

"Why," exclaimed Robin angrily, "this fellow has come as close to killing me as any man ever has. Had you not shown up right then, good Stutely, your master was done for." While they rubbed the flour from their eyes and Will Stutely and the others brushed their clothes off, Robin Hood told them the whole story:

how he had planned to play a joke on the miller, but the joke had ended up being on them.

"Quick, men, seize the miller!" Stutely cried, choking back laughter with the rest. Several rushed the miller, seized him, and tied his arms behind his back with bowstrings.

"Ha!" Robin cried, when they brought the trembling miller to him. "Murder me, would you? By my faith"—here he stopped and stood glaring at the miller. But Robin could not stay angry; first his eyes twinkled, and then he broke into a laugh.

When they saw their master laugh, the yeomen who stood around could hold back no longer, and a mighty shout of laughter arose from all. Many laughed so hard they rolled on the ground.

"What is your name, good fellow?" Robin at last asked the miller, who stood gaping in amazement.

"Sir, I am Midge, the miller's son," he said in a frightened voice.

"Well, Midge," merry Robin exclaimed, clapping him on the shoulder, "you are the mightiest Midge I have ever met. Will you leave your dusty mill and come join my band? By my faith, you are too bold a man to spend your life grinding flour."

"Truly, if you will forgive me for hitting you, not knowing who you were, I will be glad to join you," the miller answered.

"Then today I have gained the three boldest yeomen in all Nottinghamshire," Robin said. "We will go to the great oak tree and have a merry feast in honor of our new friends. And maybe a cup or two of good wine will help my poor joints and bones, though it will be some time before I feel right again." With that, he led the way into the forest.

That night fires crackled in the woods, for though Robin and the others—except for Midge, the miller's son, of course—had many a sore bump and bruise here and there, they were not too sore to enjoy a jolly feast to welcome new members. The party lasted until well into the night, with songs and joking and laughter ringing through the forest.

Little John, however, was much better at quarterstaff than he was at keeping secrets. Bit by bit the whole story of his fight with the tanner and Robin's fight with Will Scarlet leaked out.

Robin Hood and
Allan a Dale

In one day Robin Hood and Little John had three unlucky adventures that got them sore bones. But before long, they made up for their misfortune with a good deed—although not without some more pain for Robin.

After two days Robin felt somewhat better, but his body continued to remind him that he had had a beating. It was a bright morning under the great oak tree, and Will Scarlet lay on the grass next to Robin Hood's seat. Little John was cutting a new cudgel, and many others of the band sat or lay nearby.

"We have had no dinner guests for some time," said merry Robin, "and therefore we have made no money. Good Stutely, pick six men, and go to the main road or thereabouts, to find us a dinner guest. We will prepare a grand feast here to honor whomever you bring. Take Will Scarlet with you, so you can teach him the ways of the forest."

"Thank you, good master," Stutely said, standing up, "for choosing me. I have been too idle here. As for the men, I begin by choosing Midge the Miller and Arthur of Bland—for they are strong hands at quarterstaff. Right, Little John?"

All laughed but Little John and Robin. "I can speak for Midge," Robin said, "and likewise for my cousin Scarlet. This morning I looked at my ribs and found them as many colors as a beggar's cloak."

Will Stutely chose three more men and set forth for the main road, in hopes of finding a rich guest to feast in Sherwood. All day they waited; each man had brought lunch with him, so at noon they sat down under a large hawthorn bush and had a hearty feast. After this, one stood watch while the rest napped, for it was a still, muggy day.

Even so, no guest of the type they desired happened by. Many others came and went: a group of chattering girls, a plodding tinker, a merry shepherd lad, a sturdy farmer, all unaware of the seven stout fellows hidden nearby. There were no fat abbots or rich squires or wealthy moneylenders. At last the sun grew low in the heavens, and the air grew silent except for the twitter of birds and, in the distance, the voice of a milkmaid calling the cows in for milking.

Then Stutely rose. "A plague on our luck!" he said. "We have waited all day for nothing. Let us go home."

The others arose, came out of the woods, and headed back toward Sherwood. After some distance, Will Stutely suddenly stopped. "Listen!" he said, for his ears were as sharp as a fox's. "I think I hear something." All stopped and listened carefully, though for a time only Stutely's ears could make out the sound. After a time, they too heard it: a faint, sad sound, like someone weeping.

"Ha!" Will Scarlet said, "someone is in distress nearby. This must be looked into."

"I do not know," said Will Stutely, shaking his head doubtfully. "Our master is always ready to stick his finger into a boiling pot, but as for me, I see no use in getting us into a jam. That sounds like a man's voice, unless I am mistaken, and a man should be able to deal with his own sorrows."

Then Will Scarlet spoke boldly. "What a way to talk, Stutely! Stay here if you like. I am going to see what the trouble is."

"Wait," Stutely said. "I did not say I would not go; I merely suggested we not be hasty. All right, come along," he added, leading the way.

A short distance away, they came to a clearing in which a stream spread out into a glassy pool. Next to this pool, under a willow tree, lay a young man face down and weeping aloud. His golden hair was tangled, his clothing was rumpled, and everything about him seemed filled with sorrow. From the tree above his head hung a beautiful harp of polished wood inlaid with artwork in gold and silver. Beside him lay a bow and ten or so arrows.

"Hello!" shouted Will Stutely, when they had come out from the forest. "Who are you, fellow, killing the grass with all that salt water?"

Hearing the voice, the stranger sprang to his feet and placed an arrow to his bow, ready to defend himself.

"I know that lad," said one of the yeomen. "He is a certain minstrel that I have seen around here more than once. Only a week ago I saw him skipping across the hill like a yearling doe. He was a fine sight then, with a flower at his ear and a feather in his cap. It looks like our rooster has had his feathers clipped," he added, a bit smugly.

"Bah!" cried Will Stutely, coming up to the stranger. "Wipe your eyes, man! I hate to see a tall, strong fellow sniveling. Put your bow down, man! We mean you no harm."

Will Scarlet saw the pain in the young man's

face at the harsh words. Putting a hand on his shoulder, he said in a kind voice, "You must be in trouble, lad. Pay no attention to these fellows. They are rough, but they mean well; they are too old to understand a young man's problems. Come with us, and maybe we can find a certain person who can help you with your trouble."

"Yes, come along," said Will Stutely gruffly. "I meant you no hurt, and I may be able to help you. Get your singing tool down from there and come along."

The youth did so, and with bowed head and sorrowful step, walked with them. Evening gave way to night as they wended their way through the forest, with all the nighttime sounds, until finally the night was broken by a reddish glow ahead. Soon they came to a clearing bathed in moonlight, in the center of which crackled a great fire. Steaks, pheasant, chicken, and fresh fish were roasting with delicious smells.

The little band moved across the clearing, drawing curious looks, but no one questioned them. With Will Scarlet on one side and Will Stutely on the other, the stranger came to where Robin Hood sat on a mossy seat under the great oak tree, Little John beside him.

"Good evening, fair friend," Robin Hood said, getting up. "Have you come to feast with me today?"

"I have no idea," the lad said, looking around in a daze. "For all I know, I might be dreaming."

"No," Robin said, laughing. "You are awake, as you will soon learn, and a fine feast is being prepared for you, as our guest of honor."

Still the young stranger looked about in confusion. Presently he turned to Robin and said, "I think I know what has happened to me. Are you not the great Robin Hood?"

"Bull's-eye," Robin said, clapping him on the shoulder. "That is what they call me. And since you know me, you also know that whoever feasts with me has to pay for his dinner. I trust you have plenty of money, fair stranger."

"I am afraid not," said the stranger, "I have no money at all, except half a sixpence coin. My true love wears the other half about her neck, on a silk thread."

The whole band gave a great shout of laughter, and the poor lad looked as though he would die of shame. Robin Hood turned sharply to Will Stutely. "Is this your idea of a wealthy guest?" he asked. "You have brought a lean chicken to market, I think."

"No, good master," answered Will Stutely, grinning, "I have not. Will Scarlet brought him."

Then Will Scarlet told how they had found the lad in sorrow and how he had brought him to Robin, believing that Robin might help him. Then Robin Hood turned to the youth, put his hand on his shoulder, and studied him closely.

"A young face," he said in a low voice, half to himself, "and a kind face. Maybe the handsomest I have ever seen, but to judge by your looks, lad, grief comes to the young as well as the old." At these words, though spoken gently, the poor lad's eyes brimmed up with tears. "Take heart, lad," Robin said hastily. "What is your name?"

"Allan a Dale is my name, good master."

"Allan a Dale," repeated Robin, musing. "Allan a Dale. It sounds familiar. Yes, surely you are the minstrel we have heard about lately, whose voice charms every man who hears it. Are you from the Dale of Rotherstream, over beyond Stavely?"

"Yes, I come from there."

"How old are you, Allan?" Robin asked.

"I am twenty years of age."

"Too young to suffer such trouble," Robin said kindly. Then he turned to the others. "Come on, lads, get the feast ready, except for Will Scarlet and Little John—you two stay here with me."

When the others had gone about their work, Robin turned once more to the youth. "Now, lad, sit down here beside me, relax, and tell us the trouble. Speak freely, for it sometimes helps to talk about it."

The youth told the three yeomen of his trouble, at first in broken words and phrases, then with greater ease when he saw that they listened closely. He had come from York to the valley of Rother, a traveling minstrel stopping to play at castles and halls and farmhouses. He had spent one fine evening in a farmhouse, singing and playing, and sweet Ellen of the Dale had listened to him and fallen in love with him. Now in a whisper, Allan told of how he had met her beside the banks of the Rother, and told her he loved her, and she had said the same. His heart had leapt for joy. They had broken a sixpence between them, and vowed to be true to one another.

Allan next told of how her father had found out and had refused to let Ellen see him. It had nearly broken his heart—but worse yet, only a month and a half after Allan had last seen her, he had heard that Ellen was to marry an old knight named Sir Stephen of Trent. The wedding would take place two days from now. Ellen's father seemed to think it was a fine thing for his daughter to marry a well-born knight, even though she did not wish to. Allan a Dale understood, at any rate, why a knight should wish to marry Ellen, for she was the most beautiful maiden in all England.

The yeomen listened to all this in silence,

the clatter of many jesting voices around them, and the red light of the fire shining on their faces. The poor boy spoke so simply and sorrowfully that even Little John felt a lump in his throat.

"No wonder," Robin said, after a moment's silence, "that she fell in love with you, for you surely have a silver cross under your tongue. Such a voice!"

"By the breath of my body," exclaimed Little John, seeking to cover his feelings with angry words, "I have a good mind to go and cudgel the nasty life out of the body of this vile Sir Stephen. What does the old scoundrel think—that young girls are to be bought like chickens at the market? I will teach him a thing or two."

Then Will Scarlet spoke. "It does not seem right of the girl, though, to agree so quickly to such a thing, especially to marrying such an old man. I do not like it, Allan."

"No," Allan replied hotly, "you wrong her. She is as gentle as a dove. I know her better than anyone. Although she may obey her father, if she goes through with this wedding, her heart will break and she will die." He stopped and shook his head and could say no more.

While the others were speaking, Robin Hood had been deep in thought. "I think I have a plan, Allan," he said. "But tell me first: does she have spirit? For example, if you were together in church with the engagement proclaimed aloud as the law requires, and a priest present, do you think that she would marry you despite what her father wants?"

"She certainly would," cried Allan eagerly.

"Then, if her father is the sort of man he seems to be, I will arrange for him to agree that she should marry you and not this old Sir Stephen. But there is one thing remaining: the priest. Unfortunately, the abbots and bishops are not very fond of me and are likely to be stiff-necked about it; and the lesser priests are afraid to do me a favor that might anger their seniors."

Will Scarlet said, "I know of a certain friar that—if you can get on his soft side—would do this for you even if the Pope himself disapproved. He is called the Curtal Friar of Fountain Abbey. The abbey is just a simple, cozy little place. I know it well and can guide you there. It is probably a good day's walk there and back."

"Then shake my hand, Allan," cried Robin, "and I swear to you that two days from now, Ellen a Dale shall be your wife. I will find this same Friar tomorrow and will get on his soft side, even if I have to pound one side soft."

At this Will Scarlet laughed and said, "Do not be too sure of that, good uncle, though from what I know of him, I think this Curtal Friar will gladly marry two such lovers, especially if there will be good eating and drinking afterward."

Soon the feast was ready. It was a merry meal, with jokes and stories passing freely, and all laughed until the forest rang. Allan laughed with the rest, for Robin Hood had renewed his hopes.

After all had eaten their fill, Robin Hood turned to Allan and said, "Now, Allan, we have heard much about your skill, and would love a taste of it. Can you sing for us?"

"Surely," answered Allan; he was no amateur musician that must be asked again and again. He took up his harp, strummed the strings lightly, and the group fell completely silent. Then he began to sing and play.

The tune was called "May Ellen's Wedding," and was the story of a maiden who fell in love with a fairy prince. Not a single yeoman made the least sound, for fear of missing a single note, so sweetly did Allan a Dale play and sing. When he was done, they remained totally silent, gazing at the handsome singer in awe.

Finally Robin spoke: "By my faith, lad, you are—you must not leave our company, Allan! Will you stay with us here in the sweet forest? I could not bear to see you leave."

Then Allan took Robin's hand and shook it, meeting his eyes. "I will stay with you always,

dear master," he said, "for you have shown me greater kindness than anyone in my life."

Then Will Scarlet shook Allan's hand, as did Little John. And so the famous Allan a Dale became one of Robin Hood's band.

Chapter 12

Robin Hood Seeks
the Curtal Friar

The morning after the arrival of Allan a Dale, Robin said, "I am going to find this Friar of Fountain Abbey we spoke of last night, and with me will go four of my good men: Little John, Will Scarlet, David of Doncaster, and Arthur of Bland. The rest of you wait here. Will Stutely will be in charge while I am away."

Robin Hood dressed in chain mail, topped by a steel cap and armed with a fine steel broadsword. He wore a light jacket of Lincoln green and a fine leather cap with a plume over his armor. With polished steel peeking out here and there, he was a most gallant sight. He and his men set forth, with Will Scarlet acting as guide. They walked for miles, past streams, along sunlit roads, and down sweet forest paths, singing and joking.

Sometime after noon they came to a wide, glassy stream full of lily pads. Both banks were heavily worn by the horses that tugged barges up and down the little river. Right now all was quiet; only a little breeze rippled the stream's surface. Will Scarlet led them along the horse path.

"Now, good uncle," Will Scarlet said at last, after they had walked for a long time, "just beyond that bend ahead of us the river is only thigh-deep, and may be forded. On the other side is a small house where the Friar of Fountain Abbey lives. I will lead you—though it is not hard to find."

"If I had planned to wade," jolly Robin said, "I would have worn something else. But no matter. Wait here, lads, for I wish to enjoy this merry adventure alone; but if you hear my bugle horn, come quickly." So saying, he turned and left them, striding onward alone.

Robin had just gone out of sight of his men around a bend when he stopped, thinking he heard speech. It seemed to be a conversation between two men with incredibly similar voices, ahead of him and perhaps ten feet down a steep bank along the river's shore.

"Strange," muttered Robin to himself after a while, when the voices had ceased, "for two people to sound so alike. Perhaps they are twins. I will investigate." He went toward the riverbank. There he lay down in the grass and peered downward.

Below was a cool, lovely spot shaded by a leaning river-willow. The ground was thick with feathery ferns and sweet-smelling wild thyme. Against the tree sat a stout, powerful-looking fellow—but only one. His round head had curly black hair, but the top was shaven; this, his loose robe, and string of beads proclaimed him a friar. Rosy cheeks gave way to a curly black beard and mustache, and he had a bull's neck atop shoulders nearly the size of Little John's. He had little gray eyes that seemed to laugh and to invite laughter.

By his side lay a steel cap, which he had removed for comfort. He sat with legs stretched apart, and between them was a huge meat pie made with tender onions and rich gravy. In his right fist was a great piece of brown bread for him to munch on, between hearty reaches into the pie. All was washed down with gulps from a great bottle of ale sitting beside him.

"This must be the merriest sight in all merry England," Robin said to himself. "The noise was merely this odd holy man talking to himself."

Robin lay watching as the unaware friar ate his dinner in peace. When he finished, he wiped his greasy hands on nature's sweet napkins of ferns and wild thyme, took up his bottle, and began to have a conversation with himself:

"Dear lad, you are a fine fellow and wonderful company."

"Well, you flatter me, but since no one is around to hear me say so, I like you very much too."

"Then won't you have a drink of this fine ale?"

"After you, good lad, after you."

"No, please, sweeten the drink with your own lips."

Here the friar passed the bottle from his right hand to his left. "Well, if you insist; but I drink to your health with great pleasure." Now he took a long, deep drink. "And now, my good fellow, your turn," and he passed the bottle back to his right hand.

"Thank you, fine lad, and I drink to your own good health." He took another drink—in fact, enough for two.

All this time merry Robin lay on the bank and listened, striving desperately to keep from bursting out in gales of laughter, for he would not have spoiled such a sight and sound for half of Nottinghamshire.

Then the friar began to sing a song by the name of "The Loving Youth and the Scornful Maid." He sang the part of the Loving Youth in a deep gruff voice and the part of the Scornful

Maid in a high falsetto.

After a few moments of this, Robin could contain himself no longer. A mighty roar of laughter burst from him, and as the holy friar sang on, Robin joined in on the final chorus; together they sang (or bellowed) the last few lines.

At first the stout friar did not seem to have heard Robin's laughter nor his participation in the song. But no sooner was the song done than the holy man clapped his steel helmet on his head, sprang to his feet, and roared: "Who spies on me? Come forth, you evildoer, and I will carve you like a Yorkshire meat pie!" He drew a great broadsword from beneath his robes and stood ready.

"No, put up your whittling tool, friend," Robin said, standing up with tears of laughter still running down his cheeks. "Men who have sung so sweetly together should not fight afterward." He leaped down to the bank near the friar. "I tell you, friend, my throat is parched from singing. Have you by chance any ale left in that bottle?"

"You ask boldly," the friar replied in a glum voice, "for someone uninvited. Yet I am too devout a Christian to refuse a thirsty man a drink, so help yourself." He held the bottle out to Robin.

Robin took it, put it to his lips, tipped his head back, and drank for a long time. The stout friar watched Robin anxiously and, when he was done, took the bottle and shook it. With a disapproving glance at Robin, he put it to his own lips and found it empty.

"Do you know the country hereabouts, my good holy man?" Robin asked, laughing.

"Yes, somewhat," answered the other dryly.

"And do you know of a place called Fountain Abbey?"

"Yes, somewhat."

"Then maybe you also know of a man called the Curtal Friar of Fountain Abbey."

"Yes, somewhat."

"Well then, good fellow, can this friar be found on this side of the river, or the other?" Robin asked.

"That," replied the Friar, "is a difficult question. I suggest that you consult your senses: sight, hearing, taste, and what not."

"I very much wish," Robin said, looking thoughtfully at the stout priest, "to ford this river and find this same good friar."

"Truly," replied the other piously, "it is good to see such a young man so willing to seek Godly guidance. Far be it from me to obstruct your holy quest. There is the river," he said with an expansive hand gesture.

"Yes, good father," Robin said, "but you can see that my clothes are very fine. I do not wish to get them wet. Your shoulders are strong and broad; can you not find it in your heart to carry me across?"

"Now, by the white hand of the holy Lady of the Fountain!" burst the friar in a mighty rage. "Do you, you weakling youth, you dandy, ask me—the holy Tuck—to carry you? Now I swear—" Here he paused, then slowly the anger passed from his face, and his eyes twinkled again. "But why not?" he continued solemnly. "Did the holy Saint Christopher not carry strangers across the river? Should I, poor sinner that I am, be ashamed to do likewise? Come with me, stranger, and I will humbly do as you wish." He clambered up the bank, closely followed by Robin, and led the way to the ford, chuckling to himself the whole time.

Arriving at the ford, he tied his robes up near his waist, tucked his broadsword under his arm, and bent to take Robin on his back. Then he straightened up and said, "Young man, your weapon will get wet this way. Let me carry it under my arm along with my own."

"No, good father," Robin said, "I would not burden you with anything beyond my own weight."

"Do you think," the friar asked mildly, "that the good Saint Christopher would have accepted this? Give me your weapon, that its weight may remind me to be humble."

Robin Hood unbuckled his sword and handed it to the other, who thrust it beneath his arm along with his own. Then once more the friar bent his back, took Robin on it, and stepped sturdily into the water, splashing the quiet stream in wide rings. At last he reached the other side and Robin leaped lightly from his back.

"Many thanks, good father," said he. "You are indeed a good and holy man. Please give me my sword, for I am in a hurry."

At this the stout friar looked merrily at Robin for a long time, then winked. "No, good youth," he said gently, "I am sure that your affairs are urgent, but you do not consider my own. Yours are of a worldly nature, yet mine are spiritual—a holy work, so to speak—and they lie on the other side of the stream. I can tell that you are a fine young man with great respect for the priesthood. I got wet coming across, and I fear that if I wade back across I may take ill. Since I have so humbly done what you requested, I know that you will be glad to carry me back again. Plus, this is Saint Godrick's day, and you can see that the blessed saint has put two swords in my hands and none in yours. Therefore, good youth, please be so kind as to carry me back again."

Robin Hood looked at the friar and said, "Ah, you clever friar, you have me where you want me. Never in all my life has a clergyman pulled such a trick on me. I might have known from your looks that you were not so holy as you pretended to be."

"No, young man," interrupted the friar

calmly, "do not speak so disrespectfully to me, for it would be a sad thing if you were to feel the cut of bright steel."

"Come on, now," said Robin, "the loser in a bargain at least has the right to speak freely. Give me my sword, and I promise to carry you back, nor will I lift the weapon against you."

"All right," said the friar. "Not that I am afraid of you, fellow. Here is your blade; let us proceed, for I am in a hurry."

So Robin buckled his sword on again, then he bent his stout back and took the friar upon it.

Robin Hood had a heavier load to carry in the friar than the friar had in him. Moreover, he did not know the ford, so he stumbled among the stones, stepping into deep holes and nearly tripping over boulders, with the sweat running down his face in beads. Meanwhile, the friar dug his heels into Robin's sides, as one would spur a horse, ordering him to hurry and calling him names the whole time. Robin did not answer but cautiously felt around until he found the friar's belt buckle. He loosened the fastenings. By the time he reached the original bank, his passenger's sword-belt was looser than he realized. When Robin reached shore and the friar leaped down, the yeoman grabbed hold of the other's sword, and the whole belt, sheath, and blade came away. The friar was weaponless.

"Now then," merry Robin said, panting and

wiping the sweat from his forehead, "I have you, fellow. Your blessed saint has delivered two swords into my hand, and none into yours. If you do not carry me back, and quickly, I will poke you full of holes."

The good friar said nothing for a while, but looked grimly at Robin. "Now," he replied at last, "I did not realize that you were so cunning. Very well. Give me my sword, which I promise not to draw against you except in self-defense, and I promise to carry you back across."

So jolly Robin gave the friar back his sword-belt, which he buckled more securely to his side. Then, tucking up his robes once more, he took Robin Hood on his back and stepped into the water, wading along in silence while Robin sat laughing upon his back. At last he reached the middle of the ford where the water was deepest. He stopped for a moment, and then, with a sudden lift of his hand and heave of his shoulders, shot Robin over his head like a sack of grain.

Robin flew face-first into the water with a mighty splash. "There," the holy man said, calmly turning back again to the shore, "that should cool off your spirit."

With much splashing, Robin got to his feet. Water ran all down his body, out his ears, and he spat some out of his mouth. Gathering his wits, he saw the stout friar laughing at him on the bank. Robin Hood lost his temper. "Wait, you

scoundrel!" he roared. "I am coming after you, and if I do not carve you up today, may I never lift another finger!" He splashed toward the bank.

"You need not hurry," answered the stout friar. "I will wait patiently."

When Robin reached the bank, he began to roll up his sleeves. The friar did the same, displaying great, stout arms on which the muscles stood out like humps of an old tree.

Then Robin saw for the first time that the friar also had a coat of chain mail beneath his gown. "Look out," cried Robin, drawing his sword.

"Indeed," answered the friar, with his own blade already in hand. They wasted no time beginning what soon proved to be a fierce and mighty battle. Right and left, up and down, and back and forth they fought. The swords flashed in the sun and then met with a clash that could be heard far away. This was no playful bout at quarterstaff but a grim fight in earnest. They fought for an hour or more, pausing now and then to rest, each thinking that he had never before seen such a swordsman; then they returned to the combat even more fiercely. Yet in all this time neither was able to draw blood or land even a blow with the flat.

At last Robin cried: "Hold on, good friend!" Both lowered their swords. "Before we start again, I have a favor to ask," he said, wiping the sweat from his forehead, for he no longer wished to harm such a brave fellow—nor was he sure he would win the fight.

"What do you want?" asked the friar.

"Only that you will let me blow three times on my bugle horn," Robin said.

The friar looked suspiciously at Robin Hood. "I think that this is some cunning trick. Nevertheless, I am unafraid of you, and will let you have your wish—provided you will also let me blow three times on this little whistle."

"Certainly," Robin said. And he raised his silver horn to his lips and blew three times, clear and high.

Meantime, the friar stood watching for what might show up, fingering a pretty silver whistle of the sort knights use in falconry, hanging at his belt with his rosary beads.

Scarcely had Robin's last note echoed back to him when four tall men in Lincoln green came running around the bend of the road, each with a bow in his hand and an arrow in place.

"Ha! I thought so, you cheater!" cried the friar. "Then get what you deserve!" And with that, he put the whistle to his lips and blew a shrill call. The bushes on the other side of the road crackled, and from them burst four great, shaggy hounds. "At 'em, Sweet Lips! At 'em, Bell Throat! At 'em, Beauty! At 'em, Fangs!" cried the friar, pointing at Robin.

It was fortunate for Robin that he was near a tree, or he would have had a hard time. In an instant the hounds were on him, and he had just time to drop his sword and leap into the tree. The dogs looked up at him as they would at a treed cat, but the friar quickly called them off and pointed down the road toward the yeomen who stood still in wonder. "At 'em!" he cried.

As the hawk dives on his quarry, the dogs sped at Robin's men. All but Will Scarlet drew their bowstrings to their ears and let fly. Only Will Scarlet did not shoot. But the arrows all missed, for the dogs miraculously leaped out of their path and then charged forward again.

It would have gone badly for Robin's men had Will Scarlet not stepped in front of them and met the hounds' rush. "What is this,

Fangs!" he cried sternly. "Down, Beauty! Down, you dogs! You know better than this!"

At the sound of his voice each dog shrank back quickly, then came to him and licked his hands, like all dogs who meet someone they know. Then the four yeomen came forward, the hounds leaping happily around Will Scarlet. "How is this!" cried the friar. "Are you some wizard, to turn wolves into lambs? Ha!" he cried, when they had come still nearer. "Can I trust my eyes? What is young Master William Gamwell doing in such company?"

"No, Tuck," the young man said, as the four came forward to where Robin was now climbing down from his tree, "my name is no longer Will Gamwell, but Will Scarlet; and this is my good uncle, Robin Hood, with whom I am living now."

"Good master," the friar said, looking somewhat embarrassed and reaching out his great palm to Robin, "I have often heard your name spoken, but I never imagined meeting you in battle. Please forgive me; no wonder I faced such a mighty opponent."

"Truly, most holy father," Little John said, "I am most thankful that our good friend Scarlet knew you and your dogs. My heart sank when I saw my arrow miss so badly, and those great beasts of yours coming for me."

"Be thankful indeed, friend," the friar

replied gravely. "But, Master Will, why are you now living in Sherwood?"

"Why, Tuck, have you not heard the bad news about my father's steward?" Scarlet asked.

"Yes, but I did not realize you were in hiding because of it. These are bad times," the friar said grimly.

"But we are losing time," Robin said, "and I have yet to find this Curtal Friar."

"Why, uncle," Will Scarlet said, pointing to the friar, "there he stands beside you."

"What?" exclaimed Robin. "Are you the man I have been seeking all day, and gotten soaked on account of?"

"Why, truly," the friar said modestly, "some call me the Curtal Friar of Fountain Dale; others, as a joke, call me the Abbot of Fountain Abbey; others call me simply Friar Tuck."

"I like the last name best," Robin said, "for it flows best. But why did you not tell me you were he, instead of tossing me into the water?"

"Why, you did not ask me, good master," said stout Tuck. "But what did you want with me?"

"The day grows late," Robin said, "and we cannot stay to talk. Come back with us to Sherwood, and I will tell you the whole tale as we travel."

So they all headed back toward Sherwood again, with the dogs at their heels; but it was quite dark before they reached the great oak tree.

Chapter 13

Robin Hood Arranges a Marriage

On the morning of fair Ellen's wedding, which Robin Hood had sworn would be to Allan a Dale and not Sir Stephen of Trent, the band arose in fine spirits. Last to arise was stout Friar Tuck. The birds sang joyously as each man washed his face and hands in the stream.

"Now," Robin said, after breakfast, "it is time for the day's business. I will choose twenty of you to go with me, and you, Will Scarlet, will remain here as chief in my absence." His men crowded forward, all eager to be chosen. Robin called out names until he had twenty of the finest yeomen of the band, including Little John and Will Stutely. All hurried to arm themselves with bow and arrows and broadsword. Robin himself changed into a bright coat of many colors trimmed with red and yellow ribbon, the kind a wandering minstrel might wear. He slung a harp across his shoulder.

When he returned, the entire company stared and laughed at Robin's outlandish costume. Robin also had two sacks with him.

"I find it a bit gaudy," Robin said, holding up his arms and looking down at himself, "but I think it looks fine on me. Little John, carry these two bags in your pouch, for they would not look right with this."

"Why, master," said Little John, feeling the bags, "this is gold."

"It is mine, and we can afford it," Robin said. "Get ready, lads, and hurry." When all twenty were present, he gathered them in a close rank, with Allan a Dale and Friar Tuck in the midst, and led the way.

They walked for a long time until they reached the country of Rotherstream. Here were hedgerows, broad fields of barleycorn, rolling pasture lands dotted by flocks of white sheep, and fragrant, fresh-mown hayfields. It was different from the woodlands but every bit as beautiful. Robin led his band, enjoying the sweet scents carried by the gentle breeze.

They joked and laughed as they walked along until they came to a little church that was part of the great, wealthy estates of the Priory of

Emmet: a religious organization somewhat like a monastery—although it most certainly took no vow of poverty. Here fair Ellen was to be married that morning.

Across from the church a stone wall ran along the road, and beyond it were waving fields of barley. Woodbine flowers filled the warm air with their sweet summer scent. The yeomen leaped over the wall, frightening a flock of sheep lazing in the shade, and rested from the long march in this concealed position.

"One of you must watch the church," Robin said. "Young David of Doncaster, get up on the wall and hide in the woodbine and see if anyone comes."

David obeyed, and the others either napped or chatted. All was quiet except for a few low voices and Allan a Dale's restless footsteps, for he could not stop pacing. The only other noise was the mellow snoring of Friar Tuck, obviously enjoying his sleep. Robin gazed into the trees, his thoughts miles away.

After a long time, Robin spoke: "Now tell us, young David, what do you see?"

David said, "I see the white clouds floating, and I see the barley-field waving; and now over the hill to the church I see an old friar coming with a great bunch of keys in his hands. He is coming to the church door."

Robin Hood arose and shook Friar Tuck by

the shoulder. "Get up, holy man!" he cried. With much grunting, the stout Tuck got to his feet. "Get moving, for a churchman is at the door. Go arrange to get yourself into the church, to be there when we need you. Little John, Will Stutely and I will follow you soon."

So Friar Tuck clambered over the wall, crossed the road, and came to the church. The old friar was still laboring with the great key, for the lock was a bit rusty.

"Hello, brother," Tuck said. "Let me help." He took the key from the other's hand and quickly opened the door with a powerful turn.

"Who are you, good brother?" asked the old friar, in a voice diminished by age. "Where do you come from, and where are you bound?"

"My name is Tuck, brother, and I have come to see the wedding. I come from Fountain Dale and am a poor hermit living in a tiny hut beside holy Saint Ethelrada's fountain. I would like to see this fine union and take rest in the cool shade of the house of God."

"Be welcome, brother," said the old man, leading the way into the church. Meantime, Robin Hood, in his harper's outfit, had come to the church door with Little John and Will Stutely. Robin sat down on a bench beside the door to watch, but Little John and Will Stutely went inside, the larger man carrying the two bags of gold.

After a time, Robin saw six horsemen riding slowly up the road and soon recognized two of them as high officials of the Church. One was the Bishop of Hereford, dressed in vestments of richest silk and wearing a necklace of pure gold. On top of his head rested a jeweled hat of black velvet. Orange stockings and black velvet shoes with pointed toes were on his feet, with a cross embroidered on each in gold thread.

Beside the Bishop rode the Prior of Emmet on a pony, dressed almost as richly as the stout Bishop, although not quite so brightly. Silver bells jingled on the horses' harnesses. Behind the Bishop and Prior came two of the senior friars of Emmet Priory and behind them in turn two of the Bishop's servants; for the Lord Bishop of Hereford behaved as much like a great baron as any clergyman could.

Robin said to himself in disgust, "The Bishop is apparently not too holy to dress in great wealth. If I recall right, his patron is Saint Thomas. I wonder whether the good saint favored gold jewelry, silk clothing, and fancy pointed shoes, all bought with money wrung from the sweat of poor tenant farmers and workers. Read your Bible sometime, Lord Bishop: your pride may go before a fall."

As the group came to the church, the Bishop and the Prior were joking and laughing about women, sounding more like peasants than clergymen. They dismounted, and the Bishop saw Robin standing in the doorway. "Hello, good fellow," he said jovially. "Who are you, so gaily dressed?"

"I am a harper from the north country, Your Worship," replied Robin, "and I can play like no man in all merry England. Knights and merchants, clergymen and laymen have all danced to my music, even against their will—so great is the magic of my harp. Today, my Lord Bishop, if I may play at this wedding, I vow to cause the fair bride to love her new husband with all her heart."

"Ha! Are you serious?" cried the Bishop. He looked closely at Robin, who returned his gaze boldly. "Well, this maiden has greatly entranced my poor cousin Stephen. If you can do what you say, and make her love the man she marries, I will give you anything you ask within reason. Let me hear a bit of your skill, fellow."

"No," Robin answered, "I cannot play until the time is right, even at a lord bishop's request. Only the presence of the bride and groom can properly inspire me."

"You speak boldly to me," the Bishop said with a frown, "but I guess I must put up with you. Look, Prior, here comes our cousin Sir Stephen with his lady-love."

Around a bend in the road came others on horseback. First was a tall, thin, gray-haired man of knightly bearing, dressed in black silk and a black velvet hat with scarlet trim; Robin guessed this was Sir Stephen. Beside him rode a stout Saxon farmer, Ellen's father: Edward of Deirwold. Next came a litter borne by two horses, carrying a maiden whom Robin knew must be Ellen. Behind it rode six men-at-arms, the sunlight flashing on their steel caps as they came jingling up the dusty road.

When they arrived at the church, Sir Stephen dismounted and went to help Ellen down from the litter. Robin Hood could see why a proud knight like Sir Stephen of Trent wished to marry a common landowner's daughter, for she was the fairest maiden he had ever seen. Today, however, she was all pale and drooping, like a wilted white lily. With bent head and a sorrowful look, she allowed Sir Stephen to lead her by the hand into the church.

"Why are you not playing, fellow?" asked the Bishop, looking sternly at Robin.

"Have no doubt," Robin answered calmly, "that I will make music such as Your Lordship has never dreamed of, but only when the time is right."

Looking grimly at Robin, the Bishop said to himself, "When this wedding is over, I will have this fellow whipped for his insolence."

Before long fair Ellen and Sir Stephen stood before the altar, and the Bishop himself came in his robes and opened his book. Fair Ellen looked about her in bitter despair, like a deer overtaken by the hounds. Then, in all his fluttery ribbons of red and yellow, Robin Hood strode forward to stand between the bride and groom.

"Let me look on this bride," he said in a loud voice. "What have we here? Her cheeks are pale and sad, not rosy, as a beautiful bride's should be. This wedding is wrong. How can an old man like you, Sir Knight, think to make such a young maiden your wife? It must not be, for you are not her true love."

While everyone watched, too stunned to react, Robin put his bugle horn to his lips and blew three clear blasts, echoing from floor to rafters. Immediately Little John and Will Stutely leaped forward to stand on either side of Robin Hood, drawing their broadswords. A mighty voice came from above: "Here I am, good master, ready when you need me." It was Friar Tuck, up in the organ loft.

There was a great hubbub. Edward strode forward in a rage to seize his daughter and drag her away, but Little John stepped in front of him to push him back. "Stand back, old man," he said, "this is none of your business."

"Down with the villains!" cried Sir Stephen, and felt for his sword, but he wore no weapon on his wedding day.

His men-at-arms drew their swords. It seemed as if blood would flow, but suddenly there came a bustle at the door and loud voices. Steel flashed in the light and weapons clanged together. The men-at-arms fell back before the advance of eighteen sturdy yeomen in Lincoln green, with Allan a Dale at their head. They advanced up the aisle, and Allan handed Robin Hood his own stout bow of yew.

Then Edward of Deirwold spoke in a deep angry voice: "Is it you, Allan a Dale, that has brought such a commotion into church?"

"No," merry Robin replied, "it is I, and I am proud to do so. My name is Robin Hood."

A sudden silence fell. The Prior of Emmet and his attendants gathered together like a flock of frightened sheep when they scent a wolf. The Bishop crossed himself devoutly, saying, "Heaven protect us this day from that evil man!"

"I mean you no harm," Robin said. "But here is fair Ellen's promised husband, and she shall marry him if she wishes, or some of you will be sorry."

Edward spoke up in a loud, angry voice: "No, I say! I am her father, and she shall marry Sir Stephen and no other."

Throughout all this turmoil, Sir Stephen had stood in proud and scornful silence. "You may keep your daughter," he said coldly. "After all this, I would not marry her for everything in England. I tell you truly: I loved your daughter, despite my age, and would have taken her up like a jewel from a pigsty; but I had no idea she was in love with this commoner, and that he loved her. Maiden, if you would rather marry a beggarly minstrel than a noble knight, feel free. I am ashamed to remain here among my inferiors. I am leaving." The knight turned, gathered his men about him, and walked proudly down the aisle.

All the yeoman fell silent at his scornful words, but Friar Tuck leaned over the edge of the choir loft and called out to him, "Good day to you, Sir Knight. As you know, old bones must always make room for new blood." Sir Stephen ignored the words and left the church in haughty disgust with his men.

Then the Bishop of Hereford spoke hastily, "I, too, have no business here and will leave."

Robin Hood took hold of his silken clothes, saying, "Stay, my Lord Bishop, for I want a word with you." The Bishop's face fell, but he had no choice except to remain.

Then Robin Hood turned to stout Edward of Deirwold and said, "Give your consent for your daughter to marry this yeoman, and all will be well. Little John, give me the bags of gold. Look, farmer: here are two hundred pounds. I will hand them over to you as your daughter's dowry, if you consent. If you refuse, she will be married anyway, but you will get nothing. Choose."

Edward scowled and pondered, but he was

a shrewd man—especially when it came to money. At last he looked up and said, joylessly, "Let the disobedient girl do as she likes. I had thought to make a lady of her; yet if she would rather be a poor peasant, I want nothing more to do with her. Even so, I will give my blessing when she is properly married."

"It cannot be," said one of the churchmen of Emmet. "The announcement banns have not been published, as is required, nor is there any priest here to marry them."

"What are you talking about?" roared Tuck from the choir loft. "No priest? Here stands as religious a man as you, any day of the week—and with holy orders as valid as yours, I will have you know. As for the banns, I will publish them." And with that, he performed the custom of the banns, announcing the upcoming marriage and asking if anyone knew of a reason why the wedding should not occur. No one wished—or dared—to object. Then Friar Tuck came down from the loft and performed the service, and Allan and Ellen became husband and wife.

And now Robin counted out two hundred golden pounds to Edward of Deirwold, and he gave his blessing halfheartedly. The yeomen crowded around and shook Allan's hand, while he held Ellen's in his other, dizzy with happiness.

Then at last jolly Robin turned to the Bishop of Hereford, who had watched it all in grim silence. "My Lord Bishop," he said, "remember your promise. If I would play in such a manner as to cause this fair maiden to love her husband, you promised me whatever I asked within reason. You have something on you, I believe, that you do not need. That golden chain hanging from your neck would make a lovely wedding present for this fair bride."

The Bishop's cheeks reddened with rage and his eyes flashed. He glared at Robin, but what he saw in the yeoman's eyes made him think again. Slowly he took the chain from his neck and handed it to Robin, who flung it over Ellen's head so that it hung glittering about her shoulders. Then merry Robin said, "On behalf of the bride, thank you. Indeed, you yourself look better without it. And should you ever come near Sherwood, I hope to reward you with a finer feast than you have ever had in your whole life."

"Heaven forbid!" cried the Bishop earnestly, for he knew precisely what sort of feasts Robin Hood gave in Sherwood Forest.

Robin Hood gathered his men, and with Allan and his young bride in their midst, they all turned to leave for Sherwood. On the way, Friar Tuck came close to Robin and tugged at his sleeve. "You lead a merry life, good master," he said, "but would it not be best for your men's souls to have a good stout chaplain to oversee holy matters for you? I love this life mightily."

Robin Hood laughed merrily. "Indeed, holy man. Join my band, if you wish."

The feast in Sherwood that night was like none ever seen before in Nottinghamshire.

Robin Hood Aids a
Sorrowful Knight

$\mathfrak{S}$pring soon gave way to summer, then to
the merry harvest season. One autumn day
Robin Hood sniffed the air and said, "Little
John, this is too fine a day to waste in laziness.
Take some men and go east, and I will go west,
and let us each bring back a proper guest to feast
with us tonight."

"An excellent idea," cried Little John in
delight. "I will bring you back a guest today, or
not come back myself." Each chose men and left
the forest by different paths.

Robin Hood took with him Will Scarlet,
Allan a Dale, Will Scathelock, Midge the
Miller's son, and others. Only twenty of the

band, led by Friar Tuck, remained in Sherwood to prepare the feast.

Robin's group traveled all morning, arriving by noon at Alverton Town in Derbyshire. He halted them at a normally busy crossroads with hedges alongside. "This is a good place for us," Robin said. "Behind these hedges, we can have our lunch while keeping watch." They climbed over the hedge, sat down in the soft grass, and began to eat.

After lunch, a single rider came slowly over the hill: a handsome but sad-looking knight. His clothes were of good quality, but he wore no gold ornaments; even so, he was obviously of proud and noble blood. Even his fine stallion seemed to hang his head, as though sharing his master's grief.

Watching the rider, Robin said, "That fellow seems unhappy with his fine horse and clothing. There may be something here for us; perhaps the sorrow comes from the difficulty of carrying too much money. Wait here, my men." He climbed the hedge and stood waiting in the road. When the knight approached, jolly Robin stepped forward and laid his hand on the bridle saying, "Please wait a moment, Sir Knight, for I would like a word with you."

"What are you, friend, to stop a traveler on his most gracious Majesty's highway?" the knight asked.

"That is a hard question," Robin answered. "One man calls me kind, another calls me cruel; this one calls me honest, that one calls me a vile thief. How you see me is entirely up to you, for my name is Robin Hood."

"Truly, good Robin," the knight said, a smile twitching at the corners of his mouth, "you have an interesting point of view. As for me, I like what I see, for I hear much good of you. What do you wish of me?"

"Sir Knight," Robin said, "to your credit, you have surely learned the wisdom of polite speech. If you will go with me today to Sherwood Forest, I will give you the merriest feast you ever had in your life."

"You are kind," the knight replied, "but you would find me a sorrowful, dull guest. Best let me go my way in peace."

"I might, except for one thing," Robin said. "We keep an inn deep in Sherwood, but it is far from the main roads. We get few guests, so we set out on merry travels to find them; and so, here we are. But, Sir Knight, each guest must pay his bill."

"I understand your meaning, friend," the knight said gravely, "but I am not your man, for I have no money."

"Really?" Robin said, looking at the knight carefully. "I am inclined to believe you, Sir Knight, but sadly, not all knights' word is as good as some would like others to think. I trust you will not take offense if I check for myself." While keeping hold of the bridle, he put his fingers to his lips and whistled.

Sixty yeomen came leaping over the hedge and ran to where Robin and the knight stood. "These are some of my merry men. They share all my joys, troubles, gains, and losses. Sir Knight, please tell me what money you have with you."

The knight remained silent for a long time, but his cheeks flushed with embarrassment. At last he looked Robin in the eyes and said, "I should not be ashamed, but here is the truth: in my purse are ten shillings, every penny that Sir Richard of the Lea has in the whole wide world."

Robin and his men were silent a long time. At last Robin said, "And you pledge your knightly word that this is all you have with you?"

"Yes," answered Sir Richard, "my word as a true knight: it is all the money I have. Here; check for yourself." And he held his purse out to Robin.

"Put it away, Sir Richard. Far be it from me to doubt the word of so gentle a knight. I may humble the proud, but I seek to help those who walk in sorrow. Come with us, Sir Richard, and cheer up, for maybe I can help you."

"Truly, friend," Sir Richard replied, "I believe that you mean well, though my troubles are probably beyond your help. But I will go with you." The knight turned his horse and went toward Sherwood, with Robin and Will Scarlet walking alongside and the rest of the band in the rear.

After they had traveled a while Robin Hood spoke. "Sir Knight, not to pry, but would you be willing to tell me your troubles?"

"I see no reason why not," the knight said. "They are both simple and grave. I owe a great debt to the Priory of Emmet. If I do not pay it within three days, I must hand over my castle and all my estates to them. As you surely know, what is swallowed by Emmet Priory is never coughed up again."

Robin said, "I do not understand why men of your class go through their money so quickly through rich living."

"You wrong me, Robin," the knight replied, "for the debt did not come about through wasteful living, but rather by tragedy. My son is only twenty, yet he has earned his own knighthood. Last year he went to the jousts at Chester. My lady and I watched proudly as he unhorsed each knight he faced. At last he faced a certain great knight named Sir Walter of Lancaster. My son is young, but he kept his seat nonetheless. Both lances splintered, and sadly, a splinter of my son's lance went through Sir Walter's visor and straight into his eye. He was dead before his squire could even remove his helmet.

"Unfortunately, Sir Walter had friends in high places. His relatives managed to get my son charged with murder. To keep him out of prison, I had to pay a ransom of six hundred pounds in gold. I could afford that by itself, but then came the bribes to corrupt officials. When I ran out of money, I had no other option but to go to the Priory of Emmet for a loan. They drove a hard bargain with me in my hour of need and demanded all my lands as security for the loan. Even so, I grieve for my lands mainly for the sake of my dear wife."

"But where is your son now?" asked Robin.

"He is in the Holy Land, fighting bravely in the Crusade. Sir Walter's relatives would never have left him in peace in England."

Robin was deeply moved. "You have indeed suffered. But tell me: how much do you owe Emmet?"

"Only four hundred pounds," Sir Richard said.

Robin slapped his thigh in anger. "The bloodsuckers!" he cried. "A noble estate to be lost for four hundred pounds! But what will become of you in that case, Sir Richard?"

"It will be worse for my lady than for me," said the knight, "for she will have to go live with a relative on charity, and that would break her proud heart. As for me, I will sail over the sea to the Holy Land and join my son in the Crusade."

Then Will Scarlet spoke. "But have you no friend that will help you in this dire need?"

"None," Sir Richard said. "While I was wealthy, many boasted of how they loved me. When the trouble came, my 'friends' scattered like sheep. They know I am not only poor but also that I have powerful enemies."

Then Robin said, "You say that you have no friends, Sir Richard, but many have found Robin Hood a friend in their troubles. Cheer up, Sir Knight, I may yet help you."

The knight shook his head with a faint smile, but he felt a bit better, for Robin Hood had quite a reputation.

It was almost dusk when they came to the great oak tree. Even at a distance they could see that Little John had found some guests. When they came nearer, who should they find but the Lord Bishop of Hereford! He was pacing angrily, like a fox caught in a chicken coop. Behind him were three Black Friars huddling together like frightened sheep. Hitched to the trees nearby were six horses, one with a very fancy harness, the others heavily loaded with packs and bales. In addition, Robin saw something that made his eyes light up: a medium-sized strongbox bound with heavy iron bands.

"Hello, my Lord Bishop," jolly Robin cried in a loud voice. "How fortunate you are here, for I would rather see you right now than any man in merry England." Robin Hood soon came to where the Bishop stood fuming.

When Robin was near, the Bishop demanded, "Is this the way your men treat high officials of the church? These brothers and I were passing peacefully along with our packhorses, and ten men to guard them, when a great big fellow seven feet tall jumped out. He had at least sixty men with him and commanded me—me, the Lord Bishop of Hereford!—to halt. Then my armed guards, cowards all, ran away. Then this great lout actually threatened me! He said that Robin Hood would strip me as bare as a winter hedge. He also called me vile names, such as 'fat priest,' 'man-eating bishop,' 'money-grubbing banker,' and what not, as though I were some common beggar or tinker."

The Bishop glared like an angry cat, while Robin's men laughed, as did Sir Richard. Only

Robin's expression remained grave. "I am terribly sorry, my lord," he said, "that you have been so badly treated by my band. I tell you the truth: we have great reverence for your rank in the church. Little John, get over here this instant."

At these words Little John came forward, looking sheepish. Then Robin turned to the Bishop of Hereford and said, "Is this the man who was so rude to Your Lordship?"

"It was he," the Bishop said. "A very naughty fellow."

"And did you, Little John," Robin asked sadly, "call his lordship a fat priest?"

"Yes," Little John said remorsefully.

"And a man-eating bishop?" asked Robin sternly.

"Yes," said Little John, more sorrowfully than before.

"And a money-grubbing banker?" inquired Robin in a tone of deep disapproval.

"Yes," Little John said in a voice so sad it might have made a dragon weep.

"This is terrible," jolly Robin said, turning to the Bishop, "for I have always known Little John to be a truthful man."

At this, a roar of laughter went up, while the blood rushed into the Bishop's face until it was cherry red. He choked back his words in humiliation and rage.

"No, my Lord Bishop," Robin said, "we are rough fellows, but not as bad as you think. Not a man here would harm a hair of your reverence's head. I know that our joking annoys you, but we are all equal here in Sherwood, with no bishops nor barons nor earls among us, so while you are here you must share as an equal. Get to work, my merry men, and prepare the feast while we show our guests our woodland sports."

So, while some went to build cooking fires, others ran to get their cudgels and longbows. Then Robin brought forward Sir Richard of the Lea, saying, "My Lord Bishop, here is our other guest of the day, to keep you company. All my merry men will strive to honor you both."

"Sir Richard," said the Bishop reproachfully, "it looks like you and I are fellow captives in this den of—" He caught himself abruptly.

"Speak out, Bishop," said Robin, laughing. "We speak freely here in Sherwood. You were about to say 'den of thieves.'"

"Maybe," answered the Bishop, "but Sir Richard, I am very disappointed to see you laughing at their disrespectful jokes. You are encouraging them where you should be showing disapproval."

"I meant you no harm, my Lord Bishop," said Sir Richard, "but a merry joke is a merry joke. I would have laughed at it even had it been at my own expense."

Robin Hood called on some of his men to spread soft moss on the ground and cover it with deerskins and had his guests be seated. A target was set up across the clearing, and the bowmen held an archery match. The shooting was so marvelous it would have made one's heart leap. All the while, Robin kept the Bishop and the knight company with witty conversation, so that soon one forgot his anger and the other his troubles, and both laughed again and again.

Then Allan a Dale came forth and tuned his harp, and everyone sat still and silent as his wondrous voice sang of love, war, glory, and sadness. When the great silver moon gleamed white through the tree branches, two fellows came to announce that the feast was ready, and Robin led his guests to a torchlit area. Here great smoking dishes filled the air with delightful smells. All sat down and began a long and merry feast with much noise and hubbub.

After dinner, more wine and strong ale was poured; then Robin Hood called for silence. When all had hushed, he began.

"I have a story to tell you all, so listen," Robin said. Then he began to tell about Sir Richard and his dire straits. But as he continued, the Bishop's face went from smiling and merry to serious, for he knew the story—and could imagine what might come next.

When Robin Hood was done, he turned to

the Bishop of Hereford. "Now, my Lord Bishop," he said, "would you not agree that this Prior of Emmet's conduct is wrong? Are churchmen not supposed to be humble and charitable?"

The Bishop's only answer was a moody stare at the ground.

Robin continued, "You, however, are the richest bishop in all England. Can you not find it in your Christian heart to help this needy brother?"

The Bishop did not reply.

"Very well," Robin said. He turned to Little John. "You and Will Stutely bring over those five packhorses." The yeomen obeyed, and the animals were led forward to the brightest part of the clearing.

"Who has the list of goods?" asked Robin Hood, looking at the Black Friars.

The smallest, a gentle-looking elderly man, said with a tremble, "I do. Please do not harm me."

"I never harmed a harmless man in my life," answered Robin. "Please give it to me, good father." The Black Friar handed Robin a tablet on which was chalked the bill of goods. He in turn handed it to Will Scarlet and told him to read aloud. His nephew raised his voice and began:

"Three bales of silk to Quentin, the shopkeeper at Ancaster."

"We leave that alone," Robin said. "This Quentin is honest and has succeeded through hard work." The bales of fine silk were set aside unopened.

"One bale of silk velvet for the Abbey of Beaumont," read Will Scarlet.

"What do these priests want with silk velvet?" Robin asked. "Well, even though they hardly need it, I will share. Measure it into three parts, men: one to be sold for charity, one for us, and one for the abbey." This was done.

"Forty large wax candles for the Chapel of Saint Thomas."

"That rightly belongs to the chapel," Robin said, "so lay it aside, for we will take nothing away from the blessed Saint Thomas." The candles were set aside along with honest Quentin's silk. Will Scarlet read on through the list, and Robin decided what should be done with each item: some were laid aside untouched, and many were opened and divided in three: a third for charity, a third for the band, and a third for the owners. Finally the entire ground was covered with fancy silk, golden cloth, cases of rich wines, and other luxuries, and Will Scarlet came to the last line on the tablet: "A box belonging to the Lord Bishop of Hereford."

At these words the Bishop shivered, and the box was set on the ground.

"My Lord Bishop, do you have the key?"

asked Robin.

The Bishop shook his head, hoping they would not be able to open the box.

"Will Scarlet," Robin said, "you are our strongest man. Go bring a sword and cut this box open, if you can."

Soon the fair-spoken yeoman returned with a great two-handed sword. The men stood clear as Will Scarlet struck with all his might: once, twice, and a third time. With the third blow, the iron banding burst and a heap of gold spilled out, gleaming red in the torchlight. At this sight a murmur went up among the yeomen, like the sound of the wind stirring; but no man came forward to touch the money.

Robin spoke. "Will Scarlet, Allan a Dale, and Little John: count that."

This took a long time. When all the math was done, Will Scarlet called out: "Fifteen hundred pounds in all. But there is also a paper." He looked at Robin, who nodded. "It says: 'This money is the rents, fines, and penalties from certain estates belonging to the Bishopric of Hereford.'"

"My Lord Bishop," Robin Hood said, "I will not strip you quite as bare as a winter hedge, as Little John suggested; perhaps an autumn one. You will keep a third of your money. A third of it you can easily spare us for your party's entertainment, for you are very rich. The other third you can spare for charity, Bishop, for you are known as a cruel, greedy landlord. You would do yourself and the church far more credit to spend more on charity and less on your own comfort."

The Bishop looked up, silently thankful to keep some of his wealth.

Then Robin turned to Sir Richard of the Lea and said, "Sir Richard, the church is prepared to ruin you; therefore, the church can afford to help you. The five hundred pounds laid aside for charity are for you, that you may pay your debts to Emmet."

Sir Richard looked at Robin until all the lights and the faces blurred together with moisture. Finally he said, "Thank you, friend, from my heart, for what you have done for me. Yet please do not think me ungrateful when I say: I cannot freely accept this gift except as a loan. I will take this money and pay my debts. But I pledge my most solemn knightly word: I will return this money in full within a year and a day to either you or the Lord Bishop of Hereford. I feel free to borrow, for it is fair that someone high in the church should help me, since the church has driven such a hard bargain."

"Truly, Sir Knight," Robin said, "I do not quite understand the fine points of knightly honor that apply here; but as you wish. But if you must bring back the money in time, I recommend you bring it back to me, for I believe I might make better use of it than the Bishop." Robin turned and gave orders, and five hundred pounds were counted out and put in a leather bag for Sir Richard. The rest was divided, part for the band's treasure house, and part set aside with those items to be left for the Bishop.

Then Sir Richard stood up and said, "I cannot stay any later, good friends or my lady will worry. May I go?"

"Certainly, Sir Richard," Robin Hood said, "but we will give you an escort."

Little John spoke up: "Good master, let me choose twenty strong fellows from the band, arm ourselves in the proper manner, and serve as Sir Richard's retainers until he can get others to replace us."

"Well spoken, Little John. Do so," Robin said.

Then Will Scarlet spoke: "Let us give him a golden chain to wear about his neck, as befits a noble knight, and golden spurs to wear at his heels."

Robin Hood said, "Well spoken, Will Scarlet. We shall."

Next Will Stutely spoke up: "Let us give him this bale of rich velvet and that roll of golden cloth, to take home to his noble lady as a present from Robin Hood and his merry men."

The entire band shouted noisy approval.

Robin said: "Well spoken, Will Stutely. It shall be done."

Then Sir Richard of the Lea looked all around, but his voice failed him. Finally, in a husky and trembling voice, he said, "You will see, good friends, that Sir Richard of the Lea will always remember your kindness this day. And if you are ever in trouble or dire need, come to my lady and me. The walls of Castle Lea will have to be battered down before I allow harm to come to you. I—" He could say nothing further, but turned hastily away.

Shortly Little John came forward with nineteen stout fellows. Each man wore a coat of chain mail and a steel cap and a good sword; they were a gallant sight. Then Robin came and laid a golden chain about Sir Richard's neck, and Will Scarlet knelt to buckle the golden spurs onto his heels. Will Stutely and Arthur of Bland loaded the gifts onto the stallion.

Then Little John led the knight's horse forward, and Sir Richard mounted. Before he departed, the once-sorrowful knight looked down at Robin for a long time, then suddenly drew his great sword and brought it vertically before himself in salute, as to a military superior. The forest rang with the great shout of the band as Sir Richard and his proud guard marched off through the woodland, torches bringing bright gleam to the steel they wore.

When they were gone, the Bishop of Hereford spoke in a mournful voice: "I too must be going, good fellow, for the night grows late."

But Robin laid his hand upon the Bishop's arm. "Not so soon, Lord Bishop. Three days from now Sir Richard must pay his debts to Emmet. Until then, you had better stay with me, so that you cannot make trouble for him. You will have a good time, though, for I know how fond you are of deer hunting. You have paid your bill in full, so put aside your worries and live like a bold yeoman for three days. When they are over, I promise you will be sorry to go."

So the Bishop and his convoy stayed with Robin, and in that time his lordship indeed had much sport. After three days had passed, he was indeed sorry to go. When Robin set him free three days later, he sent along a guard of yeomen, to protect the remainder of the packs and bundles from banditry.

Even so, as the Bishop departed, he vowed to himself to make Robin sorry for the day he accosted him in Sherwood.

How Sir Richard of the Lea
Paid His Debts

The long highway stretched on, gray and dusty in the sun. In the distance stood the towers of Emmet Priory. Along the highway rode a knight in a plain, gray robe, gathered in at the waist with a broad leather belt, from which hung a long dagger and a stout sword. Despite his plain dress, his noble horse was richly decorated with silk and silver bells. Twenty stout men-at-arms marched behind him.

At last they reached the great gate of Emmet Priory. The knight sent one of his men to knock at the gatekeeper's house. The latter, a lame and elderly man, hobbled out.

"Where is the prior?" asked the knight.

"He is at lunch, Sir Knight, and he expects you," the gatekeeper said, "for if I am not mistaken, you are Sir Richard of the Lea."

"I am, and I will go to see him now," the knight replied.

The keeper opened the gates, and the knight entered the cobblestone courtyard of the Priory, his men behind him with a rattle of armor and swords that startled a flock of pigeons skyward.

Meanwhile, a princely feast was in progress in the dining hall. At the head of the table sat Prior Vincent of Emmet, richly dressed and bejeweled. His favorite hunting falcon perched on the arm of his chair. On his right sat the Sheriff of Nottingham in rich purple robes trimmed with fur, and on his left sat a famous old lawyer in dark and sober clothing. Further down sat the senior brothers of the Priory.

All was merry, with much joking and laughter. The lawyer was especially happy, for his fee for the case was in his pouch: thirty-five pounds in gold. He had insisted on payment in advance, for he knew the ways of holy Vincent of Emmet.

The Sheriff of Nottingham asked, "Are you sure, Sir Prior, that you will gain the lands?"

"Definitely," Prior Vincent said, smacking his lips after a deep drink of wine. "I have had him quietly watched, and he has no money to pay me."

"True," the lawyer said in a dry, husky voice, "he will lose his lands if he does not pay. But, Sir Prior, in order to hold the lands without trouble, you must be certain you get a signed release from him."

"So you tell me," the Prior said. "But this knight is so poor that he will gladly sign away his lands for two hundred pounds of hard money."

"I believe," the lawyer said smoothly, "this knight may not show up to settle his debt today. But never fear; we will find a way to get his lands for you."

Even as the lawyer spoke, there came a sudden clatter of horse's hooves and a jingle of iron mail in the courtyard below. The Prior told one of the junior brothers to go look out the window, though he knew it could only be Sir Richard. The brother did so, and said: "I see twenty strong men-at-arms and a knight just dismounting from his horse. He is dressed in long and rather plain robes of gray, but his horse is richly decorated. They are coming this way and now are entering the great hall below."

"You see," Prior Vincent said. "This knight is so poor he can barely buy a crust of bread, yet he keeps a band of retainers and puts fancy trappings on his horse, even while he wears cheap clothing. Surely such a man should be humbled."

"But are you sure that this knight will not harm us?" asked the lawyer worriedly. "His kind are fierce when crossed, and he has a band of dangerous men with him. Perhaps you should consider giving him an extension of his debt."

"Have no fear," the Prior said, looking down at the little man. "This knight would no sooner harm you than he would an old woman."

As the Prior finished, the door swung open. In came Sir Richard, with folded hands and head bowed upon his breast. In this humble manner he walked slowly up the hall to where the Prior sat, leaving his men-at-arms at the door. He knelt before Prior Vincent and said, "Blessings be upon you, Sir Prior. I have come as we agreed."

The Prior said, "Have you brought my money?"

"I am sorry to say that there is not even one penny on my body," the knight said. The Prior's eyes sparkled, and he turned to the Sheriff and smiled.

The knight continued to kneel on the hard stones. The Prior turned to him again and asked sharply, "Then why have you bothered to come?"

The knight's cheeks flushed with anger, but he kept control. "I ask your mercy. Just as you hope for Heaven's mercy, I request yours. Please do not strip me of my lands and reduce a true knight to poverty."

"According to the law, your lands are forfeit," the lawyer said, emboldened by the knight's humility.

Sir Richard asked, "Sir lawyer, will you not befriend me in this hour of need?"

"No," he said. "The Holy Prior has paid me my fee, and I am obligated to him."

"Will you not be my friend, Sir Sheriff?" Sir Richard asked.

"This is none of my business," the Sheriff of Nottingham said, "but I will try anyway." He nudged the Prior under the table with his knee. "Can you not ease him of some of his debt, Sir Prior?"

At this the Prior smiled grimly. "Pay me three hundred pounds, Sir Richard, and I will forgive the rest of the debt."

"But you know, Sir Prior, that I can pay four hundred pounds as easily as I can pay three hundred," Sir Richard replied. "Can you not give me another year to pay?"

"Not another day," the Prior said sternly.

"And is this all you will do for me?" asked the knight.

"False knight!" cried the Prior in anger. "Either pay up, or release your lands to me and get out of my hall."

Then Sir Richard stood up. "You false, lying priest!" he raged, so angrily that the lawyer shrunk away in fear. "You know quite well that

I am a true knight. Are you so rude that you would leave a true knight kneeling this whole time in your dining-hall and not even offer him something to eat and drink?"

The lawyer said, "Let us calm down, for this is no way to discuss business. What will you pay this knight, Sir Prior, for his land?"

"I would have given him two hundred pounds," snarled the Prior, "but after that little speech, not a penny over one hundred."

"Hear this, false prior," the knight said; "I would not give you one inch of my land for a thousand pounds." He turned toward the door and beckoned to the tallest of his men-at-arms, who came forward and handed him a long leather bag. Sir Richard took the bag and poured a glittering stream of gold onto the table. "Bear in mind, Sir Prior, that you agreed to accept three hundred pounds. You shall get no more." He counted out three hundred pounds and pushed it toward the Prior.

Now the Prior was downcast. He had lost his chance at the land, needlessly forgiven a hundred pounds of the debt, and wasted thirty-five pounds more on the lawyer. He turned to the lawyer and said, "I want my money back."

"No," cried the lawyer, "I will not. It is my rightful fee."

"Now, Sir Prior," the knight said, "our business is done, so I need stay no longer in this loathsome place." He turned quickly and strode away.

All this time the Sheriff had been staring wide-eyed at the tall man-at-arms, who stood as though carved from stone. At last he gasped out, "Reynold Greenleaf!"

At this, the tall man-at-arms, who was of course Little John, turned grinning to the Sheriff. "Good day, Sir Sheriff. I shall be sure to report your kind assistance to Robin Hood. Until we meet again in Sherwood, farewell." Then he turned and followed Sir Richard down the hall, leaving the Sheriff shrunk in his chair all pale with amazement.

The merry feast was ruined. Everyone had lost his appetite except the lawyer, who was happy with his fee.

A year passed, and another mellow fall had come. The year had brought great change to the lands of Sir Richard of the Lea; the meadows had been planted and a rich crop harvested. The castle moats were refilled, and the crumbling of neglect had given way to good order.

In the brightness of the morning the drawbridge fell across the moat with a clank of chains, the gates swung slowly open, and a fine array of men-at-arms marched out behind an armored knight bearing a great lance. From the lance's point fluttered a blood-red pennant. In the midst of the troop walked three packhorses laden with parcels of many shapes. Good Sir Richard of the Lea was on his way to pay his debt to Robin Hood.

They marched along until they came near Denby, which was decorated with flags and streamers. Sir Richard turned to the nearest man-at-arms. "What is going on at Denby today?" he asked.

"Your Worship," answered the man-at-arms, "there is a merry fair with a great wrestling match. Many folk have come, for the prize is a barrel of wine, a fair golden ring, and a new pair of gloves."

Sir Richard, who loved good manly sports, said, "We should stay and enjoy the merry sport." So he turned his horse's head aside toward Denby and the fair, his men following.

Denby Town was a great hubbub of merriment. Bagpipes were playing and people were dancing. But the biggest crowd gathered around the wrestling ring, and there Sir Richard and his men headed.

When the wrestling judges recognized Sir Richard, the chief judge came down from the bench to invite Sir Richard to assist in the judging. The knight dismounted and joined the other judges on the bench near the ring.

There had been exciting wrestling that morning. A yeoman named Egbert from Staffordshire had thrown every challenger with ease, until a local Denby man named William of the Scar leaped into the ring. A tough bout followed, and at last William threw Egbert heavily. There was much shouting and shaking of hands, for the Denby men were proud of their wrestler.

When Sir Richard arrived, William was walking up and down the ring, daring anyone to face him. "Come one, come all!" he said. "If there is none in Derbyshire to come against me, let them come from Nottingham, Stafford, or York. If I do not make them all root like pigs, call me a weakling."

All laughed, but a loud voice rose above the laughter: "All right, you braggart, here is a Nottinghamshire man for you to face." A tall young man with a tough quarterstaff in hand pushed through the crowd and leaped lightly into the ring. He was not as heavy as William, but he was taller and broader in the shoulders. Sir Richard turned to one of the judges and asked: "Who is this youth? He looks familiar."

"He is a stranger to me," the judge replied.

The young man laid aside his quarterstaff, then took off his jacket and shirt. His large, sharply cut muscles were impressive.

Each man spat on his hands, clapped them onto his knees, and watched the other closely for an advantage. Like a flash they leaped together, and a great shout went up, for William had gotten the better hold. For a short time they strained and struggled, and then William gave his most cunning trip and throw, but the stranger defeated it with great skill. Then, with a sudden twist and a wrench, the stranger broke William's hold, and the Denby man found himself locked in a pair of arms like a great vise. They stood for a while, straining, great drops of sweat trickling down their faces and bodies. At last William's muscles gave out, and he gave a sob. Then the youth exerted all his strength, tripped with his heel, and threw William over his right hip. The local man went down with a sickening thud! and lay as still as death.

No shout went up for the stranger; instead an angry murmur rippled through the crowd. Then one of the judges, a relative of William of the Scar, rose with trembling lip and said to the victor, "If he dies, you will be sorry, fellow."

The stranger answered boldly, "We both took our chances. Even if I killed him, no law can harm me, for it was fairly done in the wrestling ring."

"We shall see," the judge said with a scowl. Another angry murmur ran through the crowd.

Then Sir Richard spoke gently. "No, the youth is right, and he wrestled fairly. If your man dies, no one is at fault."

But in the meantime three men had come forward and lifted William from the ground. The Denby man was not dead, just badly shaken. The chief judge rose and said, "Young man, the prize is yours. Here are the ring and the gloves, and over there is the barrel of wine to do with as you wish."

The youth had since gotten dressed and collected his staff. He bowed to the judge without a word, put on the ring, and slipped the gloves into his belt. Then he leaped lightly over the ropes, made his way through the crowd, and was gone.

"I wonder who that youth is," the judge said, turning to Sir Richard. "I have never seen our William thrown in the ring before."

"And yet this youth threw him fairly and with ease. I too wonder who he is," answered Sir Richard thoughtfully.

The knight spent a bit more time chatting with the judges, then prepared to leave. He called his men, adjusted his saddle, and mounted.

Meanwhile the young stranger had made his way through the crowd, but not without incident. There was much muttering: "Look at the rooster!" "Proud of himself, is he not?" "I think he cheated!" "He did! Did you all not see tree sap on his hands?" "He needs to be cut down to size!" The stranger ignored the taunting, striding proudly across the green toward the dancing area.

As he stood watching the dancing, a rock hit him in the arm. He turned and saw that an angry crowd of men had followed him. A great hooting and yelling arose, bringing the people out of the dancing area to see what the commotion was. At last a tall, broad-shouldered, burly blacksmith strode forward from the crowd brandishing a mighty blackthorn club.

"So you come to our fair town of Denby, you cheater, to nearly kill a good honest lad with foul tricks?" he growled in a deep voice like an angry bull. "Take that!" The blacksmith struck a blow at the youth that would have flattened an ox. His target turned the blow with his quarterstaff, then answered with a strike so vicious that the Denby man fell as if struck by lightning. When they saw their leader fall, the crowd gave another angry shout; but the stranger placed his back against the tent near the dancing area and stood ready with the staff. No one else dared come within reach of that terrible weapon. They crowded back like dogs from a bear at bay.

Then some coward threw a sharp rock from the stranger's right. It hit him in the head, staggering him and drawing a bright red flow of blood. The crowd, seeing him dazed, rushed on the young man and knocked him down.

The youth might have been badly hurt or even killed but for Sir Richard. Suddenly there were more shouts, and steel flashed in the air. Blows were given with the flat of swords, and Sir Richard of the Lea spurred his white horse, plowing through the crowd. The crowd melted away before the armed men like snow on a hot stove, leaving the young stranger all bloody and dusty on the ground.

Finding himself free, the youth stood up, wiped the blood from his face, and looked at the knight. He said, "Sir Richard of the Lea, you may have just saved my life."

"You know who I am? Who are you, young man?" asked Sir Richard. "I think I have seen you before."

"You have," the youth said, "for men call me David of Doncaster."

Sir Richard said, "I see why I failed to recognize you, David. Your beard has grown longer, and you have grown more to manhood in this past year. Come into the tent and wash the blood off. Ralph, bring him a clean jacket right away. I am sorry to see you hurt, David, but glad to repay Robin Hood's kindness. Young man, you could have been seriously hurt." The knight led David into the tent where the youth washed the blood off and put on the clean jacket.

In the meantime a whisper had gone around that this was the great David of Doncaster, holder of the mid-country champion's belt, who only last spring had thrown Adam of Lincoln in the ring at Selby in Yorkshire. By the time young David cleaned up and came out of the tent along with Sir Richard, no sound of anger was heard. The fickle crowd pressed forward to see the great wrestler, proud that he had entered the ring at Denby fair.

Then Sir Richard called out, "Friends, this is David of Doncaster. It is no shame that your Denby man lost to him. He is not angry with you, but be careful how you treat strangers from now on. Had you slain him, Robin Hood would have punished your town long and harshly for the murder of such a fine young man. I have bought the barrel of wine from him, and I now give it to you to drink as you wish; but never again attack a man for being a bold yeoman."

All shouted approval, though more for the wine than the knight's wise words. Then Sir Richard, with David beside him and his men-at-arms all around, turned and left the fair.

But at wrestling bouts for many years afterward, men who saw that great match would say: "Yes, but you should have seen the great David of Doncaster throw William of the Scar at Denby fair."

Robin Hood stood in the merry greenwood with Little John and most of his yeomen around him, anticipating a visit from Sir Richard. At last a glint of steel flashed through the brown forest leaves, and into the open rode Sir Richard at the head of his men, with David of Doncaster in their midst. The knight rode forward to Robin Hood, leaped from his horse, and shook Robin's hand in both of his.

"Why, Sir Richard," Robin said, looking the knight over, "your mood has improved since I saw you last."

"Yes, thanks to you, Robin," the knight replied, laying his hand on the yeoman's shoulder. "But for you, I would now be fighting in the Holy Land, a broken man. But I have kept my word, and have brought back your money, which I can easily repay now that I am wealthy once more. I have also brought a little gift to you and your brave men, from my dear lady and myself." Sir Richard turned to his men and commanded: "Bring the pack horses!"

But Robin stopped him. "No, Sir Richard. Please do not think me rude, but in Sherwood we do business only after we feast." He led the knight to the seat under the great oak tree, while other chief men of the band came and were seated. Then Robin asked, "Why was young David of Doncaster with you and your men, Sir Knight?"

Then Sir Richard told the whole story about the events at Denby fair. "This is why I was late, good Robin. Otherwise I would have been here an hour ago."

When Sir Richard finished, Robin stretched out his hand to grasp the knight's. He spoke in a trembling voice. "I can never repay you, Sir Richard, for I would rather lose my own right hand than see young David come to harm."

They talked a while longer, and then a merry feast began with much meat and drink. When it was over, the knight ordered the pack-horses brought forward. One of the men unloaded a strongbox and opened it. Sir Richard took out a bag and counted out five hundred golden pounds.

"Sir Richard," Robin said, "you would please us all to keep that money, as a gift from Sherwood. Right, my lads?"

All shouted "Yes!" with a mighty voice.

"I thank you all deeply," the knight said earnestly, "but please do not be offended that I cannot accept such a gift. Honor requires me to repay you."

Then Robin Hood said no more but gave the money to Little John to put away in the treasury, for he knew that a forced gift only breeds resentment.

Next Sir Richard had the packs unloaded and opened, and a great shout rang through the forest again. Each yeoman received a bow of the finest Spanish yew, inlaid with silver—yet not so as to weaken it. With the bows came quivers of leather embroidered with golden thread, each containing twenty beautiful arrows fletched with peacock plumes and tipped with bright heads that shone like silver. There were two hundred such archery outfits. To Robin Sir Richard gave a stout bow inlaid with clever workmanship in gold, and each arrow in his quiver was fitted with a gold notch.

The entire band shouted its appreciation of the fair gift and swore among themselves that they would die if need be for Sir Richard and his lady.

When it was time for Sir Richard to go, Robin Hood called his entire band, and each yeoman carried a torch to light the way through the woodlands. When they came to the edge of Sherwood, the knight shook Robin's hand once again, then was gone.

Little John Turns
Barefoot Friar

After winter came spring in all its lively glory. Under the great oak tree, Robin Hood basked in the sun like an old fox, watching Little John rolling a new bowstring. Nearby sat Allan a Dale fitting a new string to his harp.

Robin said at last, "I would rather roam this forest in the gentle springtime than be King of all merry England. I need no palace built by man, for I live in one crafted by nature."

"Yes," Little John agreed as he waxed the bowstring, "this is the life for me, even in the cold season. We have such merry winter nights at the Blue Boar. Remember the night you and Will Stutely and Friar Tuck and I spent there, with the two beggars and the strolling friar?"

"Yes," merry Robin said, laughing. "That was the night that Will Stutely tried to kiss the hostess and got a pot of ale emptied over his head."

"What a night that was," Little John said, joining in the laughter. "Friar Tuck, you have a quick ear for tunes. Do you remember the song the strolling friar sang?"

"I might," Tuck said. "Let me see." He thought for a moment, assembled the pieces in his mind, and sang merrily. It was a ballad he understood well, for it compared the life of a friar to that of the robin, with plenty to eat and able to travel as he pleased. When his rich, mellow voice died down, all clapped and shouted with laughter.

"A fine song," Little John said. "Were I not a yeoman of Sherwood Forest, I would rather be a strolling friar than anything else."

"It is truly a good song," agreed Robin Hood, "but I thought those two burly beggars led the merrier life. Remember that great black-bearded one's story of his begging at the Yorkshire fair?"

"Yes," Little John said, "but the friar's story about the farmhouse in Kentshire was at least as amusing. I believe that his life was the merrier."

"Of course, for the honor of the cloth, I must agree with my good friend Little John," Friar Tuck said.

"I still think I am right," Robin said. "I have an idea to settle this, Little John. You take a friar's gown from our chest of strange clothing, and I will stop the first beggar I meet and change clothes with him. We will each wander the country today and see what befalls us."

"A great idea," Little John said. "Let's get moving."

Little John and Friar Tuck went to the storehouse and dug around in the chest until they found a Gray Friar's robe. When they came out, a mighty roar of laughter went up. Not only had the band never seen Little John in a friar's robe, but it was too short for him by nearly a foot. In addition, his hands were folded in the loose sleeves, his head reverently downward. At his waist hung a great, long string of prayer beads.

Now Little John took up his stout staff at the end of which hung a chubby little leather bottle, the kind in which reverent pilgrims carry cold spring water—but this one contained good ale. Then Robin stood up, took staff in hand, and slipped five golden pounds into his pouch—more than enough to obtain some beggar's clothes.

When all was ready, the two yeomen strode forth. They walked down the forest path and onto the highway until it forked. One road led to Blyth, the other to Gainsborough. Here they stopped.

Jolly Robin said, "Take the road to Gainsborough, and I will take the one to Blyth. Have a safe trip, holy father. With luck you will not have to pray very hard before we meet again."

"Good day, good beggar soon-to-be," Little John said. "May you beg for money, not mercy."

And with that each stepped boldly on his way, until a green hill hid them from one another's sight.

Little John walked along, whistling. His only company was the little birds with their merry twitter. He walked up hill and down valley, the wind in his face, until he came to Tuxford crossroads. Here he met three pretty girls, each carrying a basket of eggs to market. "Where are you going, fair maids?" he asked them.

They huddled together and nudged one another until one said, "We are going to the Tuxford market, holy friar, to sell our eggs."

"How unjust!" exclaimed Little John. "Such fair young women should not have to carry eggs to market. If it were up to me, all three of you would wear the finest silks, ride milk-white horses, be attended by servants, and feast only on whipped cream and strawberries. That would better suit your beauty."

At this all three blushed and looked down. One said, "By my faith!" Another, "You are making fun of us!" The third said, "Listen to the holy man!" Even so, they looked Little John over with sidelong glances.

"Such dainty maidens as you should not carry baskets along a highway," Little John said. "Let me carry them for you, and one of you may carry my staff for me, if you are willing."

"But wait," said one. "You cannot carry three baskets at once."

"Ah, but I can," Little John replied, "and I will show you how. Here I take this great basket and tie my rosary around the handle. Then I put the rosary over my head so as to carry the basket on my chest." And Little John did so, then gave the staff to one of the maids and took a basket in each hand. Off they stepped, a merry friar in the midst of three laughing maidens. Everyone stopped to stare at the outlandish and merry sight: a huge, strapping Gray Friar, in robes too short, draped in egg baskets, and hiking along with three pretty young women. Little John did not mind, and when onlookers made sport of him, he answered just as merrily.

They walked, chatting and laughing, until they got close to Tuxford Town. Here Little John stopped and set down the baskets, for he did not wish to enter town and risk being recognized by the Sheriff's men. "Well, my lovely ladies," he said, "here our merry ways must part. But before we leave one another, we should drink to friendship." With that he unslung the leather bottle, removed the stopper, and handed it to the one who had carried his staff. Each one took a fair drink, and when it had passed all around, Little John finished what was left. Then, kissing each one sweetly, he wished them all a good day and left. But the maids stood looking after him as he walked away whistling. "What a pity," said one, "that such a strong, merry lad should be in holy orders."

"That was merry indeed," Little John said to himself as he strode along. "May I find more of the same."

After he had trudged along for a time, he grew thirsty again. He shook his leather bottle; not a sound. He put it to his lips to drink; not a drop. "Little John! Little John!" said he, shaking his head, "if you do not take care, women will be your downfall."

At last he reached the crest of a certain hill and saw below a sweet little inn lying snugly in the valley below him. A voice within him cried aloud, "Good friend, your heart's delight awaits: a comfortable rest and a pot of brown beer." So he hurried downhill to the little inn. In front of the door a clucking hen was scratching in the dust with a brood of chicks around her, and the sparrows were chattering away. Beside the door were tethered two large horses with fine saddles. Three merry fellows—a tinker, a peddler, and a beggar—sat on a bench in front of the door, drinking ale.

"Good day to you, friends," Little John said, striding to where they sat.

"And to you, holy father," replied the merry beggar with a grin. "But look; your gown is too short. You should cut a piece off the top and tack it to the bottom to make it long enough. But come sit beside us here and have some ale, if your vows permit it."

"Not to worry," Little John said, also grinning. "The blessed Saint Dunstan has given me special permission to enjoy any form of refreshment I choose." He put his hand into his pouch for money to buy ale.

"Unless I miss my guess, holy friar," the tinker said, "this shows the good Saint's wisdom, for without such permission, you would be doing a lot of penance. No, take your hand out of your pouch, brother, and let me buy you a round. Landlord, a pot of ale!"

The ale was brought and given to Little John. Blowing the foam off, Little John tilted the pot high, then higher, until it pointed skyward. When it was empty, he took it down and gave a sigh of satisfaction.

"Landlord!" cried the peddler, "bring this good fellow another pot of ale. This hearty drinker's presence does us all credit."

They talked among themselves merrily for a while. Then Little John asked, "Whose horses are those?"

"Two holy men like you, brother," the beggar said. "They are feasting inside, for I smelled chicken cooking. The landlady says they come from Fountain Abbey, in Yorkshire, and are going to Lincoln on business."

"They are a merry sight," the tinker added, "for one is as lean as a spindle and the other as fat as a pudding."

"Speaking of fatness," the peddler said, "you do not look poorly fed yourself, holy friar."

"You see what miracles the holy Saint Dunstan can do for his servants, who live on handfuls of dry peas and trickles of cold water," Little John replied.

At this a great shout of laughter went up. "A wonder indeed," said the beggar. "To watch you empty that pot of ale, I would have sworn that you had not tasted plain water for at least a couple of months. Has this same holy Saint Dunstan perhaps taught you a song or two?"

"I believe he may have," Little John said, grinning.

"Then—out of respect for the holy Saint, of course—let us hear what he has taught you," suggested the tinker.

Little John cleared his throat, complained briefly of hoarseness, then began a song about a pretty maid waiting for her lover. As he completed the first verse, the door of the inn opened and the two brothers of Fountain Abbey came out, followed by the landlord fawning on them. When they saw the singer, robed as a Gray Friar, both stopped; the short fat one frowned angrily, and the tall thin one winced as though drinking sour beer. As Little John was about to begin the second verse, the fat one exclaimed loudly, "What is this? A man of the cloth drinking in public and singing profane songs?"

"Well," Little John said, "unlike Your Worship's reverence, I do not get to drink and sing in a fine place like Fountain Abbey, so I must do it where I can."

"Your behavior is a disgrace to the cloth," the tall lean brother cried sharply.

"What!" exclaimed Little John. "A disgrace? Not nearly as much disgrace as it is for priests to wring hard-earned pennies out of poor peasants, eh, brother?"

At this the tinker and the peddler and the beggar nudged one another and grinned. The friars scowled blackly at Little John but could think of nothing further to say, so they turned to their horses. Then Little John got up and ran to where the brothers of Fountain Abbey were mounting. "Let me hold your horses' bridles for you," he said. "You were right; this is indeed a sinful place. I will leave this den of evil and go with you, for surely there will be no temptation in such holy company."

"No," the lean friar said harshly, seeing that Little John was mocking them. "We want none of your company. Go away."

"It saddens me," answered Little John, "that you want to snub me, but I have no choice. For the sake of my soul, I must flee from sin and go with you."

The fellows on the bench grinned broadly; even the landlord let slip a smile. The friars of wealthy Fountain Abbey looked at one another uncertainly; they were ashamed to ride the road with a poorly clothed, common strolling friar. They also knew that he could break their bones if he wanted to, so the fat brother spoke up in a milder tone: "No, good brother. We will be riding too fast for you to keep up."

"I thank you for being so considerate," Little John said, "but have no fear, brother. I am a good runner and can keep up for many miles."

The drinkers on the bench laughed, and the lean brother's anger boiled over: "You drunkard! You should be ashamed. Stay here in the sty with the other pigs, for you do not belong with us."

"Listen to that!" said Little John. "Landlord, you are unfit to be seen with these holy men. Get back to your alehouse, for if these most holy brothers of mine say the word, I will beat your head in with this stout staff."

Another shout of mirth went up from the bench. The landlord's face flushed from smothering his laughter, but he held it back so he would not alienate Fountain Abbey's business. The brothers, with no other choice, mounted their horses and turned toward Lincoln.

"I must go, my friends," Little John said to the drinkers. "Good day to you. Off we go!" He pushed his way between the brothers' horses and hiked off at a matching pace.

The brothers glared at Little John, then drew as far from him as possible, riding along the sides of the road and leaving the center to him. The tinker, the peddler, and the beggar ran out into the highway, each with a pot in his hand, and looked after them laughing.

While they remained in sight of the inn, the brothers walked their horses soberly, knowing how it would look if word got out that the brothers of Fountain Abbey ran away from a strolling friar. When they were over the hill, however, the fat brother said to the thin one, "Brother Ambrose, should we not pick up the pace?"

"Certainly," spoke up Little John, "for the day is passing. If it will not jolt your fat too much, by all means let us hurry."

The two friars glared again at Little John in silent fury, then spurred their horses into a trot. A mile later, Little John was still running between them, showing no sign of getting tired. At last the fat brother reined up with a groan of pain. "I was afraid of that," said Little John. Such a rough pace would surely shake your poor, old, fat belly."

The fat friar stared straight ahead and

scowled. They traveled forward at a walk, Little John in the middle of the road whistling merrily to himself, the two friars riding silently on either side.

Soon they met three merry minstrels in red, who stared to see a Gray Friar with such short robes walking in the middle of the road and two brothers riding richly-harnessed mounts but with heads bowed in shame. When they approached, Little John waved his staff and cried loudly, "Make way! Make way for men of the cloth!" The minstrels stared and laughed, but the fat friar shook with rage, and the lean one hid his face behind his horse's neck. Next they met two noble knights with hawks on wrists, then two fair ladies in silks and velvets, all riding noble horses. All stared and got out of the way. Little John bowed humbly to the ladies and said as they passed, "Good day, fair ladies, from all three of us."

Then all laughed, and one of the fair ladies cried out, "What three do you mean, merry friend?"

Little John looked over his shoulder, for they had now passed each other, and called back, "Big Jack, lean Jack and fat Jack-pudding."

At this the fat friar groaned in embarrassment; his brother stared stonily ahead. Soon they came to a crossroads. Seeing that there was no one around, the lean friar reined up and said in a quivering rage, "Look, you, we have had enough of your company and your jokes. Go your way, and let us go ours in peace."

"How is this?" replied Little John. "We were having so much fun, and now your mood is all sour. But I have likewise had enough of you today as well, though it may harm my soul to leave you. I know that you will miss me; however, as you can see, I am poor and you are rich. Please give me a penny or two to buy bread and cheese at the next inn."

"We have no money, fellow," the lean friar said harshly. "Come, Brother Thomas, let us go forward."

Little John caught both horses by the bridle reins. "You truly have no money with you at all? Please, my brothers, will you not even give me a penny to buy a crust of bread?"

"We have no money!" thundered the fat little friar with the great voice.

"None at all?" asked Little John.

"Not a pound," said the lean friar sourly.

"Not a penny," said the fat friar loudly.

"Then we must remedy that," said Little John. "I cannot let such holy men depart penniless. Both of you should get down from your horses, and we will kneel here in the road and pray to the blessed Saint Dunstan. Maybe he will send us some money to help us on our journey."

"You lout!" cried the lean friar, grinding his

teeth. "You want me, the steward of Fountain Abbey, to kneel in the dirty road to pray to some beggarly Saxon saint?"

"What a disrespectful way to speak of the good Saint Dunstan!" said Little John. "I have a good mind to crack your skull for it, so I recommend that you both get down and pray with me, before I lose my patience and forget that you are in holy orders." He twirled his staff for emphasis.

Both friars grew as pale as dough. They slipped off their horses.

"Now, brothers, down on your knees. Let us pray," said Little John. With a heavy hand on each shoulder he pushed them to their knees, then knelt between the two men. Then Little John began to plead loudly with Saint Dunstan for money. After he had addressed the Saint for some time, he told the friars to feel in their pouches and see if the Saint had sent anything. Each did but brought out nothing.

"Ha!" said Little John. "Your prayers are not working! We must have more faith." He began to pray again: "Gracious Saint Dunstan! Send some money immediately to these poor folk, or they may waste away, leaving the fat one like the thin one, and the thin one reduced to nothing. But to avoid the sin of pride, send them only one pound apiece; if you send any more, send it to me."

"Now," said he, rising, "let us see what each man has." He put his hand in his pouch and pulled out a pound and some change. "Bless the Saint! How about you, brothers?"

Again each friar slowly reached into his pouch and brought out nothing.

"Nothing?" said Little John. "Impossible. I think you have missed the good Saint's gift. Let me look." He went first to the lean friar, reached in, and pulled out a leather bag. From it he counted one hundred and ten pounds in gold. "You see," said Little John, "the blessed Saint heard your prayer. And now let us see if he heard yours, brother." He reached into the fat friar's pouch and drew out a similar bag. When he finished counting its contents, there were seventy pounds. "Saint Dunstan be praised! He has also sent you some money, good brother!" explained Little John.

Then Little John gave them each a pound and took the rest of the money and said, "You gave me your holy word that you had no money. No man of the cloth would lie; therefore clearly the good Saint Dunstan has answered my prayers. And as I prayed for you each to receive a pound and the rest for me, it is rightly mine. Good day, my brothers, and a pleasant journey to you." Little John strode away, leaving the friars standing with woeful looks. They remounted and rode away in unhappy silence.

As for Little John, he turned his footsteps back again to Sherwood Forest, whistling as he walked.

Chapter 17

Robin Hood
Turns Beggar

After jolly Robin left Little John to seek adventure as a friar, he walked in the mellow sunshine, stopping now and then to exchange merry words with country maidens or simply to appreciate the beauty of the countryside. By noon, he still had met no beggar with whom to change clothing. "If my luck does not change soon, this day will be a waste. It has been a merry walk, but I have no idea how to live like a beggar."

Soon thoughts of springtime and women and beautiful scenery gave way to visions of boiled chicken, strong ale, meat pies, and good bread. Just then, as he came around a bend in the dusty road, he saw a man sitting on a fence. A dozen or more pouches and bags hung from the stranger, and his coat was patched in many colors. He wore a tall leather cap, and across his knees lay a sturdy blackthorn quarterstaff: a jolly beggar, with dancing slate-gray eyes and curly black hair.

"Hello, good fellow," Robin said as he approached. "What are you doing here this merry day?"

The beggar winked and sang:

"I sit upon the stile,
And I sing a little while
As I wait for my own true dear, O,
For the sun is shining bright,
And the leaves are dancing light,
And the little fowl sings she is near, O.

"That is how it is with me—except that my dear is not coming any time soon."

"A sweet song," Robin said, "and I dislike interrupting it; but I have some serious questions for you, so please listen."

At this the jolly beggar cocked his head to one side and said, "Serious? I rarely pay attention to anything serious, and I suspect you are the same."

"No," Robin said, "you are mistaken. My first question is the most serious one possible: where can I find something to eat and drink?"

"I give that matter no serious worry at all,"

the beggar said. "I eat what I can find and make do with water when I cannot have ale. Why, just as you showed up, I was trying to decide whether to eat breakfast. I find that hunger makes even a dry crust most satisfying, so I think I will wait and let my appetite grow."

"You have a way with words," merry Robin said, laughing. "But do you really have only a dry crust to eat, with all those full bags and pouches?"

"Why, there might be something else in there," the beggar said slyly.

"And nothing to drink but cold water?" Robin said.

"Not a drop of anything else," the beggar replied. "Over beyond that clump of trees is a sweet little inn, but they do not care much for me. Once, when the good Prior of Emmet was dining there, the landlady set a crabapple-and-sugar pie on the windowsill to cool. Fearing that someone might have lost it, I took it with me to try and find the owner. Ever since then they have treated me poorly there, but in all honesty, they have the best ale I ever tasted."

Robin laughed aloud. "Indeed, they were very ungrateful to you. But what is in your pouches?"

The beggar peeped into the bags. "Why, here is a piece of pigeon pie, wrapped in a cabbage leaf to hold the gravy. Here is some meat and a chunk of white bread. Over here are four oatcakes and a joint of ham. Hmmm . . . here are six eggs that must have come from some chicken-coop by accident. They are raw, but if they were cooked and spread with some of this butter—"

"Enough, good friend!" cried Robin, holding up his hand. "My stomach is growling. Here is an offer: if you will share your food with me, I will go to that little inn and bring us a skin of ale to share."

"An excellent idea, friend," the beggar said, getting down from the fence. "I will share the best I have with you and bless Saint Cedric for your company. But please be sure to bring at least three quarts of ale, one for you and two for me, for I am thirsty enough to drink a river dry."

So Robin left the beggar, who spread out his feast and built a little fire to roast the eggs.

After a while Robin came back with a large skin of ale and laid it on the grass.

"Friend," the beggar said, "let me feel the weight of that skin."

"Help yourself," Robin replied, "while I check to see if that pigeon pie is fresh."

After this, they ate and drank in silence. When Robin was full, he pushed the rest away and sighed contentedly.

"And now, good friend, we come to that

other serious matter I mentioned."

"Surely," the beggar said with disapproval, "you would not interrupt a fine drink of ale with serious matters?"

"No," Robin laughed. "By all means keep drinking while I talk. Here it is: I want to try life as a beggar to see if I like it."

The beggar answered, "A fine ambition, but wanting and doing are two different matters. You must serve a long apprenticeship before you could even be a clapper-dudgeon, much less an Abraham-man. You are probably too old to get the hang of it."

"Maybe so," Robin said. "Nevertheless, I want to lead a beggar's life, and for this I need the right clothing."

"Take it from me, fellow," the beggar said, "even if you were dressed as well as good Saint Wynten, the patron of beggars, you would never make a beggar. More likely, the first authentic beggar you met would beat you up for sticking your nose where it does not belong."

"Nevertheless," Robin said, "I will give it a try. I like your clothes very much, and would like to trade mine for yours; I will also give you a pound. While I had anticipated that I might have to use my staff to convince one of your begging brothers to accept my offer, I could hardly lift a finger against you after such a fine time together."

The beggar listened with his hands on his hips, and when Robin had ended he cocked his head to one side.

"Lift a finger? Against me? Have you gone mad, man? I am Riccon Hazel, from Holywell in Flintshire, and I have cracked the heads of many a better man than you. I would give you a rap on the skull, except for the ale you have given me. You will not get one rag of my coat, even if it would save you from hanging."

"Now, fellow," Robin said, "as unpleasant as the thought is, were it not for your fine feast, I would give you the beating of your life. Watch your mouth, lad, or your luck will run out."

"No one talks that way to me!" cried the beggar, rising and taking up his staff. "Defend yourself, fellow, for I will beat you—and take every penny you have!"

Merry Robin leaped up and likewise picked up his staff. "Take my money, if you can. If you even touch me, I will freely give you all my money." He twirled his staff until it whistled.

Then the beggar swung a mighty blow at Robin, then another and another, but could not get past Robin's guard. After the third, Robin saw his chance. Before Riccon knew it, his staff was over the hedge, and Riccon himself lay flat on the grass, out cold.

"So you want my hide and my money, good fellow?" asked merry Robin with a laugh.

Riccon lay silent. Robin brought the ale-skin over and poured some of it on the beggar's head and some down his throat. Soon Riccon opened up his eyes and looked around in confusion.

Robin said, "Now, good fellow, will you change clothes with me, or do you need more persuasion? Here is one pound for your entire outfit. If you refuse, of course—" and he tapped his staff on the ground.

Riccon sat up and rubbed the bump on his head. "I thought you would be easy to beat. It appears I have no choice; but you must first give me your word as a true yeoman to take nothing but my clothes."

"I swear as a true yeoman," Robin said, thinking that Riccon had a few pennies that he would save.

The beggar drew a little knife and cut the lining of his coat. He drew out ten pounds in gold, which he set upon the ground with a wink at Robin. "Now you are welcome to my clothes. I would gladly have traded mine for yours, pound or no pound."

"Sly fellow," Robin said, laughing.

They then switched clothes. Riccon danced for joy over his fine new suit of Lincoln green, eager to live well while the money lasted. He turned and left, singing a merry song about the beggar's life.

Robin listened till the song faded into the

distance, then headed down the road in the opposite direction. It was noontime, when most people are busy with food rather than travel. Robin whistled merrily, his bags and pouches bobbing and dangling about him. At last he came to a little path that led through a meadow and uphill toward a windmill. On an impulse, he hiked into the meadow.

Before he knew it, he had company: four beggars, sitting on the ground at a fine feast. Each had a sign on his chest. One said: "I am blind." Another: "I am deaf." A third: "I am mute." The last said, "Pity the lame."

Despite their proclaimed handicaps, however, they seemed merry enough. The deaf man was the first to hear Robin, for he said, "Listen, brothers, I hear someone coming." The blind man saw him first, for he said, "He is an honest man, brothers, a fellow beggar." Then the mute man called loudly to him: "Welcome, brother; come share our feast and ale." The lame man set aside his crutch and stood up easily. "Welcome, brother," said he, offering a flask of ale.

Robin laughed out loud. "You should indeed welcome me, for my arrival seems to have produced a great miracle of healing. I drink to your happiness, brothers, for drinking to your improved health seems pointless."

All grinned, and the blind beggar, who was their chief and also the broadest-shouldered of them, slapped Robin in the shoulder and called him a merry fellow.

"Where do you come from, lad?" asked the mute man.

"I spent last night in Sherwood."

"Really?" said the deaf man. "Not for all the money we are carrying to Lincoln Town would I sleep one night in Sherwood. Robin Hood would clip my ears."

"Probably," laughed merry Robin. "But what money do you mean?"

The lame man spoke. "Our King, Peter of York, has sent us to Lincoln with this money that—"

"Wait, brother Hodge," interrupted the blind man. "I would not doubt our brother here, but we do not yet know him. Brother, what are you: Upright-man, Clapper-dudgeon, Dommerer, or Abraham-man?"

Robin looked confused, then finally said, "Well, I try to be an upright man, brother, but I have no idea what you mean by all that other nonsense. But enough jargon; how about a song from that mute fellow?"

All fell silent. After a while the blind man spoke again. "You must be joking. Answer me this: have you ever fibbed a chouse quarrons in the Rome pad for the loure in his bung?" Beggars, of course, had their own special slang; and anyone showing ignorance of the most basic terms would arouse suspicion. The blind man had first asked Robin what sort of beggar he was and was now asking if he had ever robbed anyone on the highway.

"Stop making fun of me with that gibberish," Robin said, annoyed, "or I will crack all your heads. I would do it now, except for this fine ale you have shared with me. Speaking of ale, brother, pass it down."

Instead, to Robin's surprise, all four leaped to their feet and grabbed heavy cudgels. Robin quickly picked up his own staff and put his back against a tree. "What is this? Gang up on me, will you? Stand back, you rascals, or I will beat you all black and blue! Have you gone mad? I have done you no harm!"

"You are a lying spy!" accused the blind man. "You have heard too much to be allowed to escape. All together, brothers—down with him!" Raising his cudgel, he rushed Robin like a bull; but Robin was ready. With two quick blows he sent the blind man tumbling over into the grass where he lay still.

The others stood back, scowling at Robin. "Come on, you scum!" he cried merrily. "Plenty for everyone. Who else wants some?"

The beggars' only answer was silent glares from a safe distance. Or so they thought, for when Robin saw them hesitate, he leaped forward. A powerful stroke sent the mute man to the grass, his cudgel flying away. The other two ducked and ran away in different directions. Robin laughed, especially at the lame man's impressive speed, but neither looked back and both were soon out of sight.

Then Robin turned to the two men lying on the ground. "These fellows said something about taking money to Lincoln. Perhaps this blind one, who has such sharp eyesight, has it on him. It would be a pity to leave good money to such thieving rascals." He bent and searched the blind man's ragged clothing until he found a heavy leather pouch slung under his coat. Inside were four sheepskin rolls. What he saw made him gape, for each roll contained fifty new golden pounds. "I have often heard that the Beggars' Guild was rich, but not this rich," he said aloud. "They can afford to make a generous donation to my band." Then he rolled up the money and slung the pouch under his own coat, and took up the flask of ale. "Good friends, may your signboards always be inaccurate. Thank you for being so generous, and good day to you." Robin took up his staff and went merrily on his way.

When the two beggars that had been rapped on the head roused themselves and sat up, and when the others had slunk back, they were no longer merry. They had made a rather bad trade: all their money and ale in exchange for two headaches, to say nothing of the difficulty they would have explaining how they lost the funds entrusted to them.

As for Robin, he sang as he strode along.

On Robin walked until he came to the crossroads near Ollerton. Here he grew tired and sat down to rest on the grassy bank. "I should be getting back to Sherwood," he said to himself, "but I would like to have one more merry adventure before I go home." So he waited and watched to see who might come.

At last he saw a traveler riding his direction: a thin, elderly man on an equally thin horse. While Robin laughed at the amusing sight, he recognized the wayfarer as a rich grain merchant from Worksop. More than once, this particular merchant had bought up all the grain, driving up the price so high that poor people starved. Naturally, almost everyone hated him.

After a while, the grain merchant came riding up to where Robin sat. Merry Robin stepped forth, in all his rags and tatters, his bags and pouches dangling about him. He laid his hand on the horse's reins and called the old man to halt.

"Who are you, fellow, that dares stop me on the King's highway?" the lean man demanded in a dry, sour voice.

"Pity a poor beggar," Robin said. "Give me a penny, to buy a piece of bread."

"Never!" snarled the grain merchant. "Your kind belong in prison or at the end of a rope rather than strolling around free on the highways!"

"That is no way to talk," replied Robin. "We are brothers, for do we not both take our money from poor people who can hardly spare any? Does either of us make his living doing good? Has either of us ever done honest work, or actually earned a penny? We are the same, except that you are rich and I am poor. Therefore, I ask again: please give me a penny."

"How dare you!" cried the grain merchant in a rage. "If I ever catch you in town where the law can lay hands on you, I will have you whipped. As for your penny, I swear that I have not got a single coin in my pouch. Even if Robin Hood were to accost me, he would not find any money. Only a fool would travel so near to Sherwood with money in his pouch, and I am no fool."

Merry Robin looked to make sure no one was coming, then stood on his tiptoes and said quietly to the grain merchant, "Do you really believe that I am a beggar? Did you ever see a beggar this clean? In truth, I am as honest and wealthy as you. See?" Robin took out the pouch and dazzled the greedy broker's eyes with the beggars' gold. "Friend, these rags hide an honest rich man from the eyes of Robin Hood."

"Put up your money, lad," cried the other quickly. "If you think that beggar's rags will hide you from Robin Hood, you are a fool. He would strip you to the skin, for he hates a sly beggar as he hates a fat priest—or a grain merchant."

"Really?" Robin said. "Had I known, I might not have come around here dressed like this. But I must be going, for I have important business. Where are you headed, friend?"

"To Grantham, but I will spend the night at Newark, if I get there in time."

"Why, I also am going to Newark," merry Robin said. "Two honest men should stay together for safety in Robin Hood's country. If you do not mind, I will travel along with you."

"Well, now that I know you are a fine wealthy fellow, and not a miserable beggar, I do not mind," said the grain merchant.

"Then let us be going, for the hour grows late," Robin said. The old man spurred his horse into a trot, and Robin ran alongside, barely able to contain his laughter.

They traveled along until they reached a hill on the outskirts of Sherwood. Here the lean man slowed his thin horse, to conserve its strength going up the slope. Then he turned in his saddle and spoke to Robin for the first time since they had left the crossroads. "Here is your greatest danger, friend, for here we are nearest to the lair of that vile thief Robin Hood. Soon we will come again into open, honest country."

"I am worried," Robin said. "I wish I were carrying as little money as you, for today I fear Robin Hood will rob me blind."

The other winked at Robin. "In fact, I am carrying nearly as much as you, but it is hidden so well that all the rascals in Sherwood could never find it."

"You are joking," Robin said. "How could you hide two hundred pounds?"

"Ah, young man, you have a lot to learn. Since you are a good honest fellow, I will tell you something I have never before told anyone, so that you may be safer from the likes of Robin Hood. See these huge wooden shoes I am wearing?"

"Yes," laughed Robin, "your feet are awfully big for a thin elderly fellow."

"No, seriously," said the grain merchant. "This is no joke. Each of these shoes conceals a fine little box, which is revealed by twisting out a nail and opening the front like a lid. Inside each box is ninety golden pounds, wrapped in hair to prevent clinking."

Robin broke into a roar of laughter and took hold of the reins, stopping the undernourished horse. "I must say, good friend, you are the slyest old fox I ever saw. In his shoe soles, he says!" He laughed so hard he nearly fell down.

The grain merchant stared in shock. "Not

so loud, you madman! Remember where we are! Let us get moving, and you can laugh when we are safe and sound at Newark."

"No," Robin said, wiping away the tears of laughter. "I think I will go no further, for I have good friends nearby. Go forward if you will, good fellow, but you must go barefoot. I have taken a liking to your shoes, so I suggest you take them off."

At these words the grain merchant grew pale as a linen napkin. "Who are you, to say this?"

Merry Robin laughed again and said, "Men here call me Robin Hood. And as you have given me advice about Robin Hood, I will give you a bit about him in return: the sooner you give him your shoes, the sooner you will reach fair Newark Town."

The thin old man shook with fear, nearly falling off his horse, and then silently removed his shoes and let them fall to the road. Robin kept hold of the reins as he picked them up. Then he said: "Normally, I ask my business contacts to come feast in Sherwood with me, but out of gratitude for our journey together, I will decline this time. My men might not be as gentle with you as I have been, for every honest man hates a grain merchant, and I do not control their every move. Never again come this close to Sherwood, or you may someday find an arrow through your ribs. Have a good day." Robin slapped the horse's flank, and it bore the terrified old man away. He was never again seen near Sherwood Forest.

Robin turned and went into the forest, carrying the grain merchant's shoes.

That night in sweet Sherwood the red fires flickered brightly as the yeomen listened to Robin Hood and Little John tell of their adventures. The woods rang over and over again with shouts of laughter.

When all was told, Friar Tuck spoke up. "Good master, you have had a merry time, but I still maintain that the life of the barefoot friar is the merrier of the two."

"Not I," Will Stutely said. "Our master has had more fun, for he has had two fights at quarterstaff in one day."

So some of the band agreed with Robin Hood and some with Little John.

Robin Hood Shoots
Before Queen Eleanor

The road stretched white and dusty in the hot afternoon sun. A handsome, yellow-haired youth on a milk-white horse was riding toward Sherwood Forest. What a sight he was: dressed in silk and velvet, with flashing jewels and a fancy dagger at his belt. He was the Queen's page, young Richard Partington. He had come up from famous London Town on a mission from her Majesty: to seek Robin Hood in Sherwood Forest.

It had been a long hot ride from Leicester Town, and young Partington was glad to see a sweet little inn ahead. In front of the door hung a sign with a picture of a blue boar. He reined up and called loudly for some Rhine wine, for Queen's pages did not generally drink country ale. Five strong fellows, two in Lincoln green, watched from the bench under the spreading oak in front. Beside each leaned a great heavy oak staff.

The landlord brought a bottle of wine and a long narrow glass, which he held up to the page as he sat upon his horse. Young Partington poured the bright yellow wine, raised the glass, and cried, "To the health and long happiness of my mistress, noble Queen Eleanor. May I soon do her wishes by locating a certain bold yeoman called Robin Hood."

At these words all stared, but the two yeomen in Lincoln green whispered together. Then one of the two spoke up and said, "Sir Page, what does our good Queen wish of Robin Hood? My question is not idle, for I know this yeoman somewhat."

"In that case, good fellow," young Partington said, "it will be a great service to both him and our royal Queen to help me find him."

Then the other yeoman, a handsome fellow with a tanned face and curly nut-brown hair, said, "You have an honest look, Sir Page, and our Queen is kind and true to all brave yeomen. My friend and I might safely guide you to Robin Hood, for we know where to find him. But I will tell you plainly: not for all merry England would we have harm come to him."

"Do not worry, for I bring no harm, merely a kind message from our Queen."

Then the two yeomen looked at one another again, and the tall man said, "I believe it is safe, Will." The other nodded. "We believe you, Sir Page, and will do as you ask."

Partington paid for the wine, and the yeomen came forward and led him toward Sherwood.

In the cool shade of the great oak tree lay Robin Hood and many of his band, listening in silence to the wondrous music of Allan a Dale. There came the sound of horse's hooves, and then Little John and Will Stutely came into the clearing, young Richard Partington riding between them. As they approached Robin Hood, all the band stared at the noble young page. Robin rose to meet him, and Partington leaped from his horse and removed his cap of crimson velvet. "Welcome, fair youth!" cried Robin. "What brings a young noble to our poor forest of Sherwood?"

Young Partington said, "If I am correct, you are the famous Robin Hood, and these are your bold band of outlawed yeomen. I bring greetings from our noble Queen Eleanor. She has heard much about you and wishes to meet you in person. She promises that if you will come soon to London Town, she will do all in her power to guard you against harm and will send you back safe to Sherwood Forest again.

"Four days from now, in Finsbury Fields, our good King Henry is holding a grand shooting match. The most famous archers of merry England will be there. Our Queen desires that you compete and is confident that you will win. In token of her goodwill, she sends you this golden ring from her own hand, and I now give it to you."

Robin Hood bowed his head, took the ring, kissed it loyally, and slipped it on. "I would rather lose my life than this ring. Sir Page, I will obey our Queen's command and go with you to London. But before we go, I will feast you here with the very best we have."

"There is no time," the page said. "I must ask that you get ready to go right away. Our Queen also promises that anyone accompanying you will be equally welcome."

"Very well," Robin said. "I choose three of my men to go with me: my right-hand man Little John, my cousin Will Scarlet, and my minstrel Allan a Dale. Get ready, lads, for we leave soon. Will Stutely, you shall be the chief of the band while I am gone."

Little John and Will Scarlet and Allan a Dale ran excitedly to get ready, while Robin also prepared. When they came back, they were a fair sight. Robin was dressed from head to toe in blue, and Little John and Will Scarlet in good Lincoln green. Allan a Dale wore scarlet from cap to pointed shoes. Each man wore beneath his cap a little steel helmet and under his jacket a shirt of fine chain mail. When all were ready, young Partington mounted up again, the yeomen shook hands all around, and the party of five set out.

By mid-morning of the fourth day they came at last to the towers and walls of famous London Town.

Queen Eleanor sat in her royal chamber, lit by the sweet sunshine through the open windows, enjoying the perfume of the roses growing in the garden below. Her ladies-in-waiting sat and stood about her, chatting quietly.

A lady came in and told the Queen that her page, Richard Partington, and four yeomen awaited her pleasure in the court below. Queen Eleanor happily ordered them shown into her presence.

Robin Hood and Little John and Will Scarlet and Allan a Dale entered the royal chamber. Robin kneeled before the Queen with his hands folded upon his chest, saying simply, "I am Robin Hood, and I have come at your command. I will serve and obey you, even if it costs me every drop of my blood."

But good Queen Eleanor smiled pleasantly on him and told him to rise. Then she had them all be seated, and rich food and noble wines were brought to refresh them after their rapid journey. When they had eaten their fill, she asked them to tell of their merry adventures. They told her all the tales of their adventures, including the story of the Bishop of Hereford and Sir Richard of the Lea, and how the Bishop had spent three days in Sherwood Forest. The Queen and her ladies laughed in delight at the image of the stout Bishop roaming the woods in yeoman-like sport with Robin and his band.

When they had told all that they remembered, the Queen asked Allan to sing, for his fame had reached even to her royal ears. So Allan took up his harp, strummed the strings sweetly, and sang. As had happened so many times under the great oak tree, all was silent even for a while after Allan finished.

In this way they passed the time until the hour of the great archery match. Finsbury Fields were a fine sight, for along the end of the meadow stood ten decorated booths representing each company of the King's archers, topped by its captain's flag. The place was a beehive of activity, with attendants running about carrying ale or bundles of bowstrings or armloads of arrows.

On each side of the archery range were rows of seats, and in the center of the north side was a raised platform for the King and Queen, shaded

by bright-colored canvas and hung with stream-
ing silken pennants. Their Majesties had not yet
arrived, but many spectators had. One hundred
and sixty yards from the shooting-line were ten
targets on raised mounds of earth. Each target
had a white center, then a black ring, then a red
outer ring. In the very middle of the white center
was a blue dot one inch wide. From each mound
flew a flag matching the color of the company
whose target it was. All was ready for the coming
of the King and Queen.

At last a great blast of bugles sounded, and
into the meadow rode six heralds with silver
trumpets. Behind these came King Henry on a
gray stallion, his Queen beside him upon a milk-
white mare. They were flanked by the yeomen
of the guard, sunlight flashing off their steel halberds. Behind them followed the Royal Court in
a flow of bright colors, silk and velvet, waving
plumes and flashing jewels: a gallant sight.

The people stood and shouted and the
sound was like a storm breaking on the Cornish
coast. The King and Queen reached their place,
dismounted, climbed up the platform and sat
down on thrones decorated with purple silks.

When all was quiet a bugle sounded, and
the archers came marching from their tents:
eight hundred of the finest yeomen in the
world. When they reached the area in front of
the royal platform, the King beamed with pride

at the sight of such a gallant band. Then he ordered his chief herald, Sir Hugh de Mowbray, to proclaim the rules. Sir Hugh stepped to the edge of the platform and announced:

"Each man shall shoot seven arrows at his company's target. Of the eighty in each company, the three who do best shall shoot three more times. The winners will represent their companies in the final competition, and will again each shoot three times. The best shot among them shall have first prize: fifty golden pounds, a silver bugle horn inlaid with gold, and a quiver of ten white arrows tipped with gold. The second prize shall be one hundred of the fattest deer that run on Dallen Lea, to shoot whenever he wishes. The third prize shall be two barrels of fine Rhine wine."

When Sir Hugh finished, all the archers waved their bows aloft and shouted. Then each company turned and marched back to its place.

Now the shooting began, the captains going first. It took a long time, for over five thousand arrows were to be shot. When it was over, the judges inspected the targets, each of which bristled with arrows like a hedgehog's back. They announced the names of those who had shot the best, and a great cheer arose for the favorite archers of the crowd. Ten fresh targets were put up, and silence fell as the remaining archers once more took their places.

This time the shooting was quicker, for each company shot only nine times. When the shooting was done, the judges did their work once more and soon proclaimed the best bowmen of each band. Gilbert of the White Hand's company had done the best, all three of his arrows hitting the white center. But brave Tepus and young Clifton had done nearly as well, and the others were close behind.

It was still anyone's game to win. The ten remaining archers went to their tents to rest and change bowstrings, for neither aim nor equipment must fail them now.

While the crowd buzzed with anticipation, Queen Eleanor turned to the King and asked, "Do you think that the yeomen here are the very best archers in all merry England?"

"Certainly," said the King with a contented smile. "They are the best archers in all merry England, indeed in the whole world."

"What if," Queen Eleanor asked, "I found three archers to match the best three yeomen of your guard?"

"Then you would have outdone me," the King said, laughing, "for there is no archer on earth who can equal Tepus and Gilbert and Clifton."

"Well," the Queen said, "I know of three yeomen—in fact, I have seen them recently— whom I would gladly match against your best three. I could summon them here to shoot today, but I will only do so if you will offer safe conduct to any man I invite."

The King laughed loud and long. "Truly, you are involved with strange matters for a queen. Bring these three fellows, and I will promise faithfully to give them free pardon for forty days, in which they may come and go as they wish in safety. If they outshoot my men, they will win the prizes. But seeing as you have developed this sudden interest in sports, would you care for a bet?"

"Why, certainly," said Queen Eleanor, laughing. "I am not very familiar with such matters, but I will try anyway. What stakes do you propose?"

The merry King laughed again. "I will bet you ten barrels of Rhine wine, ten barrels of the best ale, and two hundred bows of finest Spanish yew, with quivers and arrows to match."

All nearby smiled, but Queen Eleanor bowed her head and said quietly, "I will take your bet, for I can think of good uses for these items." She turned to look about those in the court. "Now, who will back me?"

Everyone was silent. "Will you, my Lord Bishop of Hereford?"

"No, your Majesty," said the Bishop hastily. "Men of the cloth should not gamble."

"Especially those who are very fond of their

money," said the Queen with a smile. A ripple of laughter went around, for the Bishop's stinginess was legendary.

Turning to the King, Queen Eleanor said, "Since no one will back me, I will bet this jeweled belt that I am wearing. It is surely worth at least as much as the wine and ale and bows that you are betting."

"I accept," the King said. "Send for your archers. But here come the others; let them shoot, and I will match the winners against all the world."

The Queen beckoned young Richard Partington and whispered something in his ear. The page bowed and left. Those remaining nearby wondered what it meant and which three men the Queen might have in mind.

Now the ten archers of the King's guard took their places again, and the great crowd was silent as death. Each man shot with great care; the only noises were the twanging of bowstrings and the thwacks of arrows hitting the targets.

When the last shaft had sped, a great roar went up; and the excellent shooting deserved it. Once again Gilbert had put three arrows in the white; Tepus came second with two in the white and one in the black ring next to it; but Clifton had narrowly lost third place to Hubert of Suffolk. All the archers around Gilbert's booth cheered, tossing their caps aloft and shaking hands.

In the midst of all the hubbub, five men came walking across the lawn toward the King's pavilion. The first was Richard Partington, whom most knew, but the others were strange to everybody. Beside the page walked a yeoman in blue, and behind came three others, two in Lincoln green and one in scarlet. This last yeoman carried three strong bows, two fancifully inlaid with silver and one with gold.

While these men approached, the King dispatched a messenger to summon Gilbert, Tepus, and Hubert. The crowd ceased shouting and stood up to try to see what was going on.

When Partington and the others arrived before the King and Queen, the four yeomen knelt and removed their caps to her. King Henry leaned forward and stared at them closely, but the Bishop of Hereford started as though stung by a wasp. He opened his mouth as if to speak, then saw the Queen smiling meaningfully at him. He blushed with remembered humiliation and was silent.

Then the Queen leaned forward and spoke clearly. "Locksley, I have bet the King that you and two of your men can outshoot any three of his. Will you do your best for my sake?"

"Yes, your Majesty," replied Robin Hood. "If I do any less, I swear never again to draw a bow."

Although Little John had been somewhat bashful in the Queen's chamber, the feeling of green grass under his feet emboldened him again, and he said, "Blessings on your Majesty's sweet face. If any man alive would not do his best for you, I would crack his worthless skull!"

"Hush, Little John!" said Robin Hood hastily and quietly, but good Queen Eleanor laughed aloud, and a ripple of merriment washed through the booth.

The Bishop of Hereford and the King did not laugh. King Henry turned to the Queen and asked, "Who are these men?"

The Bishop could no longer contain himself. "Your Majesty, that fellow in blue is an outlawed thief of the mid-country, one Robin Hood. The tall, uncouth one is called Little John; the other in green is a backslid gentleman known as Will Scarlet. The minstrel in red is a rogue named Allan a Dale."

At this speech the King's brows knit in anger, and he turned to the Queen. "Is this true?" he asked sternly.

"Yes," the Queen said, smiling, "as the Bishop should know, for he and two of his friars spent three days in merry sport with Robin Hood in Sherwood Forest. I hardly thought that the good Bishop would betray his friends. But remember your promise: you promised these good yeomen safety for forty days."

"I will keep my promise," said the King, in a deep and angry voice, "but after forty days, this outlaw had best take care." Gilbert and Tepus and Hubert had arrived in the meantime and stood listening and wondering. The King turned to them and said to them: "I have promised that you will shoot against these fellows. If you win, I will fill your caps with silver pennies. If you fail, you shall lose your prizes, which I will give to those that shoot against you. Do your best, lads, and if you win now you will be rewarded."

The King's archers went back to their booths. Robin and his men went to their assigned shooting-places, chose their best arrows, and strung their bows.

But when the King's archers went to their tents, they told their friends what had happened and that these four were the famous Robin Hood and three of his band: Little John, Will Scarlet, and Allan a Dale. The news spread like flame on dry grasses, and soon the entire crowd knew that they were about to see the famous mid-country yeomen in action.

Six fresh targets were set up, and Gilbert and Tepus and Hubert came out of the booths. Then Robin Hood and Gilbert of the White Hand tossed a coin to see who should shoot first. Gilbert won and called upon Hubert of Suffolk to lead.

Hubert took his place, fitted a smooth arrow, and drew the string carefully. The arrow lodged in the white. Again he shot, and again he hit the center. His third shot landed in the black, but less than an inch from the white. A shout went up, for it was Hubert's best shooting so far that day.

Merry Robin laughed and said, "That will be hard to beat, Will, for it is your turn. Show them how we shoot in Sherwood."

Will Scarlet took his place. But he was too cautious and spoiled his first shot. It hit the red outer ring. "Lad, lad," Robin said, "you held the string too long! Have I not often told you that overcaution spoils the shot?" Will Scarlet paid attention, and his next two shots struck well within the center, but stout Hubert had outshot him.

The crowd cheered for the guardsman who had defeated the stranger. The King said grimly to the Queen, "If your archers shoot no better than that, you are likely to lose the bet." But Queen Eleanor smiled, for she looked for better things from Robin Hood and Little John.

Now Tepus took his place to shoot, and he made the same error as Will Scarlet. His first arrow hit the center, but the second landed in the black. The third was tipped with luck, for it hit the small blue dot in the very center of the white. "That is the sweetest shot of the day," said Robin Hood, "but even so, friend Tepus, I think your cake is burnt. Little John, your turn."

Little John stepped up and shot his three arrows quickly without once lowering his bow arm. All three of his arrows hit the white center, very close to the blue dot. There was no shout, though it was the best shooting so far that day. The Londoners did not like to see bold Tepus lose, even to an archer as famous as Little John.

Next Gilbert of the White Hand took his place and shot carefully. For the third time in one day he put all three shafts into the white center.

"Well done, Gilbert!" said Robin Hood, clapping him on the shoulder. "With your skill, lad, you should be a free and merry ranger like us. You belong in the forest, not inside the gray walls of London Town." With that Robin took his place, drew out an arrow, inspected it carefully, and did the same with two more.

Then the King muttered in his beard, "Now, blessed Saint Hubert, if you will jog that rogue's elbow so as to make him hit even the black ring, I will donate a hundred and sixty wax candles to your chapel." But perhaps Saint Hubert's ears were plugged, for he seemed not to hear the King's prayer.

When merry Robin was satisfied with his three arrows, he inspected his bowstring, then placed an arrow in it. "Yes," he said to Gilbert, who stood nearby, "you should pay us a visit in merry Sherwood." Robin drew the bowstring to his ear. "In London"—here he shot—"there

is nothing to shoot at but crows and jackdaws; in Sherwood, our targets are the noblest deer in England." The arrow lodged not more than half an inch from the blue dot.

"By my soul!" cried Gilbert. "Are you the devil in blue, to shoot like that while talking?"

"No," laughed Robin, "not that bad, I trust." He place a second arrow, pulled it back and shot. Again his arrow struck next to the dot, on the opposite side of it from the first. With his third shot, he sent an arrow into the blue dot right between the other too, so close that their feathers touched. They looked from a distance like one single, thick arrow.

A low murmur ran through that great crowd, for never before had London seen such shooting. All saw that the King's archers were fairly beaten. Gilbert shook Robin's hand and admitted that he could never hope to match Robin Hood or Little John. But the infuriated King would not accept this. "No!" he exclaimed. "Gilbert is not yet beaten! Did he not also hit the center three times? I have lost my bet, but he has not yet lost first prize. I command them to shoot again, and again, until either he or that rascal Robin Hood comes off best. Sir Hugh, go tell them to shoot another round, and another, until someone loses." Sir Hugh, seeing royal anger, obeyed quickly and without a word. When he reached Robin Hood and Gilbert, he told them what the King had said.

"If it will please my gracious lord and King," merry Robin said, "I will shoot all day and night. Take your place, Gilbert lad."

Gilbert did so, but this time he failed. A little sudden wind arose, and his arrow missed the center—though just barely.

"Your eggs are cracked, Gilbert," Robin said, laughing. He shot, and once more his arrow hit the white center.

The King arose, scowling about him. Anyone caught smiling would have been very sorry. Then the royal entourage left, the King in the foulest of foul moods.

After the King had gone, all the yeomen of the guard and many spectators came crowding around Robin and his men to get a look at the famous men talking with Gilbert. Soon the three judges came forward, and the chief judge began the awards ceremony.

"The first prize belongs to you," the judge said to Robin. "Here are the silver bugle, the quiver of ten gold-tipped arrows, and a purse of fifty pounds." He turned to Little John. "The second prize is yours: a hundred of the finest deer of Dallen Lea, to shoot whenever you wish." Last he turned to Hubert. "You have held your own, and you therefore keep your prize: two barrels of good Rhine wine, to be delivered whenever you wish." Then he called on the other seven of the King's archers who had last shot and gave each eighty silver pennies.

Then Robin spoke: "This silver bugle I keep in honor of this shooting match; but you, Gilbert, are the best archer of all the King's guard. To you I freely give this purse of gold, and I wish it were ten times as much, for you are a true yeoman. To each of the ten who shot last, I give one of these gold-tipped arrows. Keep them, so that if you ever have grandchildren, you may tell them that you are the very boldest yeoman in the whole world."

All shouted aloud in appreciation of the compliment. Then Little John spoke: "Good friend Tepus," said he, "I do not need these deer of Dallen Lea, for we have plenty in our own country. Fifty I give to you to shoot as you wish, and I give five of the rest to each band."

Another great shout went up, and many tossed their caps high and called Robin and his yeomen the finest of fellows. While they did so, a tall burly yeoman of the King's guard came up and caught Robin by the sleeve, saying, "Good master, I have a message for you. It is a pretty silly thing for one yeoman to say to another, but a young peacock of a page named Richard Partington was looking for you, and when he could not find you, he told me to bring it to you, word for word. It comes from a certain lady you know, and if I recall correctly—let me see—it was: 'The lion growls. Beware your head.'"

"Really?" said Robin, for the message was obviously a warning from the Queen: the King was infuriated. "Thank you, good fellow, for you have done me greater service today than you realize." Then he called his three friends together and told them that it was time to go, for merry London Town was about to become unsafe for them.

They said their farewells and made their way through the crowd. After this, they left London Town and started north.

Chapter
19

The Chase of
Robin Hood

Robin Hood and the others had been traveling homeward for less than an hour when the
Queen's warning proved both true and timely. Six
yeomen of the King's guard bustled through the
remaining crowd, under orders to arrest Robin
and his men. It was dishonorable of the King to
break his promise, but the Bishop of Hereford
had persuaded him. It happened this way:

After the match, the King fumed all the way
from the archery grounds to his council chamber. With him went the Bishop of Hereford and
Sir Robert Lee, but for a time no one spoke. At
last the Bishop of Hereford spoke in mournful
tones: "It is too bad, Your Majesty, that this vile
outlaw is getting away. Once he is safe in

Sherwood Forest, he can continue laughing at both king and king's men."

The King looked grimly at the Bishop. "You think so?" he said. "Just wait. Forty days from now, I will seize this outlaw even if I must tear down all of Sherwood to find him. The laws of the King of England will not be evaded by a friendless, penniless vagabond!"

In a silky, cautious voice the Bishop continued: "Forgive my boldness, Your Majesty, for I wish the best for both England and her King. Even if my gracious lord uprooted every tree in Sherwood, there are other places for Robin Hood to hide. Cannock Chase is not far from Sherwood, and there is the nearby Arden Forest and many other mid-country woodlands where catching Robin Hood would be like catching a rat in a cluttered warehouse. No, my gracious lord, once he sets foot in the woods, he will be forever outside and above your royal law."

The King tapped his fingertips on the table in frustration. "What do you suggest, Bishop?" he growled. "Did you not hear me pledge my word to the Queen? Your talk is useless."

"Far be it from me," the cunning Bishop said, "to imagine what I would think and do in Your Majesty's place. But with all due respect, were I the King of England, I would think: 'I have promised my Queen; for forty days, I will allow the cleverest outlaw in all England to come and go. Now he is in my grasp! Will I then foolishly adhere to such a hasty promise? Moreover, the Queen is not aware of the grave matters of governing the state. This Robin Hood is a passing fancy of hers, like a daisy picked on a whim and discarded when it wilts. Must I let him slip away, that he may return to his habit of scoffing at my authority?' This, Your Majesty, is what I would say to myself in your place."

The more the Bishop talked, the more persuasive the King found him. After a while, the monarch turned to Sir Robert Lee. "Sir Robert, go send six yeomen of the guard to capture this Robin Hood and his three men."

Sir Robert Lee, a gentle and noble knight, was disappointed to see the King break his promise, but this was clearly no time to argue. Instead, in hopes of protecting his sovereign's honor, he went first to the Queen. He told her what had happened, so that she might send Robin Hood word of his danger. Only then did he command the yeomen of the guard to arrest the outlaws. As a result, the yeomen of the guard arrived at the archery field too late.

It was late afternoon when Robin Hood, Little John, Will, and Allan headed for home. By the time they reached Barnet Town, some ten or twelve miles from London, the moon shone bright and full in the eastern sky. On the far side of Barnet, they came to a little inn shaded with roses and woodbines, and Robin said, "Let us rest here for the night, now that we are well away from London Town and the King's anger. We could all use some good food and drink and comfort after this busy day. What do you say, lads?"

"Good master," Little John replied, "you always seem to know what I want. Let us go in."

Will Scarlet said, "Uncle, I wish we were further along the road before stopping for the night. But if you think it best, then let us stay here."

They went in and called for the best food and drink in the house. A lovely young maiden set before them a fine feast, with two bottles of good wine to wash it down. Little John, who had a way with women and loved their smiles as he did food and drink, kept winking at her, earning him merry sidelong glances and soft giggles. It was a merry dinner party indeed, and when the four were done eating, they lingered over the wine. As they relaxed, the landlord came in and said that a young page named Richard Partington, of the Queen's household, wished to see the lad in blue right away.

Robin arose quickly, told the hovering landlord to give him privacy, and went out to speak with the page. Robin found young Richard Partington sitting on his horse waiting for him.

"What news do you have, Sir Page?" Robin said. "I trust that it is not bad."

"It is bad enough," young Partington said.

"That vile Bishop of Hereford has stirred up the King against you. His Majesty sent men to arrest you at Finsbury Fields; not finding you there, he sent forth a thousand armed men along this very road. They are to capture you, if they can, or at least prevent you from getting back to Sherwood. The Bishop commands this force, and you can guess what sort of justice to expect from him: a long rope. The men have fanned out, and two bands on horseback are not far behind me on this road. You had better get going, unless you want to spend tonight in a cold dungeon. The Queen sent me to tell you."

"Now, Richard Partington," Robin said, "this is the second time that you have saved my life, and I will never forget it. As for that Bishop of Hereford, if I ever catch him near Sherwood again, he will regret it. Tell our good Queen that I will leave right now and will let the landlord think that we are going to Saint Albans. When we are on the road, however, I will go one way and will send my men another, so that if one falls into the King's hands the others may escape. With luck we will all reach Sherwood safely. Farewell, Sir Page, and thank you once again."

"Farewell, bold yeoman," young Partington said, "and a safe trip home to you." They shook hands, and the lad turned his horse back toward London, while Robin went back inside the inn. There he found his yeomen sitting in silence waiting for him, along with the nosy landlord, curious to know what the Queen's Page wanted with this stranger in blue.

"Up, my merry men!" said Robin. "This place is not safe. Let us go forward once more and not stop until we reach Saint Albans." He paid the landlord and they left.

When they were beyond the town, Robin stopped and told them about his conversation with young Partington and how the King's men were hot on their heels. "Let us part company here," he instructed. "You go east, and I will go west, staying off the main highways. Do not go north until you have gotten well to the east. Will Scarlet, you are the most cunning, so you take the lead. I will see you all back in sweet Sherwood." They shook hands, embraced, and parted company.

Shortly after this, twenty of the King's men came clattering up to the door of the inn at Barnet Town. They quickly dismounted and surrounded the place. The captain and four others barged into the yeomen's former room—too late. "I thought they were bad men," said the landlord, when the men-at-arms told him who they sought. "But I heard that rascal in blue say that they were heading for Saint Albans. If you hurry, you might catch them on the highway." The captain thanked him heartily, called his men to mount up, and galloped toward Saint Albans on a wild goose chase.

Little John and Will Scarlet and Allan a Dale left the highway near Barnet and traveled east until they came to Chelmsford, in Essex. Then they turned north, passing through Cambridge and Lincolnshire to Gainsborough Town. From there they turned southwest, reaching at last the northern borders of Sherwood Forest. They completely evaded the King's men. The journey took eight days, but when they reached home, they found that Robin had not yet arrived.

Robin was not as fortunate as his men. Leaving the great northern road, he turned west, past Aylesbury to fair Woodstock in Oxfordshire. He then turned north, passing through Warwick Town and arriving at Dudley in Staffordshire. This took seven days. When he believed he was far enough north, he headed east along the back roads. Not far from Sherwood, he came to a place called Stanton, and joyfully believed he would soon smell the fresh greenwood air once again. As Robin found, a lot can go wrong at the final moment.

When the King's men found themselves foiled at Saint Albans, with no idea where to seek Robin and his men, they waited for further orders. Soon another band of horsemen came, and another, until all the moonlit streets were full of armed men. Between midnight and dawn another band arrived, along with the Bishop of

Hereford. When he heard that Robin Hood had again slipped away, he immediately gathered his bands and hurried his force north. He left a party behind in Saint Albans, to send along any other groups that might straggle in.

Four days later, in the evening, the Bishop reached Nottingham Town. There he divided his men into bands of six or seven and sent them out to block every highway and country road east, south, and west of Sherwood. The Sheriff of Nottingham called out all his men to help the Bishop, for here was his best chance ever for revenge. Will Scarlet and Little John and Allan a Dale had just missed the King's men east of Sherwood; the day after they passed, the roads they had traveled were blocked. Had they delayed even a little, they would surely have fallen into the Bishop's hands.

Unaware of any of this, Robin whistled merrily as he walked along the road beyond Stanton. At last he came to a little stream crossing the road and stopped to cup his hands and drink the clear, sparkling water.

As he bent to drink, something hissed past his ear and splashed into the streambed beside him. If any man alive knew the sound of an arrow, it was Robin Hood. He bounded to his feet and leaped across the stream, plunging into the forest without stopping to investigate.

Even as he jumped into the forest six more

arrows rattled into the branches after him. One hit his jacket and would have gone deeply into his side, but the tough coat of fine chain mail turned it aside. Behind the volley of arrows came a squad of the King's men in great haste, and they leaped from their horses and went after Robin on foot. But Robin knew the ground better than they, and between crawling, ducking, and quick dashes across clearings, he soon left them far behind. Before long he came to another road about eight hundred yards from the one he had left, and stopped for a moment to catch his breath. He could still hear the shouts of the seven men as they crashed uselessly through the brush like hounds put off the scent. Then he tightened his belt and ran swiftly east down the road toward Sherwood.

Robin had not gone quite half a mile when he crested a hill and looked down. Beneath him was another band of the King's men sitting in the shade along the road. They did not see him. He turned quickly back the way he had come, to take his chances with the seven men in the thicket. Soon he was safely past them—or so he thought. As he ran, he heard a great shout behind him: the seven had come out onto the road, a quarter mile behind him. The chase was on again.

Robin ran like a greyhound, mile after mile, stopping only when he was over the Derwent River and close to Derby Town. When he had lost them, he sat down under a hedge to rest in the cool shade and long grass. "By my soul, Robin," said he to himself, "that was the narrowest miss of your whole life. The feather of that arrow actually tickled my ear. This running, though, has given me a huge appetite. I wish I had some food and drink. I pray Saint Dunstan to send me some meat and beer, and soon."

As if in answer to Robin's prayer, a cobbler named Quince, from Derby, came plodding along the road. He had just delivered a pair of shoes to a nearby farmer. In his pouch he had a boiled chicken and a bottle of stout beer, a bonus from the grateful farmer for the fine shoes. Good Quince was an honest fellow, but his wits were as thick as raw dough. The only thing that was in his mind was, "Forty-two and one half pence for your shoes, good Quince—forty-two and one half pence for your shoes." This thought rolled around inside his head like a pea rolls around in an empty pot.

"Hello, good friend," Robin said from beneath the hedge when Quince was near. "Where do you go so merrily on this bright day?"

The cobbler stopped, and seeing a well-dressed stranger in blue, he spoke politely: "Good day, fair sir. I have come from Kirk Langly, where I have been paid forty-two and one half pence for my shoes. And you, stranger in blue— what are you doing down under that hedge?"

"Well," merry Robin said, "I sit down here to drop salt on the tails of golden birds, but so far today you are the nearest thing to a bird I have seen."

The cobbler's eyes and mouth opened big and wide. "Golden birds?" he said. "I have never seen such a thing. And you find them under these hedges, you say? Are there many of them, good fellow? I would like to find some myself."

"Of course," answered Robin, "they are as thick here as fish in the sea."

"Amazing!" the cobbler said in wonder. "And you can catch them by dropping salt on their pretty tails?"

"Yes, but this salt is hard to get. One must boil a quart of moonbeams in a wooden platter, and even that makes only a pinch. But tell me, my good man, what is in that pouch by your side?"

The cobbler stopped to think for a moment, quite unable to consider two matters at once. At last he remembered: "Why, there is a bottle of good March beer, along with a fat boiled chicken. A fine feast awaits Quince the cobbler this day."

"Tell me, good Quince," Robin said, "would you be interested in selling them to me? I will give you these bright blue clothes, plus ten shillings, for your clothes and leather apron and beer and chicken. What do you say?"

"You cannot be serious," the cobbler said.

"My clothes are coarse and patched, and yours are fine and very pretty."

"I mean it," Robin replied. "Take your jacket off and I will show you. I like your clothes very much; also, I will share the beer and chicken with you." Robin began to slip off the blue jacket. Seeing Robin serious, the cobbler began pulling off his clothes also. Each put on the other's clothing, and Robin gave the honest cobbler ten bright new shillings. Quince admired his new outfit while Robin said, "I have been many things in life, but never have I been an honest cobbler. Come, friend, let us eat, for my stomach is begging for chicken." Both sat down and began a hearty feast, which lasted until the bones of the chicken were picked bare.

Then Robin stretched his legs out in comfort and said, "I can tell from your voice, good Quince, that there is a fair song or two somewhere in your head. Will you sing me one?"

"I have a song or two," the cobbler said. "They are poor things, but you are welcome to one." Moistening his throat with a swallow of beer, Quince prepared to sing.

Just as he began, the stout cobbler's music was interrupted by six horsemen, who burst upon them where they sat. Quickly and roughly they seized the honest craftsman. "Ha!" roared the leader of the band with joy. "We have caught you at last, you rascal in blue! Now, my lads, the good Bishop's bounty of eighty pounds is ours today. Do not think to play foolish with us, you cunning rogue! We know who you are, you old fox, and you are coming with us to have your tail snipped off."

The poor cobbler gazed all around him in shock, his mouth wide open and speechless. Robin also gaped and stared in wonder, just as the cobbler would have done in his place. "My goodness!" he said. "What have I walked into? Surely this is a good, honest fellow."

"Hardly an honest fellow, you clown!" said one of the men. "This is none other than that famous rogue, Robin Hood."

The cobbler stared and gaped more than ever, his wits thrashing about his head in confusion. As he looked at Robin Hood and saw the yeoman looking much like what he knew himself to be, he began to doubt reality. Maybe, Quince thought, he was indeed the great outlaw. In a slow, wondering voice he said: "Am I really? I had thought—no, Quince, you are mistaken—can it really be? It must! I must indeed be Robin Hood! I never thought that I would ever go from being an honest craftsman to a great yeoman."

"Shame on you men!" Robin Hood said. "Look what your ill treatment has done, confusing the poor lad so. As for me, I am Quince, the cobbler of Derby Town."

"Truly?" Quince said. "Then, indeed, I am somebody else and can be none other than Robin Hood. Take me, fellows; but let me tell you: you have laid hands on the bravest yeoman that ever walked the woodlands."

"Play madman, will you?" said the leader of the band. "Giles, fetch a cord and tie his hands behind him. When we get him back before our good Bishop at Tutbury Town, his wits will come back in a hurry." They tied the cobbler's hands behind him and led him off with a rope.

When they were gone, Robin laughed until the tears rolled down his cheeks. He knew that no harm would come to the honest fellow. It was too bad he could not see the Bishop's reaction when simple Quince was brought before him as Robin Hood. Then he stepped east again toward Nottinghamshire and Sherwood Forest.

But Robin Hood had been through much. His journey from London had been hard and long, over a hundred and forty miles in one week. He now meant to travel nonstop until he had come to Sherwood, but he had not gone ten more miles when he felt his strength finally fading. His feet felt like lumps of lead, and he sat down to rest, then tried to press on. After traveling a couple of miles he gave up. He was near a little inn, and summoned the landlord to ask for a room, though it was barely sundown. There were only three rooms in the place, and one was already taken; the landlord showed him to the worst of the two that remained. Robin did not care; he was exhausted enough to sleep on a pile of broken rocks. He took off his clothes and fell asleep as his head touched the pillow.

Not long after Robin went to bed, a great dark cloud peeped over the hills west of the inn. Soon it became a thunderstorm, blasting the night with flashes of lightning and rumbling thunder. Two rich businessmen, not caring to be caught in it, stopped at the inn. They stabled their horses and then called for the best food and drink in the house. When they were full, they went wearily to their room, complaining about having to share a bed but soon losing their troubles in sleep.

The wind began to shake the inn with great gusts. As though it had brought a guest, the door opened, and in came a high-ranking friar of Emmet Priory in fine robes. He called to the landlord to stable his mule and likewise asked for the inn's best. A stew with dumplings was brought, along with a bottle of ale, and the holy friar plunged into the feast. Soon nothing was left in the platter but a little pool of gravy.

In the meantime the storm intensified. Rain began to accompany the wind, rattling down in showers and lit by bright flashes of lightning. Thunder rolled across the skies.

At last the holy friar had the landlord show him to his room. To the friar's great and vocal dismay, his only option was to share a shoddy room with a common cobbler, but it was better than sleeping in the storm. The friar of Emmet Priory came to his room and looked Robin over and felt a little less annoyed; at least he was not sharing a bed with a rough, unwashed fellow. He took off his robes and huddled into the bed, while Robin rolled over in his sleep and made room. The friar soon joined Robin in blissful and ignorant sleep.

When dawn came, Robin opened his eyes and looked over. Who lay next to him but a shaven-headed man, obviously in holy orders, and still sound asleep! Robin wondered how the holy man had landed here. He got up softly, so as not to waken the other, and saw the friar's clothes lying on a bench. He smiled and said, "Good Brother Whatever-your-name-is, since you have felt free to borrow my bed, I will just borrow your clothes in return. He put on the holy man's robe and rosary, but kindly left the cobbler's clothes in their place.

Then he went out into the inn's front room. The stableman looked at him in wonder, for friars of Emmet were not known as early risers. Keeping this thought to himself, he asked Robin if he wanted his mule brought from the stable.

"Yes, my son," Robin said, thinking quickly.

"And hurry, for I am late." The stableman obeyed, and Robin climbed onto the mule and went happily on his way.

As for the holy friar, he awoke in a foul mood. His rich, soft robes were gone, as was his purse with ten golden pounds. In exchange he had only patched clothes and a leather apron. He raged and swore like any layman, but neither his raging nor the landlord could help; he had to be at Emmet on business that very morning. Worse still, it was muddy from the rainy night and his mule was gone. He must wear the cobbler's clothes or travel naked; either way he must walk. Swearing revenge on every cobbler in Derbyshire, he put on the cobbler's clothing and set out.

The holy friar's day soon worsened. He had not gone far before he was caught by a squad of the King's men, who marched him off with little dignity toward Tutbury Town and the Bishop of Hereford. He tried to convince them that he was a holy man, and showed his shaven head, but the men would hear none of it and prodded him along through the mud.

Meanwhile merry Robin rode along contentedly, passing safely by two bands of the King's men. Sherwood was near, and his heart danced within him. Suddenly he met a noble knight in a shady lane. Robin halted his mule quickly and leaped off its back. "Sir Richard of the Lea," he cried, "well met! I would rather see your good face today than that of any other man in England!"

Then he told Sir Richard the whole story and that now at last he felt safe, being so close to Sherwood. But when Robin finished, Sir Richard shook his head sadly. "You are in greater danger now than ever, Robin. Before you lie bands of the Sheriff's men blocking every road and checking every traveler. The King's men are behind you, and by now they know of your new disguise. I would gladly shelter you in Castle Lea, but we would lose, for the force now in Nottingham would storm it."

Robin's heart sank; he felt like a fox with the hounds at his heels and his den's entrance blocked. Sir Richard bent his head to think.

Presently Sir Richard spoke again. "There is only one thing to do, Robin. Go back to London and throw yourself on the mercy of our good Queen Eleanor. Come with me to my castle, and I will dress you as one of my retainers. Then I will go to London Town with a troop of men, including you, and seek audience with the Queen. This is the only way you will ever get back to Sherwood."

Robin went with Sir Richard of the Lea, for he knew that the noble knight was right. Castle Lea was not far, and soon they were on the road to London, an armed knight with his fine band of men-at-arms walking alongside.

Queen Eleanor walked in her royal garden among the sweet roses, kept company by six of her ladies-in-waiting. Suddenly a man leaped to the top of the wall from the other side, hung for a moment, then dropped lightly to the grass. The ladies screamed in surprise and fear, but the man ran to the Queen and kneeled at her feet. She saw that it was Robin Hood.

"Why, Robin," she cried, "you have come into the very jaws of the raging lion! If the King finds you here, you are in serious trouble. Do you not know that he has men all over the land hunting you?"

"Yes," Robin said, "I know that the King seeks me, so I have come. Surely I will be safe, for he has given his royal word to Your Majesty. Moreover, I know Your Majesty's kind and gentle heart; I place my life freely in your gracious hands."

"I understand, Robin Hood," the Queen said. "You have every right to be disappointed in me, for I have not done all I should have to keep you safe. You must have been in great danger indeed to come here. Once more I promise you my help, and will do all I can to send you back safely to Sherwood Forest. Wait here." She left Robin in the garden of roses and was gone a long time.

When she came back Sir Robert Lee was

with her, and the Queen's cheeks were hot and her eyes bright, as though she had been yelling at somebody. Sir Robert came forward to where Robin Hood stood and said in a cold, stern voice, "Our gracious King has eased his anger toward you, fellow, and has promised once more that you shall leave in safety. In addition, he has promised to send one of his pages to go with you to see that you are left alone.

"You can thank your patron saint that our noble Queen is your good friend; were it not for her persuasion and arguments, you would be a dead man. Let this whole mess teach you two lessons. First, be more honest and do not cause so much trouble. Second, be more careful in your comings and goings. A man who walks in the dark may get away with it for a time, but he eventually falls into a pit. You have put your head in the angry lion's mouth and escaped by a miracle. Do not try it again." So saying, he turned and left Robin.

For three days Robin remained in London in the Queen's household. After that the King's head page, Edward Cunningham, came to get him. Page and outlaw headed north toward Sherwood. Now and then they passed bands of the King's men returning to London, but none of those bands stopped them, and at last they reached the sweet, leafy woodlands.

Robin Hood and
Guy of Gisbourne

For some time after the great shooting match, Robin followed part of Sir Robert's advice: he came and went less boldly. He may not have been more honest, at least not as the Sheriff would see it, but he stayed closer to Sherwood.

This period brought changes to England, for King Henry died and noble King Richard ascended to the throne. The events of the outside world hardly affected Sherwood's shades. Robin Hood and his men lived as merrily as ever, hunting, feasting, singing, and practicing woodland sports.

One summer's day dawned fresh and bright, with a chorus of birds singing loud enough to awaken Robin Hood. Little John and the rest also arose, had breakfast, and started on the various duties of the day.

As Robin Hood and Little John walked down a forest path, where the breeze made the leaves dance, Robin said, "I am restless this fine morning, Little John. Let us each go out and seek adventures, then entertain the band with them tonight."

"That sounds good," Little John said. "Here are two paths; take the right-hand one, and I will take the one to the left. Each of us will walk straight ahead till he tumbles into some merry doing or other."

"Yes," Robin agreed, "let us part here. But be careful, Little John, for I would not have harm come to you for all the world."

"Listen to you!" Little John replied. "You get into worse messes than I do."

Robin Hood laughed. "That is because you have a blundering, hard-headed way that seems to get you out of most troubles in good shape. Let us see who does best today." They shook hands, and each went his own way.

When he was well out of Little John's hearing, Robin came to a broad woodland road arched with tall trees. He could not have imagined that on this lovely road awaited the harshest adventure of his entire life.

As he walked, enjoying the birds' songs, he saw a stranger ahead sitting under an oak tree.

The man seemed not to notice Robin, who halted to observe the stranger. Never had Robin seen such a horrible looking character: dressed from head to toe in horsehide, with the hair still on it, including a hood made from the horse's head. The unfortunate horse's ears stuck up from it like horns. A heavy broadsword and a sharp dagger hung from the stranger's belt. A quiver of smooth arrows was slung on his back, to go with his stout yew bow.

"Hello, friend," cried Robin, coming forward at last. "Who are you? And what is that costume? I have never seen anything like it. It is a good thing I have a clear conscience. Otherwise I might suspect that you were a messenger from the Devil, come to summon me to Hell for a conference."

The wild man pushed back his hood and turned to glare at Robin. He had fierce, hawkish black eyes and a hooked nose above a thin, cruel mouth. Robin was appalled: here was evil in the flesh.

"Who are you, rascal?" he said at last, in a loud, harsh voice.

"Cheer up, brother," merry Robin replied. "You sound like you had vinegar and nettles for breakfast this morning."

"If you do not like my words," the other said fiercely, "then go away, for my deeds match them."

"Oh, but I do like them, you sweet, pretty thing," Robin said, squatting down on the grass in front of the other. "Your speech is clever and pleasing."

The other said nothing at first but glared at Robin like a fierce dog about to go for the throat. Robin gazed back in wide-eyed innocence without even the shadow of a smile. They stared at each other like this for a long time until the stranger finally broke the silence: "What is your name, fellow?"

"What a relief!" Robin said. "I began to fear the sight of me had stricken you mute. As for my name, it may be this or that, but as you are the stranger here, perhaps you should tell me yours first. And why do you wear that dainty clothing?"

The other broke into a short, harsh roar of laughter. "For a fool, you are bold indeed! I am not sure why I do not just run a sword through you, like I did to someone just two days ago for giving me half as much back talk as you. I wear this clothing, idiot, to keep warm and because it is good protection against a sword-thrust. As for my name, most have heard of me. I am Guy of Gisbourne, the outlaw from Herefordshire.

"Recently the Bishop of Hereford sent for me and asked me to do a favor for the Sheriff of Nottingham. The Sheriff was offering two hundred pounds and a free pardon.

"So I came straight to Nottingham Town to see the Sheriff. Apparently there is an outlaw around here, one Robin Hood. No one in Nottingham is man enough to face him, so they had to send to Herefordshire. I do not mind killing him, for I would kill my own brother for half as much money."

Robin listened, sick to his stomach, for he had heard much about the bloody and vile deeds of Guy of Gisbourne. He held his peace, however, for a reason. "Oh, yes," he said, "I have heard of your gentle doings. I am sure Robin Hood would enjoy meeting you."

Guy of Gisbourne gave another harsh laugh. "It will be a merry thing for a bold outlaw like Robin Hood to meet Guy of Gisbourne. Well, not so merry for Robin Hood, perhaps, for he will die."

"But what," Robin asked, "if this Robin Hood turns out to be the stronger? I know him well, and people hereabouts think him a mighty yeoman."

"By your standards, perhaps he is," Guy of Gisbourne said, "but your poor sty of a county is not the whole world. I will stake my life that I am the better man. He is supposed to be an outlaw, but I hear that he has never drawn blood in his life, except when he first came to the forest. He is rumored to be a great archer, but I would challenge him any day."

"Some people do say that," Robin Hood said, "but we of Nottinghamshire are famous for our archery. I myself dabble in it. Would you like to have a shooting match with me?"

Guy of Gisbourne looked at Robin with wondering eyes, then roared with laughter until the woods rang. "I like your bold spirit, fellow. Few men dare talk to me this way. Put up a little wreath for a target, lad, and I will shoot against you."

"In these parts, only little boys shoot at wreaths," said Robin. "Let me put up a good Nottingham target for you." Robin went off to a hazel thicket and whittled a wand about twice as wide as a man's thumb, sharpened the point, and thrust it into the ground in front of a great oak tree. Then he measured off eighty paces, bringing him back to where the wild man sat. "There," Robin said. "That is what we shoot at hereabouts. Split that wand, if you are truly an archer."

Guy of Gisbourne stood up. "You madman! The Devil himself could not hit that!"

"Maybe, and maybe not," merry Robin said. "We will never know until you try."

The horsehide-clad outlaw gave Robin a suspicious, evil look, but decided that he meant no offense. Without speaking he strung his bow and shot twice. He missed the wand by nearly a foot the first time and by six inches the second.

Robin laughed loudly. "You were right. The Devil himself can not hit that target. Good fellow, if you are no better with the broadsword than the bow, better hope you do not meet Robin Hood."

Guy of Gisbourne glared savagely, growling, "You have a merry tongue, rascal. Be careful with it, or I might cut it out."

Robin Hood strung his bow in silence, though his heart quivered with anger and loathing. He shot twice. The first arrow came within an inch of the wand, and the second split it right down the middle. Without waiting to hear the other's reaction, he flung his bow on the ground. "There, you murdering beast!" he yelled. "So much for your skill at manly sports. And now, take a last look at the daylight, for you have spoiled this world long enough. Today you die—for I am Robin Hood!" His bright sword flashed into the sunlight.

Guy of Gisbourne's first reaction of deep shock gave way immediately to rage. "So you are Robin Hood?" he snarled. "Glad to meet you, wretch! Pray, if you are the praying sort, because it will soon be too late." He drew his sword in turn.

Now came the fiercest fight that Sherwood ever saw. No mercy would be given; each man knew that he or the other must die. They fought up and down until the sweet green grass was crushed flat under their heels. More than once the point of Robin Hood's sword felt soft flesh, and soon the ground began to be sprinkled with bright red drops. None of them came from Robin.

At last Guy of Gisbourne made a fierce and deadly thrust at Robin Hood. Robin leaped back lightly, but in doing so caught his heel in a root and fell heavily on his back.

"Now, Holy Mary aid me!" he muttered, as the other leaped at him grinning with rage. Guy of Gisbourne stabbed savagely downward at Robin, but Robin caught the blade in his bare hand and turned it aside. It cut his hand badly but plunged deep into the ground. Before his enemy could pull the sword all the way out, Robin leaped to his feet, his own sword ready.

Now Guy of Gisbourne despaired, and he looked around like a wounded hawk. Robin saw his opening, leaped forward, and gave his foe a backhanded slash under the sword arm. Guy of Gisbourne let go of his sword and staggered back. Before he could recover, Robin took one more step forward and ran his sword all the way through the evil man's body. Guy of Gisbourne spun on his heel, cried out in agony, and fell motionless on his face in the green grass.

Then Robin Hood wiped his sword clean and put it away. Coming to where Guy of Gisbourne lay, he folded his arms and said to

himself: "This is the first man I have killed since I shot the King's forester so long ago. I often regret that day, even now, but I do not regret this one. This was like the killing of a mad, frothing dog. If the Sheriff of Nottingham is going to send this sort of scoundrel after me, I think I will put on these disgusting clothes and seek out his worship. Maybe I can make a payment on the debt I owe him."

Robin stripped the hairy, bloody garments off the dead man and put them on. Then he strapped the other's sword and dagger around his waist. In his hand he carried his own sword, both bows, and his bugle horn. He drew the hood over his face and set out toward

Nottingham. As he walked along, those who saw him hid in terror, for they had heard much of Guy of Gisbourne.

While Robin had been having this adventure, Little John walked through the forest paths until he came to the edge of the woods. Before him were fields of barley and grain smiling in the sun. He turned up the road, soon passing a little thatched cottage in a cluster of crabapple trees. He heard something. Was it someone weeping? A quick listen told him that the sorrowful sound was coming from the cottage, so he went inside.

There he saw a gray-haired woman sitting beside a cold hearth, weeping bitterly. The tall, gruff yeoman was moved. He went to the old woman, patted her kindly on the shoulder, and asked her to tell him her troubles. "Perhaps," he said, "I can ease them in some way, so take heart, good woman."

The sad woman shook her head, but all the same, his kind concern soothed her pain somewhat. She told him the reason for her grief: her three tall, fair young sons had been taken away to be hanged.

The family had grown short of food, and the oldest son had gone out and shot a deer in the moonlight. The King's rangers had followed the blood trail to her cottage and found the deer meat in the cupboard. Neither of the younger brothers had betrayed the oldest, but he had confessed in an attempt to shield them. The foresters had taken all three away in spite of the confession, for the Sheriff had sworn to stamp out poaching by making a fatal example of the first rogue caught doing so. They had said they were taking the three youths to the King's Head Inn, where the Sheriff was staying that day, awaiting the return of a fellow he had sent into Sherwood after Robin Hood.

Little John listened, shaking his head sadly now and then. When the poor woman finished, he said, "This is indeed bad news. I wonder, though, who is looking for Robin Hood? And why? I wish he were here to advise us, but there is no time to be lost if we are to save your sons. Good lady, have you any clothes I can put on in place of this Lincoln green? If I am caught in these by the Sheriff, I will probably hang before your sons."

The old woman still had some clothes belonging to her husband, who had passed away two years before. She brought these to Little John, and he made a wig and false beard out of raw wool to cover his own brown hair and beard. He then put on the deceased man's tall hat, took up his staff and bow, and hastened toward the King's Head Inn.

A mile or more from Nottingham Town, near the southern borders of Sherwood Forest, stood the cozy inn bearing the sign of the King's Head. The place was bustling, for the Sheriff and twenty of his men awaited Guy of Gisbourne's return. There was much fuss and hiss of cooking, and the Sheriff was feasting merrily on the inn's best food and drink. His men sat or lay out front, whiling away the time with ale and conversation.

To this inn came the King's rangers, driving the widow's three sons before them with their hands tied behind their backs. They were marched to the room where the Sheriff sat eating. They stood trembling before him as he scowled sternly at them.

"So," he said, in a great, loud, angry voice, "poaching the King's deer, are you? I will hang all three of you, as a warning to others. Too long has our fair county of Nottingham been a breeding place for outlawry, and I intend to stamp it out for good, beginning with you three."

One of the poor fellows opened his mouth to speak, but the Sheriff roared at him: "Silence! Take them away. I will deal with this when I finish feasting." So the three poor youths were marched outside to await their fates.

After a while the Sheriff came out, called his men about him, and said, "These three poachers shall be hanged shortly, but doing so here would bring bad luck to a good inn. We will take them over into the forest, to hang them on the very trees of Sherwood itself. Let those vile outlaws of Robin Hood see what to expect from me when I catch them." The Sheriff and his men mounted up and set out for the woods, encircling the poor youths.

Soon they came to a large oak tree at the edge of the forest, and nooses were fastened around the young men's necks. The Sheriff's men flung the rope-ends over the oak's thickest branch. The three youths fell to their knees and asked the Sheriff for mercy, but he only laughed. "Too bad there is no priest here for you to pray with. Since we have none, you shall just have to take your sins to Saint Peter, like three peddlers, and see if he will let you into Heaven or not."

While all this had been going on, an old man had come near and stood leaning on his staff, watching. His hair and beard were all curly and white, and across his back was a bow that looked much too strong for him to draw. As the Sheriff looked around just before ordering his men to hoist up the youths, he saw the old man and beckoned him to come over, saying, "Come here, old father. I want to speak with you."

Little John came forward. Something about him seemed familiar to the Sheriff, and he said: "I think I have seen you before. What is your name, father?"

"Please, Your Worship," said Little John, in a cracked old man's voice, "my name is Giles

Hobble, at Your Worship's service."

"Giles Hobble, Giles Hobble," muttered the Sheriff to himself, searching his brain. "I do not recall your name, but it does not matter. How would you like to earn six pennies this morning?"

"I would be glad to," said Little John, "for I am no wealthy man, to turn away an honestly earned sixpence. What would Your Worship like me to do?"

"It is simple," the Sheriff said. "Here are three men in serious need of hanging. I will pay you twopence apiece to hang them, for I do not like asking my men-at-arms to serve as hangmen. What do you say?"

"Well," Little John replied, still in the old man's voice, "I have no experience hanging men, but I may as well earn the sixpence as anyone. But, Your Worship, have these naughty fellows been allowed to pray?"

"No," said the Sheriff, laughing, "but you can handle that also if you wish. Just hurry, because I want to get back to the inn."

So Little John came to where the three youths stood trembling. He put his face to the first fellow's cheek as though listening to a prayer, and whispered softly into his ear: "Stand still, brother, when I cut your bonds. When you see me throw away my false beard and wig, take off that noose and run for the woods." Then he slyly cut the cords that bound the youth's hands. The young man gave no hint. Little John went to the second fellow and did the same, and then the third. The Sheriff and his men-at-arms sat laughing and waiting, paying little attention.

Then Little John turned to the Sheriff. "Please, Your Worship," he said, "may I string my bow? I would like to help these fellows along the way, once they are swinging, with an arrow in the ribs."

"Yes," the Sheriff said, "but like I told you before, hurry up and get it over with."

Little John put the tip of his bow to his instep and strung the weapon with surprising ease for an old man. Next he drew a good smooth arrow from his quiver and placed it. Then, checking behind him, he ripped off the wool disguise and bellowed, "Run!"

Quick as a flash the three youths flung the nooses from their necks and sped like arrows toward the deep woods, Little John at their heels. At first the Sheriff and his men were too stunned to act, but the yeoman had not gone far when the Sheriff realized who it was. "After him!" he roared in a mighty voice of fury and embarrassment.

Little John heard the Sheriff's words and saw that he could not reach the forest first, so he stopped and turned with his bow at the ready. "Stand back!" he cried fiercely. "The first man that takes a step forward or touches a bowstring, dies!"

The Sheriff's men stood still, for they knew it was no idle threat. The Sheriff roared at them, calling them cowards and urging them to charge as a group; they would not budge an inch. Little John backed slowly away toward the forest.

When the Sheriff saw his enemy about to escape, years of rage overcame his good sense. With a great shout he rose in his stirrups and spurred his horse into a charge. Little John drew back his deadly bowstring, but disaster struck. Before he could shoot, the good bow that had served him so long split in his hands. The arrow fell harmlessly at his feet.

Seeing this, the Sheriff's men gave a shout and charged after their master. The Sheriff caught up with the yeoman before he could vanish into the woodlands. Leaning forward, the Sheriff struck a mighty blow with the flat of his sword. Little John ducked, but not far enough to avoid a stroke on the head. He fell to the ground, knocked senseless.

"How fortunate," said the Sheriff, when the men arrived and found that Little John was alive, "that I have not slain this man in my haste! Thieves should hang, and I would rather lose five hundred pounds than miss out on it. Go, William, and get some water from that fountain to pour over his head."

The man obeyed, and soon Little John opened his eyes and looked around in a daze.

They tied his hands behind him, hoisted him onto a horse facing backward, and strapped his feet together under the mount's belly. In this way they took him back to the King's Head, exulting in the capture. But the widow's three sons had gotten safely away and were hidden in the woodlands.

Soon the Sheriff was back inside the inn, delighted that he had finally captured Little John. With a deep drink of wine, he said to himself, "This time tomorrow, the rogue shall hang on the gallows in front of Nottingham gates, and I will finally be even with him." Then he had second thoughts. "Except, of course, that it all depends on that foul Guy of Gisbourne capturing or killing his master. If he fails, there is no telling what that cunning Robin Hood might do. Perhaps I should hang this rascal sooner rather than later." With that he pushed his chair back, went outside to gather his men, and said, "I can not wait a whole day to see this rogue hang. We shall do it now, from the very tree where those young poachers would have hanged had he not stepped between them and the law. Get ready."

Once more they sat Little John on the horse, facing backward, and led his mount back toward the edge of the forest. As they came to the large oak tree, a man spoke. "Your Worship, someone is coming. It looks like that Guy of Gisbourne you sent out to find Robin Hood."

The Sheriff shaded his eyes and looked eagerly. "Indeed, it is. Let us hope that he has killed the master thief, just as we will soon kill his henchman!"

When Little John heard this exchange he looked up, and his heart sank. Not only were the man's shaggy clothes all covered with blood, but he carried Robin Hood's bugle horn and bow and broadsword. His face was hidden under the devilish hood.

"Guy of Gisbourne!" cried the Sheriff, when Robin Hood came near. "How was your luck? Man, your clothes are all bloody!"

"If you do not like my clothes," Robin said in a harsh voice like that of Guy of Gisbourne, "you can shut your eyes. This is the blood of the vilest outlaw who ever walked the woodlands. I have killed him today, though I also was wounded."

Then Little John spoke for the first time since his capture. "You bloody wretch! I know you, Guy of Gisbourne, for everyone knows about your evil deeds. Have you slain the kindest and best man that ever lived? You are a fitting tool for this coward Sheriff of Nottingham. I am glad to die, nor do I care how, for life means nothing to me!" Salt tears rolled down his tanned cheeks.

The Sheriff of Nottingham clapped his hands for joy. "If this is true, Guy of Gisbourne, your fortunes have just taken a turn for the better!"

"Of course it is true," snarled Robin. "Here are Robin Hood's sword and bow and bugle horn. Do you think he would have given them to Guy of Gisbourne as presents?"

The Sheriff laughed aloud. "This is a great day! The great outlaw dead and his right-hand man in my hands! You deserve a special reward, Guy of Gisbourne; what will it be?"

"Just this," Robin said. "I enjoyed killing the master and would like to kill his man. I ask that you hand this fellow over to me, Sir Sheriff."

"You are a fool!" cried the Sheriff. "I would have given you a knight's ransom in gold. I do not like this much, but I will keep my promise. Take him."

"Thank you kindly," cried Robin. "Take the rogue down from the horse, men, and lean him against that tree. I will show you how we slaughter a hog where I come from!"

Some of the Sheriff's men shook their heads. They did not care for Little John's life, but to see him butchered in cold blood disgusted them. "Do as he says," growled the Sheriff. The men obeyed.

While they were doing this, Robin Hood strung both his bow and that of Guy of Gisbourne, so cleverly that no one noticed him stringing both. Then, when Little John stood against the tree, he drew Guy of Gisbourne's sharp dagger. "Back off, you rascals!" he cried. "Have you no manners, to crowd in on my pleasure? Further!" The men moved away, some even looking aside so as not to watch. Robin put his face close to Little John's as if to gloat and taunt him.

"Come!" said Little John. "Here is my heart. I will gladly die by the same hand that butchered my dear master. I know you, Guy of Gisbourne!"

"Hush, Little John!" Robin whispered. "Twice you have claimed to know me, but you obviously do not. Can you not recognize me in this evil clothing? Just in front of you are my bow, arrows, and broadsword. When I cut your bonds, take them."

Little John's heart leaped, but he gave no sign. "Now! Get them!" cried Robin Hood, slicing the bonds. Little John leaped swiftly forward and took up the bow and arrows and broadsword. At the same time Robin Hood threw back the hood and bent Guy of Gisbourne's bow with one of the killer's sharp, barbed arrows. "Stand back!" he cried sternly. "The first man who touches a bowstring is dead. I have killed your assassin, Sheriff, and you could be next." Seeing that Little John too was now armed, Robin put his bugle horn to his lips and blew three shrill blasts.

When the Sheriff of Nottingham saw whose

face it was beneath Guy of Gisbourne's hood and heard the bugle ring, he was sure that he was about to die. "Robin Hood!" he roared, and wheeled his horse in the road and went off in a cloud of dust. The Sheriff's men saw no reason to stay around, and spurred their horses after him.

The Sheriff had a fine mount, but the horse could not outrun an arrow. Little John's bowstring twanged. When the Sheriff dashed in through the gates of Nottingham Town at full speed, he had a gray goose-feathered arrow sticking out of his rear. For a month afterward, the poor Sheriff could sit only on the softest cushions available.

When Will Stutely and a dozen or more stout yeomen burst from the woods, they saw no enemies—only a little cloud of dust in the distance.

Then they all went back into the forest again, where they found the widow's three sons, who ran to Little John and shook his hand. But they could no longer roam the forest on their own, so they promised to return and join the band that night, after they told their mother of their deliverance.

Chapter 21

King Richard Comes
to Sherwood Forest

Only two months had passed since Robin Hood and Little John's close calls with the Sheriff and his assassin. All Nottinghamshire was in a great stir, for King Richard the Lion-Hearted was to visit Nottingham Town in the course of a royal journey through merry England. People were at work everywhere: constructing and decorating arches for the King to pass under, preparing a grand banquet at the Guild Hall, and crafting a suitable throne for the monarch. His Majesty was to sit side by side with the Sheriff at a feast.

Finally the much-anticipated day dawned, bright and sunny. People from town and country alike crowded the streets, packed so tightly the Sheriff's men could barely hold them back far enough to let the King through.

"Watch your elbows! Stop stepping on my feet!" cried a great, burly friar to one of these men. "Show me more respect, or by Our Lady of the Fountain, I will crack your skull even though you are one of the mighty Sheriff's men."

At this laughter arose from a number of tall yeomen in Lincoln green scattered through the crowd. One nudged the holy friar with his elbow. "Quiet, Tuck," he said. "You promised to hold your tongue today, did you not?"

"I did," grumbled the other, "but I did not expect to have some clod trample my toes like a bunch of acorns in the forest."

Then the clear sound of many bugle horns echoed down the street. The bickering ceased as people craned their necks in the direction of the sound, crowding more than ever. Soon a gallant force of men came gleaming into sight, and the throng began to cheer until their voices became an enthusiastic roar.

First came twenty-eight heralds in velvet and golden cloth, each playing a trumpet bearing the royal coat of arms. Next were a hundred noble knights on heavy warhorses, fully armed. Each knight's page walked beside him bearing his helmet. The sun blazed brilliantly off their armor. After these came the mid-country barons and nobles in their finest clothing. Then came a great force of men-at-arms with spears and halberds, and in their midst were two riders. One was the Sheriff of Nottingham in his robes of office. The other, a head taller than the Sheriff, wore simple but elegant robes and a heavy gold chain about his neck. His hair and beard were golden and his eyes the blue of the summer sky. As he rode, he bowed left and right to acknowledge his people. A mighty roar of voices followed him as he passed, for this was Richard, King of England.

Then above all the shouting a great voice roared: "Heaven and its saints bless you, our gracious King Richard! And likewise Our Lady of the Fountain!" King Richard looked toward the sound and saw a very tall, strapping priest standing in front of all the crowd.

"By my soul, Sheriff," said the King, laughing, "you have tall priests here. Even if Heaven were deaf, I suspect I would now receive blessings, for that great fellow over there would make a statue of Saint Peter himself listen. I wish I had an army of his kind."

The Sheriff gave no answer, but his face turned white. He had to grasp his saddle to keep from falling, for he recognized the shouter: Friar Tuck. Behind him were Robin Hood, Little John, Will Scarlet, Allan a Dale and others of the band.

"What is wrong?" the King asked hastily.

"Are you ill, Sheriff? You look terribly pale."

"No, Your Majesty," the Sheriff said. "It was a sudden pain that will soon pass." He was too ashamed to tell the King that Robin Hood dared come within the very gates of Nottingham Town. For their part, Robin and his men rejoiced that England had such a noble king.

Evening had come; the great feast in the Guild Hall was done. The lords, nobles, knights, and squires all sat enjoying wine. At the head of the table, on a throne hung with cloth of gold, sat King Richard with the Sheriff of Nottingham beside him.

The King said to the Sheriff, "I have heard much about the deeds of certain outlaws around here. Their leader is called Robin Hood, and they are said to live in Sherwood Forest. Can you tell me more about them, Sir Sheriff? I hear you have had several dealings with them."

The Sheriff of Nottingham looked down gloomily. The Bishop of Hereford, seated nearby, bit his lip. The Sheriff said, "I can tell Your Majesty little about the deeds of these naughty fellows, but they are surely the boldest lawbreakers in all England."

Then young Sir Henry of the Lea spoke. He was a great favorite with the King, under whom he had fought in the Crusade. "May it please Your Majesty, when I was away in the Holy Land I often heard from my father. He told me many stories of this Robin Hood. If Your Majesty wishes, I will share one with you."

King Richard laughed and told Sir Henry to proceed. The young knight told how Robin Hood had helped Sir Richard of the Lea with money borrowed from the Bishop of Hereford. Again and again the King and others roared with laughter, while the poor Bishop blushed with fury and humiliation. When Sir Henry of the Lea was done, others present followed his lead by telling other tales concerning Robin and his merry men.

"This is as bold a rascal as I have ever heard of," King Richard said. "I must do what you cannot, Sheriff: clear the forest of him and his band."

That night the King was relaxing in the finest lodgings in Nottingham. With him were young Sir Henry of the Lea and two other knights and three barons of Nottinghamshire. His Majesty was still thinking about Robin Hood. "I would freely give a hundred pounds to meet this Robin Hood and to see how he lives in Sherwood Forest."

Sir Hubert of Gingham spoke up with a laugh: "Your Majesty's wish would be easy to satisfy, although expensive. If Your Majesty were willing to lose one hundred pounds, I could arrange for you not only to meet this fellow but to feast with him in Sherwood tomorrow."

"I would be willing, Sir Hubert," the King

replied. "But how will you do this?"

"Very simply," Sir Hubert said. "Your Majesty and six of us here will dress in Black Friars' robes, and Your Majesty shall conceal a purse of one hundred pounds beneath your gown. We will then attempt to ride from here to Mansfield Town tomorrow. Unless I am mistaken, we will meet and dine with Robin Hood before the day is out."

"I like your plan, Sir Hubert," the King said merrily. "Tomorrow we will try it."

Early the next morning, the Sheriff came to greet his King. His Majesty told the Sheriff of the merry adventure planned for the day. The Sheriff was aghast. "My gracious lord and King, you have been badly advised! You do not realize what this will mean. The outlaw you seek has no respect for king nor king's laws, Your Majesty, and I fear for your safety."

"Was I not told last night," replied the King, "that, except for the evil Guy of Gisbourne, this Robin Hood has not drawn blood since he became an outlaw? And all honest men should thank him for the death of Guy of Gisbourne. Was I misinformed, Sheriff?"

"No, Your Majesty," the Sheriff said, "that is the truth. Nevertheless—"

"Then," interrupted the King, "why should I fear meeting him, having done him no harm? This is not dangerous at all, but a merry adventure.

Perhaps you would like to join us, Sir Sheriff?"

"No, Your Majesty," the Sheriff said hastily. "Heaven forbid!"

Seven Black Friars' robes were brought for the King and his companions. The hoods hid their faces well. His Majesty hung a purse of one hundred golden pounds under his robe, and they went out to where seven mules stood waiting. The King ordered the Sheriff to say nothing about their doings, and the royal party mounted and left.

They traveled on, laughing and joking, past recently harvested fields and scattered clumps of forest. Soon the trees grew denser, and a few miles later the party was well within the forest. They rode on without meeting anyone who seemed like Robin Hood, eventually coming near to Newstead Abbey.

"I wish I were better at remembering important things," the King said. "We forgot to bring anything to drink. Right now I would give fifty pounds for something to quench my thirst."

No sooner had the King spoken than from the underbrush stepped a tall fellow with yellow beard and hair and merry blue eyes. "Truly, holy brother," he said, taking hold of the King's reins, "it would be a poor Christian indeed who would refuse your fair offer. We keep an inn nearby, and for fifty pounds we will not only give you a generous drink of wine, but also as noble a feast as you have ever had." The man gave a shrill whistle, and the bushes on either side of the road crackled to yield up sixty strong yeomen in Lincoln green.

"What sort of naughty rogue are you?" the King said. "Have you no respect for holy men?"

"Not in this case," merry Robin Hood said. "All the holiness belonging to rich friars like yourselves could fit into a thimble. My name is Robin Hood. You may have heard it before."

"How dare you!" King Richard said. "I see that the tales are true: you are a bold fellow with no respect for the law. Please let me and my brothers travel forward in peace."

"I cannot," Robin replied. "It would be very bad manners to let such holy men travel onward with empty stomachs. But since you offer so much for a little drink of wine, I am sure you can afford a stay at our inn. Show your purse to me, reverend brother, rather than have me strip off those robes and find it myself."

"Do not use force," the King said sternly. "Here is our purse, but do not lay hands upon our person." Then as now, it was absolutely forbidden to lay hands upon the King of England without his consent. King Richard drew out and offered his purse.

"Who do you think you are, the King of England, to speak like this?" merry Robin said. "Will, check this purse."

Will Scarlet took the purse and counted out the money. Then Robin had him keep fifty pounds for themselves, and put fifty back into the purse. This he handed to the King. "Here, brother. Thank your Saint Martin that you have fallen into the hands of good-hearted rogues like us. Others might have taken it all. Now, how about putting back your hood, so I can see your face?"

"I cannot," the King said, drawing back. "We seven have vowed not to show our faces for twenty-four hours."

"Then keep them covered," Robin said, "for I would never ask you to break your vows."

Robin then called seven of his yeomen to lead the mules, and the mock friars were taken into the depths of the forest. They soon came to the clearing in front of the great oak tree.

Little John, also leading sixty yeomen, had likewise gone out in search of rich guests that morning, for with so much travel afoot in Nottinghamshire there must be many fat purses on the roads. Friar Tuck and about forty yeomen stayed behind in Sherwood. When Robin's group arrived, these men rose to greet them.

"By my soul," merry King Richard said, when he had dismounted, "you have a fine band here, Robin. King Richard himself would be glad of such a bodyguard."

"These are not all of them," Robin said

proudly. "Sixty more are away on business with my good right-hand man, Little John. As for King Richard, all of us would give our lives for him. You churchmen cannot be expected to understand our King, but we yeomen love him. His brave doings remind us of our own."

Friar Tuck came bustling up. "Good day, brothers," he said. "I am glad to welcome fellow holy men to this sinful place." Then he winked and added, "I do believe that these roguish outlaws would have a hard time of it without Holy Tuck to pray for them."

"Who are you, mad priest?" the King said in a serious voice, smiling beneath his hood.

Friar Tuck looked around the band. "Never again say that I have a quick temper. This rascal of a friar calls me a 'mad priest,' yet I do not hit him. My name, fellow, is Friar Tuck—the holy Friar Tuck."

"That is enough, Tuck," Robin said. "Now perhaps you might go and bring these thirsty brothers of yours some wine. They have paid handsomely, so bring them our best."

Friar Tuck grumbled but did as asked. A great barrel was brought, and wine was poured for all the guests and for Robin Hood. Then Robin held his cup high. "I propose a toast. To good King Richard of great fame: confusion to all his enemies."

All drank the King's health, including the

King. "Perhaps, good fellow," he said, "you just drank to your own confusion."

"Never," merry Robin replied. "We of Sherwood are more loyal to our King than the clergy are. We would give our lives for him, while you would be content to sit in your abbeys and priories, no matter who sits on the throne."

The King laughed. "Perhaps King Richard's welfare means more to me than you realize. But enough of that. For our money, can you show us some merry entertainment? Your men are said to be legendary archers, and I would like to see your skill."

"Surely," Robin said, "we love to show our guests yeomanlike sports. Lads, set up a wreath down at the end of the clearing."

The target was set up a hundred and twenty paces distant: a wreath of leaves and flowers a foot and a half wide, hung on a stake in front of a thick tree trunk. "There, lads," Robin said. "Each of you shoot three arrows at it. To make things more interesting, anyone who misses with a single arrow shall be thrown by our great wrestler, young David of Doncaster."

"Listen to him!" said Friar Tuck. "Master, you hand out falls like a young maiden's love-taps. Obviously you are sure to hit the target yourself, or you would not be so generous with penalties."

First Will Stutely shot and put all three of

his arrows inside the wreath. "And a good thing," laughed Stutely, "for I notice that some crafty soul has had young David stand next to that boggy spot." Next came Midge, the Miller, and he also put all three shots into the wreath. Then followed Wat, the Tinker, but bad news for him! One of his arrows hit two inches outside the wreath.

"Come here, fellow," David of Doncaster said in his young, friendly voice. "I owe you something that I must pay." Stout Wat came forward to stand in front of David, his expression sheepish, trying for secure footing on the squishy grass. David rolled up his sleeves, braced, took his stance, then made his move. With the swiftness and power that had made him a champion, the young wrestler slipped a heel behind Wat's and an arm across the Tinker's chest. With a great SPLAT! the older man was hurled to the earth. Water and mud flew all about; what the soft spot offered in cushioning it took away in dignity. Wat sat up, slightly dazed, unhurt but completely soaked and muddy. The forest rang with the band's laughter. King Richard laughed until the tears came.

And so the band shot in turns, some getting off scot-free, others thrown into the mud for missing. Last of all Robin took his place, and all were silent as he shot.

The first arrow split a piece from the stake

holding up the wreath; the second hit within an inch of it. "What skill!" King Richard said to himself. "I would give a thousand pounds for this fellow to be one of my guard!" And now Robin shot for the third time, but his luck was bad. The arrow had a crooked feather and wavered aside to strike an inch outside the wreath.

A great roar went up, with many of the yeomen rolling in the grass and shouting with laughter, for they had never before seen their master miss so. Robin flung his bow to the ground in irritation. "Curse it! That arrow had bad fletching. I felt it as it left my fingers. Give me a clean arrow, and I will split the stake with it."

The yeomen laughed louder than ever. "No, good master," Will Scarlet said in his soft voice, "you have had your fair chance, and missed cleanly. The arrow was as good as any other shot today. David is waiting for you, for he wishes to pay you what he owes."

"Go, good master," roared Friar Tuck, "with my blessing. You have felt free to give out David's gentle tosses. You have earned your fair share."

"No," merry Robin said. "I am king in Sherwood, and no subject may lay hands on the king. But even our great King Richard can yield without shame to the holy Pope, and so I will yield to this holy friar. He seems to be in authority, and I will take my punishment from him." He turned to the King. "Please, brother, will you give me my penance?"

"With all my heart," merry King Richard replied, rising from his seat. "You kindly relieved me of the heavy weight of fifty pounds, and I would like to thank you properly. Stand well clear, lads."

"If you can truly throw me," Robin said, "I will give you back your money. But if you fail, brother, I will take the rest of your money in return for your boasting."

"So be it," the King said. His Majesty rolled up his sleeves, showing arms that made the yeomen stare. Robin stood next to the boggy area with his feet apart, braced and smiling. Then the King balanced himself, grappled Robin, and hooked his heel. Down went Robin into the muddy water, sending a great splash of it all around. Any man nearer than the length of two longbows was splattered with mud, the King himself receiving a generous dose.

The yeomen laughed until their sides ached, for they had never seen such a mighty throw in their lives. Robin sat up and looked around, muddy water rolling out of his yellow hair and beard. After a while, still gazing around at his laughing yeomen, he looked down ruefully at his once-clean suit of Lincoln green. "Will

Scarlet," he said, "give this fellow back his fifty pounds. I want nothing more of either his money or him, and a plague on his arms! I should have taken my punishment from David instead. I believe my very ears are full of mud, so hard was I thrown."

While the band was still laughing, Will Scarlet counted out the fifty pounds, and the King dropped it back into his purse again. "Thank you, fellow," he said, "and if you ever want the front of your clothes to match the back, come to me and I will help you free of charge."

Even as the King finished speaking, many voices were heard. From the brush burst Little John and the rest of the men, along with Sir Richard of the Lea. They ran across the clearing, and Sir Richard shouted to Robin, "Make haste, dear friend! Gather your band and come with me! King Richard left Nottingham Town this very morning to look for you in the woods. I do not know how he will come, for I heard only a rumor, but I know it to be true. Bring all your men quickly, and come to Castle Lea, to hide out until your danger passes. But who are these strangers?"

Merry Robin was finally getting up. He said, "These are certain gentle guests that came with us from over by Newstead Abbey. I do not know their names, but I have at least come to know this powerful rogue's strength this morning. It has cost me muddy clothing and fifty pounds!"

Sir Richard looked closely at the tall friar, who drew himself up to his full height and gazed directly back at the knight. Then Sir Richard's cheeks grew pale. Quickly he leaped from his horse's back and fell to his knees.

At this the King threw back his hood, and all the yeomen recognized him also, having seen him in Nottingham. Every man knelt in silence. King Richard looked around grimly, then brought his glance back to Sir Richard of the Lea.

"How is this, Sir Richard?" he said sternly. "How dare you step between me and these fellows, let alone offer your knightly castle as a hideout for the most famous outlaws in England?"

Then Sir Richard of the Lea raised his eyes to meet the King's. "Far be it from me," he said, "to offend Your Majesty, but I would rather risk Your Majesty's anger than to allow harm to come to Robin Hood and his band. I owe them life, honor, everything; can I then desert them in their hour of need?"

Before the knight was done speaking, one of the mock friars near the King came forward and knelt beside Sir Richard. He threw back his hood to reveal himself: young Sir Henry of the

Lea. Sir Henry took his father's hand and said, "Here kneels one who has served you well, King Richard. As you know, I stepped between you and death in the Crusade. I stand with my dear father, and I also say: I would freely shelter this noble outlaw, Robin Hood, no matter how angry it made you, for my father's honor and welfare mean more to me than my own."

King Richard looked from one knight to the other. At last the frown yielded to the start of a smile. "Sir Richard," said the King, "you speak with knightly courage; I do not fault you for it. Your young son takes after you in actions as well as words, for he did indeed save my life in the Holy Land. For his sake, I would pardon you for worse deeds than harboring outlaws. Arise, all of you, for I will do you no harm today. It would be a pity to ruin such a merry time with unkind deeds."

All rose, and the King beckoned Robin Hood to him. "Well, are your ears too full of mud to hear me?"

"Only death could plug my ears to Your Majesty's voice," Robin said. "As for Your Majesty's throw, I would say this: my sins may be many, but I think they are now paid in full."

"You think so?" said the King with a bit of sternness. "Those ears might have been shut permanently, but for three things: the loyalty you have professed for me, my love for a brave yeoman, and my sense of mercy. Do not talk lightly of your sins, good Robin. But brighten up, for your danger is past. I hereby give you and your entire band a royal pardon. However, I cannot let you continue to roam the forest, doing as you have done.

"You have said you would willingly serve me. I accept; you shall come back to London with me, along with that bold, strapping Little John and your cousin Will Scarlet and your musician Allan a Dale. As for the rest of your band, we will have their names recorded as royal rangers. It makes far more sense to have them as law-abiding caretakers of our deer in Sherwood than to have such men at large, outlawed for poaching. But you promised me a feast. Get it ready, for I would like to see how you live in the woodlands."

Robin told his men to prepare a grand feast. Great fires soon burned brightly, filling the air with the delicious scent of roasting meat. In the meantime, the King told Robin to call for Allan a Dale, for His Majesty desired to hear the famous minstrel. Soon Allan came up with his harp.

"Indeed," King Richard said, "if your voice matches your looks, we will be well entertained. Let us have a taste of your skill."

Then Allan touched his harp lightly, and all hushed while he sang a sad song of love: a man speaking to his daughter, who had been to a river and kissed a marvelous man in white—then died just as she finished telling her father of it.

When Allan a Dale was done, King Richard sighed and said, "By my faith, Allan, your voice moves my very heart. But I do not know what to make of this sad song. I would rather hear you sing of love and battle. Also, I do not fully understand what it means; can you tell me?"

"I do not know myself, Your Majesty," Allan said, shaking his head, "for that is how it often is: sometimes I just sing, without needing to understand."

"Well," the King said, "never mind. But I tell you, Allan: you should sing more about love or war, for you are the best singer I ever heard."

Now a yeoman came forward to say that the feast was ready. Robin Hood brought King Richard and his party to where it lay spread out on white linen cloths on the grass. His Majesty the King sat down and ate and drank, and when he was done he swore that he had never had a better feast in all his life.

That night the King lay in Sherwood Forest on a bed of soft green leaves, and early the next morning he set out for Nottingham Town. Robin Hood's entire band escorted him. The Sheriff had no idea what to say when he saw Robin Hood in such high favor with the King, but his bottled fury turned to poison in his heart.

The next day the King left Nottingham Town. Robin Hood and Little John and Will Scarlet and Allan a Dale shook hands with all the rest of the band, swearing that they would often come to Sherwood and see them. Then each mounted his horse and rode away with the King.

In spite of Robin Hood's promise it was many years before he saw Sherwood again.

After a year or two in London Little John came back to Nottinghamshire. There he lived a law-abiding life near Sherwood and achieved great fame as the quarterstaff champion of all England. Will Scarlet returned to the home he had fled. The rest of the band did their duties as royal rangers. Only Robin Hood and Allan a Dale stayed long in the King's service.

Robin's great archery made him a favorite with the King. He rose rapidly in rank, soon becoming chief of all the yeomen. In reward for his loyalty and service, the King made him a nobleman: the Earl of Huntingdon. Robin went off to war with King Richard, but even when he was in England, he was always too busy to visit

Sherwood. Allan a Dale and his fair wife Ellen followed Robin Hood and shared in all his ups and downs.

Eventually, King Richard died in battle, as one might expect of a lion-hearted king. After a time, Robin Hood was done with foreign wars. He came home to England, and with him came Allan a Dale and his fair Ellen. It was springtime when they arrived, with green leaves and small birds singing happily—just as they had done in fair Sherwood when Robin Hood roamed merry and free. The sweetness and joy of the time made Robin long to see the woodlands once more.

So Robin went directly to King John, who had succeeded Richard the Lion-Hearted, and asked permission to visit Nottingham. His Majesty granted the wish but commanded Robin not to remain in Sherwood more than three days. And so Robin Hood and Allan a Dale set out for Sherwood Forest.

They spent their first night in Nottingham Town but avoided the Sheriff, for his worship's grudges against Robin Hood had not lessened. Early the next day they mounted their horses and set out for Sherwood. As they approached the forest, Robin felt that he knew every stick and stone he saw. There, now, was a path he had often walked with Little John; over there was the way he had gone to seek a certain friar to perform a wedding.

As they rode, they shared memories of familiar places and deeds, growing more wistful by the moment. At last they came to the large clearing and the broad, spreading great oak tree that had long been their home.

Neither spoke. Robin looked around this well-loved space, seeing much that was old and much that was new. Where there had once been much bustle there was now only quiet solitude. Yearning welled up in Robin all the way to his blue eyes and then out, as he wept for the carefree life of Sherwood.

He had brought his old bugle horn, and now he longed to sound it once more. He raised it to his lips and blew; the sweet, clear notes resounded through the forest and echoed back to him.

By chance, that very morning, Little John was walking through the forest on some errand when the faint, clear notes of a distant bugle horn came to his ear. He halted and bent to listen. The note rang again, thin and clear, and then a third time. Then Little John gave a great, wild cry of yearning and joy and grief all mingled together. He dashed into the thicket like a wild boar, ignoring the thorns and briars. All that mattered was to reach the great oak tree.

Finally he burst forth into the clearing in a shower of broken twigs and saw Robin and Allan a Dale. Little John rushed forward and knelt at Robin's feet with great shaking sobs; neither Robin nor Allan could speak, but stood looking down at Little John with tears rolling down their cheeks.

At this moment, seven royal rangers led by Will Stutely rushed into the clearing and shouted with joy at the sight of Robin. Shortly after came four more, winded from running, among them Will Scathelock and Midge the Miller. They hurried to embrace Robin, tears in their eyes.

After a while Robin looked around him and said huskily, "I swear that I will never again leave these dear woodlands. I have been away from them and from you too long. I lay aside the name of Robert, Earl of Huntingdon, and take once again that nobler title: Robin Hood, the Yeoman." A great shout went up, and all the yeomen shook one another's hands for joy.

The news that Robin Hood had come back to live in Sherwood spread like wildfire all over the countryside. Before a week had passed, nearly all of his old yeomen had returned. But the news also reached King John, and he was furious. His Majesty swore that he would not rest until he had Robin Hood in his power, dead or alive.

At court there was a certain knight, Sir William Dale, a gallant soldier who knew Sherwood Forest well. His Majesty ordered Sir William to take an army of men and find Robin

Hood, and furthermore, to enlist the Sheriff and all his men-at-arms in the chase. The Sheriff needed no urging. Sir William and he set out in obedience to the royal command. For seven days they hunted up and down—but failed to find Robin Hood.

Had Robin Hood been as peaceful as before, the whole affair might have ended without much trouble, but years of warfare under King Richard had changed him. To run away like a fox from the hounds wounded his pride, and so Robin and his yeomen met Sir William and the Sheriff and their men in the forest. A bloody fight followed, and the first man slain was the Sheriff of Nottingham, who fell from his horse with an arrow in his brain before ten arrows had been fired. Many a better man than the Sheriff soon followed him in death. At last Sir William Dale retreated from the forest, himself wounded and most of his men dead. Dozens of good men were slain that dark day.

But even though Robin Hood had driven off his enemies in a fair fight, it lay heavily on his mind, and he brooded. He came down with a fever; he rested, but it got worse. After three days he called Little John over. Robin wanted to go see his cousin, who was the Prioress of Kirklees Nunnery in Yorkshire. She was skilled in drawing blood, which in those days was the standard treatment for bad health. He asked

Little John to help him travel, so they set out leaving Will Stutely as captain of the band until they returned.

Traveling slowly and easily, they came at last to the Nunnery of Kirklees. Robin's cousin owed him much, for King Richard had gotten her appointed as Prioress to show his affection for Robin Hood. But gratitude is easily forgotten. When she heard that her cousin had thrown away his earldom and gone back to Sherwood, she feared that she too might suffer from royal anger.

When Robin came to her and asked for her help, she acted glad to be of service—but with treachery in mind. The nunnery had a high, round tower with winding stone stairs, and the Prioress met the men at the foot of the stairs. Robin was allowed up, but not Little John. The poor yeoman turned away from the door, but did not go far; he sat down in a little clearing nearby to keep watch, like some great, faithful dog turned away from the door where his master has entered.

After the women had gotten Robin Hood upstairs, the Prioress sent everyone else away. First she tied a little cord tightly about Robin's upper arm, as was normal. She then opened a blood vessel—but she did not choose a blue vein near the surface in the standard way. Instead, she cut down to a deep artery, where bright red blood leaps straight from the heart. Robin had no idea anything was wrong; the blood flowed, but not fast enough to worry him.

The vile deed done, the Prioress left her cousin, locking the door behind her. All day the blood ran from Robin Hood's arm. After a time he realized something was very wrong, but nothing he could do would stop the flow of blood. Again and again he called for help, but his cousin ignored him and Little John was out of earshot. So he bled and bled until he felt his strength slipping away.

Finally he tottered to his feet to lean against the wall where his bugle horn hung. He blew it three times with what little strength he had. Little John heard the faint notes, and his great heart was sick with dread. He ran to the nunnery and banged on the door, bellowing to be let in. The door was of massive oak, barred from the inside and studded with spikes. The nuns called through the door and they told Little John to go away.

Little John went mad with grief and fear for his master's life. Looking wildly about, he spotted a heavy rock. He bent, raised the massive rock over his head, and charged; a yard from the door, he hurled it with insane might. The door splintered, sending the terrified nuns shrieking away. Little John stormed in without a word and ran up the winding stone steps to his master's room. This door too was locked, but one violent shove from Little John's shoulder burst the locks like brittle ice.

There he saw his own dear master leaning against the gray stone wall barely able to stand, his face terribly pale. With a great, wild cry of love and grief and pity, Little John leaped forward and caught Robin Hood in his arms. He lifted his chief as a mother lifts her child and laid him tenderly on the bed.

Now the Prioress hastened in, frightened at what she had done and dreading the revenge of Little John and the rest of the band. With a bit of skilled bandaging, she quickly stopped the bleeding under Little John's grim watch. When she finished, the huge yeoman growled at her to leave, and she did so in terror.

After she left, Little John spoke cheerfully to Robin, saying that it was all a minor fright and that no strong yeoman would die from the loss of a few drops of blood. "Why, in a week you will be roaming the woodlands as boldly as ever."

But Robin shook his head and smiled faintly. "My dear Little John," he whispered, "Heaven bless your kind, rough heart. But, dear friend, we will never roam the woodlands together again."

"We will so!" said Little John loudly. "Who dares even say that any more harm shall come to you? Am I not here? Let me see who dares touch—" Here he stopped, choked up. At last he said in a deep, husky voice, "If you are harmed by this day's doings, I swear by Saint George that I will burn this evil place to the ground. As for these women," he snarled, "they will be very sorry!"

But Robin Hood took Little John's rough, brown fist in his pale hands. "Since when, my good right-hand man, have you ever thought of harming women, even in revenge?" Robin said in a low, weak voice. He continued to talk and whisper until finally Little John promised not to harm the nuns or their building, no matter what. Then silence fell, and Little John sat with Robin Hood's hand in his, gazing out the open window, trying to swallow back the great lump in his throat. The sun dropped slowly to the west in a blaze of red glory.

Then Robin Hood, in a faltering voice, asked Little John to raise him to look out once more upon the woodlands. The yeoman lifted Robin in his arms, and he gazed with a wide, lingering look at the lovely sight. Hot tears rolled one by one from Little John's eyes, for he knew that the time of parting drew near.

Next Robin asked his friend to string his stout bow for him and choose a good arrow from his quiver. Little John managed to do so without jostling his beloved chieftain.

Robin's fingers wrapped lovingly around his

good bow. He smiled faintly as he placed the arrow on the part of the string that his fingers knew so well. "Little John," he said, "Little John, my dear friend, whom I love better than anyone in the world, I ask you to dig my grave where this arrow lands. Lay me with my face toward the East, Little John, and see that my resting place remains green and beautiful and undisturbed."

Now Robin Hood sat upright. His strength seemed to come back to him, and he drew the bowstring to his ear with the assurance of old. With a twang! the arrow sped out the narrow window. As the shaft flew, his hand sank slowly with the bow till it lay across his knees, and his body likewise sank back again into Little John's loving arms; but something had left that body along with the arrow.

For some minutes Little John sat motionless. Then he laid Robin gently down, folded his hands, and covered up the face. He turned and left the room without a sound.

On the steep stairway he met the Prioress and some of the senior sisters. To them he said in a deep, quivering voice, "Go within twenty feet of that room and I will tear down your miserable nunnery over your heads, stone by wicked stone. Remember my words, for I mean them." Then he left them, and they watched him run rapidly through the falling dusk until he was swallowed up by the forest.

The early gray of the dawn was just beginning to lighten the eastern sky when Little John and six men came rapidly across the open ground toward the nunnery. They saw no one, for the sisters were all hidden away in terror. Through the wrecked doorway and up the stone stairs they ran, and a great sound of weeping was heard. After a while this ceased, and then came the scuffling and shuffling of men's feet carrying a heavy weight down the steep, winding stairs. They went outside, and from the forest's dark edges came a great wail, as though many hidden men poured out sorrow.

And so died Robin Hood, at Kirklees Nunnery in fair Yorkshire, without malice in his heart toward his betrayers. He ended his days as he had lived them: with mercy for those who make mistakes and pity for the weak.

It is said that on a stone at Kirklees, there is an inscription:

> **Here underneath this little stone**
> **Lies Robert, Earl of Huntingdon;**
> **No archer was as he so good**
> **And people called him Robin Hood;**
> **Such outlaws as he and his men**
> **Will England never see again.**

He died December 24, 1247.

In time his yeomen scattered, but they came to no harm. A more merciful sheriff, one with no grudge against them, succeeded the slain one. They lived here and there throughout the countryside in peace, so that many lived to hand down these tales to their children and their children's children.

Afterword

The Merry Adventures of Robin Hood is an entertaining and heartwarming adventure story. But it is also a story about personal growth. Robin Hood is a character who changes for the better as a result of his experiences in life.

The first life-changing experience for Robin teaches him the need to think before he acts. This event comes when he is mocked by a group of the King's foresters (Chapter 1). Angered by the men, Robin turns to leave. The drunken forester who started the confrontation shoots at him, missing his head by only three inches. Robin answers with an arrow of his own and kills the forester. At that moment, Robin's life changes forever. " . . . his heart was sick with the realization he had slain a man. 'Poor devil," he cried, "your wife will weep today! . . . I shot in haste, but I will grieve forever!" And Robin does feel grief for years to come. Long after that killing, the Sheriff sends three hundred men into Sherwood Forest to capture Robin Hood (Chapter 4). Robin says he wants to avoid a fight because, "I killed a man once, and I hope never to do so again, for it gnaws at my soul." The killing of the forester has taught him to think more carefully about his actions.

The next event that marks a change in Robin demonstrates a further shift from a care-free life to a more serious and thoughtful life. In Chapter 11, Robin meets Allan a Dale, who is heartbroken because his true love, Ellen, is being forced to marry an older man. Robin kindly tells the grieving lad that he is "too young to suffer such trouble." A few moments later he tells Allan, "Now, lad, sit down here beside me, relax, and tell us the trouble. Speak freely, for it sometimes helps to talk about it." Over the next two chapters, Robin puts his energy into reuniting Allan with his beloved Ellen. Up to this point we have seen the Robin Hood who loves a friendly fight with quarter-staffs or who loves to play a good joke on the Sheriff of Nottingham. This gentle, fatherly tone is a new dimension to the character.

In Chapters 14 and 15 Robin undertakes an even more serious task. When he learns that Sir Richard of Lea is about to lose everything he has to the Priory of Emmet, he takes action to help the knight. And Robin Hood's kindness to Sir Richard is repaid when Sir Richard saves David of Doncaster from being killed by an angry mob at Denby fair. Sir Richard's action moves Robin Hood almost to tears: "Robin stretched out his hand to grasp the knight's. He spoke in a trembling voice. 'I can never repay you, Sir Richard, for I would rather lose my own right hand than see young David come to harm.' This is a more mature and sensitive Robin than we saw in the first half of the book. He clearly has changed from the hotheaded youth who killed the forester years earlier.

The next major event that marks a change in Robin Hood's life comes when Queen Eleanor invites him to participate in King Henry's grand shooting match in London. King Henry has promised Robin Hood and his companions safety for forty days so that they can participate in the contest. But the King breaks his word and orders the capture of Robin Hood and his three men as they return to Sherwood Forest. It is only with the help of Queen Eleanor that Robin Hood avoids capture and execution. As Sir Robert Lee explains to Robin, "You can thank your patron saint that our noble Queen is your good friend; were it not for her persuasion and arguments, you would be a dead man." As a result of this incident, Robin begins to recognize the limitations of his own power. We are told that, "after the great shooting match, Robin . . . came and went less boldly."

Robin Hood's next adventure has an even greater impact on his life. Early in Chapter 20, Robin Hood meets Guy of Gisbourne. This fierce and violent man is an evil monster. He is "dressed from head to toe in horsehide, with the hair still on it, including a hood made from the horse's head. The unfortunate horse's ears stuck up from it like horns." Guy "glared at Robin like a fierce dog about to go for the throat." His laugh is a "harsh roar." He makes Robin "sick to his stomach, for he [Robin] had heard much about the bloody and vile deeds of Guy of Gisbourne." Robin compares Guy to "a mad, frothing dog." Ultimately, he defeats the monster. Afterward he disguises himself in "the hairy, bloody garments" of the dead man. Robin is no longer a lighthearted adventurer who dresses up like a priest or a butcher or a beggar. This is "the harshest adventure of his entire life."

After killing Guy of Gisbourne, Robin Hood says, "This is the first man I have killed since I shot the King's forester so long ago. I often regret that day, even now, but I do not regret this one." Until this point, Robin Hood has refused to kill anyone. But Guy of Gisbourne represents a greater evil than he has ever faced before and he can kill the man with no regret. That is a significant change from the Robin Hood who hoped never to kill a man again.

This new level of recognition signals that Robin Hood is ready to move beyond Sherwood Forest. He has outgrown his "merry, carefree life, dining on deer and oatcakes and honey washed down with good ale." Only two months after Robin kills Guy of Gisbourne, King Richard the Lion-Hearted comes to Sherwood Forest. After defeating Robin Hood in a wrestling match, King Richard grants Robin and his men a royal pardon. No longer an outlaw, Robin serves King Richard well and is rewarded with the title of Earl of Huntingdon. But after King Richard is killed in battle, Robin returns to Sherwood Forest. Many members of his band gather again. Robin's long stay in Sherwood Forest angers the new king, who sends an army to help the Sheriff of Nottingham find Robin and take him back to London. The result is the bloodiest battle in the entire book: The first man slain was the Sheriff of Nottingham, who fell from his horse with an arrow in his brain before ten shots had been fired. Many a better man than the Sheriff soon followed him in his death. At last Sir William Dale retreated from the forest, himself wounded and most of his men dead. Dozens of good men were slain that day.

But Robin finds no pleasure in this defeat of his lifelong enemy and his victory over those who would take him away from his beloved Sherwood Forest. The event "lay heavily on his mind, and he brooded. He came down with a fever; he rested, but it got worse." It is almost as if Robin Hood has been made sick by the violence and killing he has participated in.

In the final moments of his life, Robin Hood is dying as a result of a betrayal by a Prioress who has bled him. In spite of her actions, Robin makes Little John promise not to seek revenge. How was Robin able to feel no "malice in his heart" toward his betrayers? The answer lies in the qualities of "mercy for those who make mistakes and pity for the weak." Having once made the horrible mistake of killing a man in a moment of anger, he understands and forgives others who make mistakes.

In conclusion, Howard Pyle has written a wonderful entertainment that is also the celebration of an enduring character who we not only can enjoy but also can respect and admire.